Uncaged

Andrea Stephens

D0707312

NTP Publishing
A Division of NeuroPivot Transformational Programs, LLC

NTP Publishing
A Division of NeuroPivot Transformational Programs, LLC

Paperback ISBN: 978-1-7370240-0-2
Ebook ISBN: 978-1-7370240-1-9

Library of Congress Control Number: 2021909117

First Edition

Editing and Book Production by Ashley Mansour, LA Writing Coach
Cover Design by Olivia Robinson
Interior Layout by Carla Green, Clarity Designworks

www.neuropivot.com

To every single person who has had a part
in making my life the beautiful masterpiece
that it is today. Without all of you,
this book wouldn't have been possible.

Brendakay,
Thank you very much
for your encouragement + support.
It has meant alot to me.
+ Thank you for being a part of my
friendly Universe! 😊

-Andrea Stephens

There are two ways you can live:
You can live as if nothing is a miracle,
Or you can live as if everything is a miracle.
—*Albert Einstein*

∽ ONE ∼

*P*anting for breath, looking at her watch, Jasmine hurried up the last flight of stairs to her apartment. *I swear,* she said under her breath, *I hate walking up these steps. They can be such a waste of time.*

Jasmine reached the top stair and walked a few steps down the cement platform to door 3B. She took her key out of the pocket of her black running tights, unlocked the door, and walked straight to the calendar that hung on the side of her refrigerator. She took the pen from its designated spot and marked an X through January 9—5 miles.

She held her head high as a congratulatory smile spread across her face, placed the pen back in its proper spot, and opened the freezer to pull out the necessary ingredients for the day's scheduled smoothie. She glanced over her recipe card, then pulled out frozen blackberries, frozen raspberries, and—she stood on her tiptoes to scan the entire freezer—no blueberries, only mangos.

"Mangos it is," she accepted, as she plopped the ingredients on the counter and opened the refrigerator. She peeked around in the fridge. "No spinach?" She opened the yogurt container. "And, a tablespoon of yogurt." She scowled. "Water will have to do."

I need to run by the supermarket on my way home from work, she thought, reminding herself.

She then made a sour face at the thought of having to lug her groceries up the three flights of stairs as she dumped the ingredients in the blender and turned it on. While the fruit pureed, Jasmine threw away the empty frozen fruit bags and added more smoothie ingredients to her grocery list.

Running late, she sat down at the small kitchen table to pull off her running shoes and drink her smoothie. As she bent down, her arm accidentally bumped the cup, spilling the freshly poured liquid all over the floor. "Come ON!" Jasmine complained. "I don't have time for this!" she griped. "I swear, life has it out for me. Nothing ever goes right. Why can't I ever catch a break?"

"Happy Birthday, Jasmine," she wished herself with bitter irony as she bent down to clean up the watery mess. "Why should I expect my thirtieth birthday to start any other way?"

"Thirty!" she added in disbelief, holding a dirty washcloth in her hand. "How in the world am I thirty? Where the heck did ten years go? And how did thirty years get me *here*?! I'm supposed to be living the American dream, with my camera in one hand, and my lover in the other."

Jasmine plopped on the floor in frustration and looked around her apartment. All she saw were the bare white walls she'd never taken the time to paint. A small white bookshelf, mostly stocked with photography books she'd not cracked open in years, a couch, recliner, bare mantel, and a TV stand equaled all her apartment's meager living room furnishings. *Some dream you've got here Jasmine*, she jeeringly thought, half-suppressing a laugh.

She exhaled noisily, as she continued cleaning up the mess on the floor. "This is so disgusting," she ranted out loud, as she ran the washcloth to the sink to avoid it dripping on the floor again.

Feeling the disappointment of her current situation rising, Jasmine swallowed the lump forming in her throat, and wiped away a slight tear from her eye.

Curious, she let her mind wander, recalling memories from past experiences. For one moment, she forgot all about the time and, like a deck of shuffling cards, allowed images from her life to whirl through her mind.

Why have bad things always happened to me? she questioned silently.

Because God is angry with you, a voice instantly answered back.

Jasmine lowered her head like a child who received a failing grade.

For real, though, it doesn't matter how hard I try, somehow, God is never pleased with me.

The loud noise of a glass bottle breaking jolted Jasmine back into reality at her little IKEA kitchen table where she sat.

How can one neighbor be so loud? she wondered, as she cupped her head in her hands and then swept both of them across her forehead, as if trying to wipe away the flashbacks that had just trampled through her mind.

That's strange. I haven't thought of those things in years.

She had dwelt more on the memory that hit her the hardest—the verbal abuse she'd endured from her mom the last time she had gone home for a visit.

I do not have time to be thinking about Mom right now. I must stay focused on my presentation.

Jasmine then picked herself up from the table, along with the cup that held the remains of her smoothie, and groaned as she noticed the time on the only clock she had in her apartment, realizing that she needed to hurry and get dressed for her big day at work.

A slightly worried smile materialized on her face as she thought about the presentation she was finally going to deliver. Deeply sighing, Jasmine sharply breathed in as she began down the short hallway toward her bedroom, carrying the smoothie cup in her hand.

Standing at her bathroom sink, she finished the rest of her bland drink and wrinkled up her face as she rinsed out the cup. *Gross, that did not taste good at all*, she thought, as she swallowed the last few drops. *It's probably just as well that most of it ended up on the floor.*

"So, Garrett Gunther," Jasmine stated aloud, bringing her mind back to the day's main issue. "Today is my day to impress you," she announced, shuffling through her closetful of clothes hurriedly.

"The head honcho. The big boss. The vice president of sales. The man I've been trying to impress for years." She tossed her brown hair behind her.

Jasmine pulled her black straight skirt and hot pink blouse out of her closet, then walked over to the mirror and held the clothing up to her body. Her head tilted and lip snarled as she scrunched up her face.

"Ugh. This looks tacky."

Jasmine hurriedly returned to her closet to find something more adequate to wear.

"This one, perhaps?" she queried, while she quickly sidestepped back to the mirror.

Her head tilted again. "I guess it can't hurt to try it on."

She wriggled into the chosen dress, then glanced at herself in the mirror. *Ugh! Is this* too *much?* she questioned silently, as she turned sideways to look at her perfectly chiseled hips, straining against the dress material.

Shawn's image instantly popped up in her mind. *Shawn might like it*, a voice chimed in. Jasmine's face lit up in a smile at the mere thought of Shawn.

"Why do guys have to be so confusing?" she grimaced. *He has been acting oddly out of character lately*, Jasmine thought.

Asking me indirect questions like he has something on his mind. How am I supposed to know if he's into me?

"Hi Shawn, do you like me? Like, *like me*, like me?"

I don't think that's how it works, Jasmine, the voice replied.

Abruptly taking a breath to snap herself out of her thoughts of Shawn, Jasmine remembered that she was in a hurry. "Today," she confidently boasted as she forced her nylons up, "I will put Karen in her place. She has stolen one too many projects from me, and it ends today!"

She smiled in premature glory at the thought and headed to the bathroom to don her makeup. She finished placing the final touches of highlighter on the tips of her cheekbones, then stepped back to examine her finished look before choosing a lip color.

What is going on? I thought I would feel better than this today.

Applying her ruby red lipstick, Jasmine pressed her lips together. The pit in her stomach grew, as she wondered, *Am I nervous? Scared? Is it because I turn thirty today?*

As Jasmine stepped over to examine her completed look in her full-length mirror, she caught herself strangely looking into her deep espresso-brown eyes. *Who are you?* She felt as if she was looking at a stranger. She stared back at the stranger for a few minutes before turning away.

She smacked her cheeks lightly, as if to snap out of the trance she'd been in all morning. *Wow, turning thirty is hitting me harder than I expected.*

Jasmine felt, however, as if something was off. Things were finally looking up and were finally starting to go her way, but in this moment, something didn't feel right.

She spoke to the stranger she was staring at in the mirror. "Things are going to change," Jasmine determinedly told her. "Starting today, my life will be different."

Jasmine's affirmation was interrupted by the sound of her phone buzzing on the counter. She picked it up and read the text.

Happy Birthday. Hope you have a good day.

It was from Sara, Jasmine's only sister.

She raised an eyebrow. *Why do you even bother continuing with these awkward birthday texts?*

Jasmine continued to stare at her phone, mulling over how to respond. Yet, the more she thought about what to say, the more fake she felt. *Let's face it*, she thought, *we both know you could care less if I have a good day.*

TY. It's going to be great, she texted back.

Jasmine glimpsed at the time on her phone, then slipped her nylon-covered feet into her sleek black heels, and headed towards the door. She collected everything she needed for the presentation and then opened the door. Glancing back once more to make sure she had everything she needed for this make-or-break day of her career, she scanned the apartment, shut the door behind her, made sure it was locked, and started toward the stairs with nervousness coursing through her body.

As she began her descent, she mumbled to herself with each step about how difficult it was to walk down the stairs in heels. "Why couldn't I find an apartment that didn't have me walking up and down stairs with holes in them every day?" Jasmine questioned aloud. It figured the only ones available when she showed up in town were walk-ups. "Sometimes, it feels like life has it out for me."

Finally reaching the bottom, she walked across the broken pavement in the parking lot to her aluminum-gray, two-door Honda. "I can't wait until I have enough money for a new car," she said, as she opened the long passenger door and awkwardly bent down to place her bags in the front seat. Her heel tilted and she struggled to keep her balance on the uneven pavement. "As if it isn't hideous enough," she added as the car door squeaked shut.

Jasmine wasn't a fan of Baltimore traffic, but on this particularly cold morning, she was perfectly happy to spend the twenty-minute commute in the car. In spite of her nervousness, she visualized in her mind the way the events of the morning would unfold.

A conceited smile spread across her face as she saw herself walking past the less important people sitting in their cubicles as they worked away on their menial tasks—those she would soon be directing. Jasmine, with her leather computer bag in hand, would confidently trot down the hallway toward the conference room where only special people were allowed.

Garrett would be sitting at the head chair, and would motion his hand to welcome her inside when she arrived. She would feel like part of an elite club.

At the table would be Brett, her immediate supervisor, and Derek, Liam, and Sylvia. Trying her best to retain her composure, Jasmine would silently remind herself, *I am here! I am one of them! I made it!*

Garrett knows who I am, and I am finally a Somebody!

The sound of a honking horn brought Jasmine back to reality. She was still on the road, driving to work. Without even knowing why, or at whom, she honked back, showing her disdain for being brought out of her imagination. She preferred to stay in her own world, sitting in a room with important people.

It was probably too good to be true anyway, she grimaced. *Wouldn't that be funny; something finally working out for Jasmine Stone.*

Her foot pressed the gas pedal with force as she sped past the cars in the left lane. Then she glanced at the time—fifteen minutes left. More nervous energy coursed through her body, and she clung to the steering wheel as she resituated herself in her seat.

Why are you so nervous? This is what you've always wanted, the voice inside her said.

Well, actually, camera design is what I always wanted, but this potential promotion is what I've been working toward for a long time.

But you know you always sabotage everything.

"It's not me!" she responded in an irritated tone. *You know who REALLY sabotages everything.* Jasmine took a deep breath, with her hands on the wheel, trying to shake off the voice that was talking inside her head.

Your life is not your own; it belongs to God.

Jasmine cut off the thought as a deep resentful sigh coursed through her body. She wanted to ignore the words that she'd repeatedly heard as a child in her church class. As she drove, she attempted to drown out the voice and pay closer attention to the road, but it returned.

Yes, I know. It belongs to that Big Bully up in the Sky.

Jasmine instantly regretted allowing the voice to pop into her head again. She felt guilty and afraid that God would now sabotage her presentation for thinking such a thing.

Get it together, Jasmine, she coached herself nervously. *Get it together.*

She braced herself at the stop light just before the parking lot.

You can do this, she thought, looking into the rearview mirror. *Today is your day.*

The light turned green and Jasmine turned her attention toward the road, taking deep breaths as she pulled into the parking lot.

∽ TWO ∽

"You have got to be kidding me," Jasmine gasped, through half-clenched teeth, as she pulled into the lot. "What in the world is Karen doing standing outside the entrance, talking to Brett?" she fumed. "Look at that little Chatty Kathy," she added, squinting her eyes and mimicking Karen's expressions as she whipped her car to the back of the parking lot, her mouth moving up and down, mocking her. "What the heck is she up to now?"

Did she start the conversation with Brett or did he start it with her? And what could they possibly be talking about? Jasmine was getting increasingly worked up with each passing second.

"Why the heck does Karen have to be working here any-way?" she muttered as she craned her head to look backwards and reverse into her parking spot. "Of all the places in the world that she could have chosen to work, she picked Nuevo Design. Why do I always have to put up with people like her no matter where I go?" she mumbled as the driver's door squeaked open and she climbed out.

After she shut the car door, she quickly glanced at her reflection in its window. She bent down and examined her hair to make sure it was still in place. Then she tiptoed around the car over to the passenger side, careful not to let her heels hit the pavement.

Guess what, honey? Jasmine yanked her bags out of the front seat. *This is my playground, sweetheart, and let's make one thing clear: Garrett assigned ME to represent the Johns Hopkins design project. I'm in charge of this presentation.*

Jasmine made her way to the building entrance, barely able to walk in her effort not to ruin her shoes. Her animosity toward Karen continued to grow. *You have bulldozed your way into one too many of my assignments, and this is NOT one I'm willing to give up.*

The eight-story building stood in front of her. Passing the last vehicle on the lot, her nerves leaving her more and more on edge, she watched as Karen threw back her head, laughing at something Brett said.

She rolled her eyes. *You have sabotaged me for far too long. In less than an hour, I will be in the conference room with Garrett Gunther and the others, without you.*

Jasmine wobbled as swiftly as possible to the entrance, and her resentment grew with every angry step she took.

"Getting your morning tattle in, Karen?" Jasmine taunted. "It must be rough needing to gossip your way to the top and still get rejected." She brushed by, almost knocking her shoulder against Karen's in an attempt to establish dominance. "I'll see you in the conference room with Garrett, Brett," Jasmine announced. "I've put together a killer presentation you all will love!" Jasmine was speaking as if she had already become one of *them*. It felt good. She closed her eyes for a second as she proceeded inside, and imagined herself finally stepping ahead.

Jasmine dominantly walked through the lobby, clicking her heels firmly on the tile flooring, alerting everyone around that she was not happy. She stopped at the elevator and scanned her badge to enter.

I've got to find out what they were talking about, Jasmine thought as she stepped on. She pushed the button for the fifth floor and waited, thankful to be alone for a few seconds to take a few deep breaths.

Something didn't feel right.

Was she pestering Brett about her boring life, or had Brett needed to discuss something with her? The self-assured smirk on Karen's face said it was probably the latter.

The elevator dinged and opened. Jasmine felt a slight sense of relief when the first person she spotted after getting off was Corbin, the administrative assistant. He was always an invaluable source of information. She decided to task him with finding out what they were talking about.

"Hey," Jasmine whispered.

Corbin looked at her and pointed to himself, obviously wondering if Jasmine was talking to him.

"Yes, you." She motioned him to come closer.

"Hey Jasmine, what's up?"

"Did you happen to see Karen talking to Brett outside?"

"No," he answered slowly. He seemed to be waiting for her next question.

"Darn it," said Jasmine, disappointed. "She looked like she was up to something."

"Gossip? Should I investigate?"

"Please? Can you find out what that busybody is up to? I have a feeling it's nothing good, and let me tell you, if this Johns Hopkins project leads to promotion, she is *not* taking that from me this time. That promotion is *mine*. I've worked far too long and hard for it to be taken away from me by a conniving gossip."

"I'll do my best," he assured.

"And hurry," she instructed him, storming off to her cubicle. As she pulled her computer and papers out of her bag, she felt a headache coming on.

Not now!

She sat down at her desk and reached for one of the bottles of Excedrin that she kept in her desk, popping two into her dry mouth to keep her headache at bay. *I need to be functioning at my absolute best right now*, she thought, swallowing the pills without water.

What is going on with me? Jasmine blinked her eyes, trying to focus. She sat back in her chair to catch her breath. Instead of digging into the business that awaited her on

Monday mornings, she paid attention to the bunch of people mindlessly mulling about, getting ready for yet another busy workweek. She was baffled by things she had never taken the time to consider before. So many people crawling around the mess of cubicles, hallways, and doorways. Some were scrolling on their computers at their desks, while others were standing about talking. Some were eating breakfast. Lonnie, one of eight employees that she managed, was eating so fast that he was almost choking. Jasmine scrunched up her face as she watched him.

Gross.

Her headache was getting worse. She took in a deep breath and her eyes fluttered shut. Another breath. She sat still and alienated from everyone around her, while taking in for the first time the scent of several different coffee blends filling the air. There were other smells that she hadn't taken the time to notice before either—obvious ones, along with the coffee. Sugary pastries. Freshly dabbed perfume. Paper and toner. Pencil shavings and pen ink. It all seemed to hurt her head even worse. She felt her face grow hotter, and her head started to spin.

What is going on with me? Jasmine asked herself yet again, as she scratched her itchy neck. She leaned her elbows on her desk and placed her head in her hands, trying to ground herself.

She pressed her hands against her head even tighter, as if to drown out the voice inside her. "This can't happen today, Jasmine," she told herself.

"Do not screw this up for me, God," Jasmine whispered in a threatening tone. *I know You get to push around Your human minions and make them succumb to whatever You want while we have no say in the matter, but please leave me alone today. I know You get a certain pleasure in sabotaging and ruining people's lives, but please, I am begging You, leave my life alone today. Spend Your day picking on someone else. Maybe try Karen for a change?*

She crossed her arms on her desk and tucked her head into one of the folds. She rested there with her eyes closed, not sure if she should keep acknowledging her thoughts or if she should be getting ready for her day like everyone else. With her head down, she began to notice sounds swirling around her, making her dizzy. She heard laughter, papers rustling, and shoes walking along the thinly carpeted floor. Footsteps. More footsteps. They seemed to be getting closer.

Before she could sit up, a drumroll on the side of her desk startled her. "Wake up, Jas! Big day today. No time for naps!"

It was Shawn, the head of the marketing team for Nuevo Design. "Well, don't you look professional today!" he added before she was fully upright. He then saw her face for the first time. "Oh my gosh, Jasmine, are you OK?"

"Headache," she muttered, pressing her temples with each middle finger and flashing a pained look on her face.

Shawn nodded understandingly, as if he should have guessed that. "A migraine?" he asked, raising his eyebrows.

Jasmine scrunched her face, not wanting to think about it. "I hope not. I just swallowed two Excedrin, and I'm waiting for them to kick in."

"Take a third," he suggested. "You can't screw up the meeting today."

Jasmine faintly looked at him through squinted eyes, trying not to move too much.

"You nervous?" he probed, baring his teeth.

"Me? Never." Jasmine fibbed, trying to sound as cool as possible, but her head was swimming in a dozen different directions.

"How much time do you have?"

"About two hours."

Shawn kneeled down next to Jasmine's chair and gently placed his hand on her arm.

In spite of the pain, she felt her pulse rising in excitement with Shawn so close to her.

"Listen, put your head down on your desk and rest until the medicine kicks in."

He moved a strand of her hair behind her ear, and she skipped a breath when the back of his knuckle brushed her cheek.

"I'll come back to check on you in a few."

"Thank you," Jasmine said, wishfully smiling. She placed her hand on top of Shawn's and closed her eyes for a second to enjoy the feeling.

"You rest. I'll be back. And Happy Birthday," he winked.

He always has a way of brightening my day, she thought, watching him walk away.

He stopped at Scott's cube, the young marketing assistant. *Probably a question about their spring baseball league starting back in a few weeks.* A smile crept across her face as she watched him. He tipped his head back and laughed that gorgeous laugh of his. *He is so handsome.*

Shawn looked back at her and raised an eyebrow, then simultaneously pointed his finger and his head downward to signal Jasmine to put her head down.

Why did I screw this up for myself? she thought, as he rounded the corner. *I can't believe I didn't date him when I had the chance.*

Jasmine situated herself in her chair as comfortably as she could, placed her arms on her desk, and closed her eyes. Her mind drifted to the exact moment she had met Shawn.

It was her second week of work, and she was instructed to bring Sylvia the samples binder. She'd headed into the copy room, unsure of which binder she was looking for and where it was located.

Shawn must have noticed the distressed look on her face and known that she hadn't a clue. "You're new?" he asked sweetly.

Jasmine looked up and saw a handsome man, about six feet tall, smiling at her with a hint of a smirk. He was impeccably dressed in dark jeans that fit his body well and a maroon Ralph Lauren shirt. Her heart skipped a beat, and she instinctively cleared her throat, unsure of how to respond.

"I am," she replied nervously.

"I've seen you around. Don't let this place intimidate you. It can get crazy busy. What department are you in?"

"I'm on the sales team."

"Oh nice. Did Brett send you down here?"

"Sylvia did," she said.

"Oh, Sylvia." He bugged his eyes out. "She can be a tough one. Don't let her intimidate you."

"I don't plan on it," Jasmine responded with a snarky smile.

"Ooo, a feisty one, huh?" he asked teasingly. "Sales teams do tend to attract the feisty ones." He snickered at his own joke. "What can I help you find?"

She hesitated before answering. "I need the samples binder?"

"Oh, you're close. It's up here," he pointed, and reached up in front of her. The smell of his cologned body took her breath away, and her knees went weak. She wanted to reach out and bring him in toward her for a nice long whiff. Instead, she just smiled.

As he handed her the massive binder, he reached out his hand. "Shawn Miroda," he said, expecting her name in return.

"Jasmine. Jasmine Stone."

"Angelic name." He held her hand longer than necessary, and his gaze lingered longer than she expected. Enough to make her cheeks turn pink.

"Nice to meet you," she replied, breaking the gaze and looking toward the ground. "I'd better get this to Sylvia."

"Let's hang out sometime."

Jasmine's stomach did a somersault. "Sure." She could feel her cheeks flushing.

She felt a poke on her shoulder and opened her eyes to see Shawn kneeling down next to her, holding out a glass of water with a concerned look on his face. "Oh!" Jasmine exclaimed, struggling to reorient herself. "Thank you so much. You didn't have to do this for me."

"You look a hundred times better now," Shawn remarked, with a relieved look on his face.

"I feel a hundred times better." She sat up to drink the water.

"Are you ready to knock this meeting out of the park?"

Jasmine gave him a thumbs-up to avoid as much head movement as possible. "I'll do my best." She held his gaze for a few extra seconds.

Shawn leaned in closer to her as if he had something important to say. "Listen, I want to take you out after work to celebrate your big day."

Jasmine's face lit up, but she winced in pain. "Ah, sure! I would love to."

"And ... I have some news."

"Some news?" She tilted her head and squinted her eyes at him inquisitively.

Shawn's facial expression seemed strange. "Yes, some news."

"What's the news?" she asked excitedly.

"It has to wait until dinner. You can't be distracted right now."

"You can't torture me like that! Can you at least give me a hint?"

"Um …," Shawn tossed his head back and forth and then bit his cheek. "It has to do with me and you," he offered. "And work," he added.

Me and you, and work, Jasmine contemplated.

"Okay …," she responded, "I'm even more curious now," looking at him with squinted eyes and furrowed brows.

Is he going to ask me out? she wondered.

"So, it's a yes?"

"Sure. Dinner tonight. What time?"

"Let's say six. At Bygone's."

Jasmine's face lit up. *Dinner at Bygone's? With Shawn? This is definitely a date!*

"You mean like top-of-the-Four-Seasons-Hotel, twenty-ninth-floor Bygone's?"

"The one and only."

"I won't have time to go home to change."

Shawn tilted his head at her. "No need to change," he assured her in his carefree way. "You look lovely just the way you are."

Jasmine melted inside and gazed into his eyes.

They were interrupted by her cell phone buzzing. Jasmine let his eyes go and picked up her phone.

Happy Birthday Jasmine. Mom and I miss you.

"It's my dad painfully wishing me 'happy birthday,'" she informed, placing her phone back on the desk and returning her focus to Shawn.

He must have noticed the annoyed look on her face because he questioned, "How long has it been since you've been home?"

"Seven years," she said heavily, instantly remembering the reason but choosing not to entertain it.

"What did your mom have to say when she called?"

Her face scrunched up in curiosity and her eyes squinted. "Surprisingly," she paused, "she hasn't been in touch yet."

"That's strange. Doesn't she usually call you early in the morning on your birthday?"

"Yes, she does." Jasmine clutched her chin. "Maybe she forgot. Or finally quit calling," she commented, with sarcasm creeping into her voice.

"She wouldn't forget about you, Jas. Who could do that?" Shawn winked.

Jasmine raised an eyebrow at him to avoid answering. She felt heat run through her body as she dwelt on the things that Shawn had just said to her. *Does he have feelings for me again? A fancy restaurant, a surprise …. He's asking me out! Is he going to ask me to be his girlfriend?*

She looked into his gorgeous nutmeg-brown eyes and smiled sweetly, as if she was already saying yes to Shawn's request to start a relationship.

"You'd better get going," he quickly said, moving away.

"Yes. I'd better." Jasmine then collected her leather shoulder bag and started down the hallway.

"Go get 'em, tiger!" Shawn called out behind her, his voice playful again.

Jasmine half closed her eyes as she continued down the hall, imagining what it would be like to wake up next to Shawn. *I wonder if he snores.*

⌁ THREE ⌁

*J*asmine stepped into the lobby of the Four Seasons Hotel, and instantly felt out of her comfort zone. She timidly scanned the magnificent lobby for Shawn.

"May I help you, ma'am?" a voice called to her from behind.

Turning around, she saw a bellhop standing politely with his hands behind his back.

"Oh! No, thank you. I'm waiting for a friend."

"You can sit there, if you'd like," he said, pointing to the extravagant seating area she had noticed when she walked in. "May I offer you something to drink?"

Something to drink! Jasmine gasped.

"No, thank you," she responded politely.

He tilted his head toward her to acknowledge her answer and retreated.

What is happening to me right now? Jasmine asked herself with excitement as she looked around at the beauty of the lobby. *This is incredible! Finally, a second chance with Shawn.*

Her mind drifted back to a past conversation she'd regretted as soon as it occurred.

Shawn approached Jasmine's table in the large breakroom. "Of all the tables in this room and you chose mine?" Shawn asked, putting down his lunch on the table and pulling out a chair.

"Um … I've been here five minutes."

Shawn winked at her. "I'm just teasing. May I join you?"

"I believe you already have."

Shawn seated himself. "Salad, huh?"

"That's kind of what it looks like," Jasmine responded, looking at her lunch.

"Were you able to book your flight to Chicago?"

"Yes, I am headed to the Design Center Showroom the week after tomorrow."

"Your *first* showroom?"

"Yes, I'm accompanying Sylvia."

"Good for you! You're moving right along here. I'm gonna miss you."

He's going to miss me?

There was an awkward pause.

"I may or may not miss you," she teased.

Shawn bore his natural smile. "I like your sense of humor." Then he added flirtatiously, "So … there are rumors floating around … that we're a thing." He looked at her with wide eyes and a smirk while he chewed his lunch.

Jasmine's stomach flipped. Her cheeks warmed, as she looked down at her salad and tucked her hair behind her ears. Shawn smirked and twisted his lips while he watched her.

"No worries. I'm off the table," she said curtly.

Wait—why would you say that? Are you crazy?

"Oh!" Shawn blurted out in surprise as he leaned back into the chair and put his fork down while looking at her. "I suppose I'm not surprised a pretty girl like you would already be taken."

"I'm not *taken* by anyone," Jasmine clarified.

Shawn tilted his head, implying he didn't understand.

"I … pretty much despise men," Jasmine responded.

Jasmine, you are crazy.

"Good to know," he commented, taking another bite. "May I ask why?"

Surprised by his question, she shrugged her shoulders, not wanting to answer. "I don't know." *Because I'm not going down that path again. I've been hurt by too many men, too many times.*

"Do you despise me?" he asked, genuinely curious.

"Well, I mean, I guess I don't despise *all* men—just the ones who feel the need to control women."

Shawn gave his head a slight shake. "I'm not that guy."

"Of course you aren't," she insulted. "None of them ever are."

"You've only known me for six months. I guess I'll have to prove myself to you."

Jasmine looked away from him, instantly regretting where she had let this conversation go.

But he's so cute! the voice inside her said. And it warned, *It's always the best-looking ones who turn out to be the worst.*

❧ —— ❧

Jasmine was brought back to reality when she saw Shawn entering through the hotel's revolving door. His thick, fawn-brown hair was styled just right, with bangs that flipped back into the perfect swoop.

He spotted her when she stood up from the bench and waved at her. His face was chiseled to near perfection, and his cheeks sunk in at just the right place. He was wearing dark denim jeans and a forest-green wool jacket over a black, V-neck T-shirt that clung to his chest.

"How do you do it?" she asked, reaching for his hand and looking up at him.

"Do what?" he asked, backing up to let go of her hand.

"How do you make your style look so easy and effortless?"

Shawn let out a short laugh. "That's kind of you."

Jasmine felt him pull away.

"I'm sorry I'm late. I was held up in traffic. What do you say we go eat?"

She watched his lips move as he spoke, allowing herself to be turned on with every word. She felt more and more sure that a relationship with Shawn was the right move. "Yes, let's. I'm super curious about what your news is," she hinted.

Shawn let out a short laugh again.

They then walked over to the elevators, waited for one to arrive, then stepped inside.

Jasmine reached for Shawn's hand and gave it a squeeze.

Shawn inquired, "Are you okay?"

"Just happy to be here with you," Jasmine replied.

Shawn gave her an awkward smile and raised his eyebrows.

They rode the elevator in silence the rest of the way up to the twenty-ninth floor.

The elevator door dinged open, and when they stepped out, Jasmine's mouth dropped open. An exquisite chandelier sparkled overhead, and its light ricocheted off the windows. Jasmine stepped over to a window ledge to take in the view of the city of Baltimore.

"Shawn, this is amazing! I've never been up here before," she said, turning around to show him her excitement. "Thank you so much!"

His broad smile indicated that he was pleased to see her enjoying herself.

"Happy Birthday!" he beamed. "You deserve it."

She followed his lead and walked to the entrance of the restaurant.

"Reservation for Shawn Miroda," he informed the hostess, who looked down at her screen. "Right this way," she motioned, after picking up two menus.

He motioned for Jasmine to walk in front of him, and she followed the hostess to a table next to a window, near the back of the restaurant. It was neatly set for two, complete with purple cloth napkins folded into gorgeous fans, wineglasses, and crystal silverware. A flickering candle sat in the table's center.

The hostess pulled Jasmine's chair out to seat her, while Shawn seated himself. She opened the menu and presented it to Jasmine with her left arm tucked behind her back. Jasmine observed as the hostess then proceeded to present Shawn his menu in the same way. "Enjoy your Bygone's experience," she said warmly.

"Fancy," Jasmine enthused to Shawn with delight.

"You seem excited. I can't wait to hear about the meeting with Garrett! I assume your presentation went well?"

This excitement has nothing to do with Garrett or my presentation, Jasmine recognized as she beamed.

"I totally nailed it," she gloated, squeezing her hand into a fist and holding it up in the air.

"I'm so proud of you, Jas. I knew you'd pull it off."

"Thank you."

"Remind me again why Garrett chose you for the presentation. Was it because of the presenting sponsorship idea for the marathon?"

"I assume it was. Ever since Garrett caught wind that I came up with the idea for the marathon, he's showed more interest in my work."

"Being noticed and acknowledged by Garrett Gunther," Shawn whistled and cocked his head, "that's quite an accomplishment. I bet you have all kinds of people jealous of you now, huh?"

"You have no idea," Jasmine admitted, looking up from the menu. "Karen, for one. That little snitch actually thinks she has a chance of competing with me on this one."

"She doesn't stand a chance," Shawn replied, reassuring her. "You're great at your job because of who you are on the inside, and that's not something someone can steal from you."

Jasmine raised her eyebrows, not fully believing him.

"What are you thinking of ordering?" he questioned. "This all looks so delicious."

"Not the pheasant or quail, I can tell you that," she joked.

"Come on, where is your adventurous spirit," he teased back. "I've decided on the grilled lobster."

"I was eyeballing that. But if you're eating that, I'll do the blue crab cakes."

"The marathon sponsorship planning is coming along wonderfully, by the way. It was a brilliant move and it's going to be amazing. You should be proud of yourself. I'm not at all surprised that idea brought you to Garrett's attention. What did he have to say about the Johns Hopkins presentation?"

Jasmine cocked her head and gave Shawn a supercilious gaze. "He *loved* it," she emphasized by proudly raising her chin. "He shook my hand, thanked me for all my 'wonderful ideas and contributions,' and said we'd talk soon."

"So, what do you think this means for you?" Shawn asked excitedly.

"Well ... I won't be crawling around with all those little cubies now. I'll be making my move closer to the top, and I'll get a real office ... with a door."

"Sounds like you plan on sticking around Nuevo Design for a while, yeah?"

"It's not the *dream*, but it's what I have." She shrugged her shoulders. "And, I have you," she flirted, rubbing her fingers gently on his arm.

Shawn looked down at the table. "You know, Jas," he paused heavily, "you've been such a good friend to me over the past several years, and I really appreciate that."

He bit his cheek and brought his gaze back to the table.

Jasmine stared at him. *Here comes the question!* she squealed inside.

"I want you to know that." He looked back to her face, while shaking his head in agreement with himself.

"Thank *you*, Shawn. You've been an amazing friend, too. You've been there for me since the beginning. You were my anchor when I first joined the company and dumped my life story on you."

Shawn cracked a smile and looked down at his hands, resting on the table.

"You showed me the ropes and helped me get around those first few months until I got the hang of things." She hesitated before continuing. "We have shared some very personal conversations, allowed ourselves to be vulnerable, and I want you to know how much I've appreciated that."

She leaned forward to emphasize her words. "You understand me, Shawn, in a way no one else does. Even my own mother."

Shawn took a deep breath and slowly let the air out, sat back in his chair and shook his head at Jasmine.

"I mean it."

The conversation paused as the server brought their drinks. Shawn tipped his head to thank her.

He turned his attention back to Jasmine while biting his cheek, his smile gone.

"Was it something I said?" she questioned, seeing the look on his face.

"It's everything you said, Jasmine."

AH! He's so sweet!

She looked at him, waiting, waiting ….

"I like seeing you happy, Jas."

"I like being happy," she said, feeling herself blush. She reached out and placed her hand on Shawn's arm. *Just ask me already!*

She gazed at his arm and imagined herself under it, her head snuggled on his chest. *How safe I would feel. Finally.* She let her thoughts continue to spiral. She saw herself placing his hand slightly above one of her breasts to let him know that she was fully committed, that she didn't want to hold back any longer.

"Are you okay, Jasmine?"

She caught herself drifting and cleared her throat quietly, as if to clear her mind of the things she was thinking about Shawn. "Yes," she paused, "I'm fine," she replied, pulling her hand back from his arm, feeling embarrassed.

Instead of telling her his news, he asked, "Have you heard from your mom yet?"

Jasmine took a deep breath. "No," she said curtly.

Seriously? I don't want to be discussing my mom right now.

"She'd usually have called you or at least texted you by now, wouldn't she?"

"Yes, usually. Don't know. Don't care. Let's not talk about my mother, okay?" She couldn't help it; she was starting to get irritated by the way Shawn was dragging out 'his news.'

"What do you want to talk about?" he asked.

"You!" she said her tone sharp. "That's why we're here, right? You have something you want to tell me?" Jasmine's last words had turned more flirtatious, and she rubbed her hands together.

Shawn seemed relieved to see the server heading in their direction with the food.

"Smells delicious," he said.

Jasmine reached for her knife and fork. "Yes. Delicious," she commented.

And, I'm not talking about the food! "Now, can we talk about your big news? Unless you'd rather do that at your place," she added boldly with her head cocked. "Over dessert."

Shawn's laugh sounded uncomfortable, and he looked away from her face, tilted up in an encouraging smile. "No," he said, and she could tell he was nervous. "I'll tell you now."

He took a deep breath. "Okay. So, the big news ...." He put down his silverware and rubbed his hands together. "Two things," he said.

"Ooo two things!" Jasmine said coyly.

"This is so hard!" Another deep breath.

Jasmine waited, poised to smile with excitement and happiness.

Okay, so, first off, do you remember about five years ago, when we got so frustrated with the company changes and vowed that one day, we would find 'real' jobs?"

"Yeees," said Jasmine slowly, wondering where in the world he was going with the question.

"Yet day after day, 'one day' turned into over five years."

"Yeees," she said again.

"Well … my uncle Jim's wood-turning business has taken off and he needs a marketing expert." He paused, then added, "And ... he's asked me to come help him."

Jasmine stopped midbite and stared at him in disbelief, unable to speak.

These weren't the words she'd been anticipating for the last several hours.

"Wow," was all she could get out before swallowing, clearing her throat, and putting down her fork. "What was the second thing?"

She braced herself as she stared at the heavenly man sitting across from her, feeling him about to slip through her grasp.

"Do you remember my old girlfriend, Sheila?"

"Yeees." There it was again, that unsure, feeble word.

"She and I," he scratched above his ear, "reconnected. We've gotten back together again."

Jasmine choked.

"I knew you'd be happy for me," he said. "You were the one who encouraged me to do it—to get back together with her."

Jasmine stared at him until she felt able to speak. "Shawn, that was like two years ago."

"Yes, I know, but it took me a while to realize it was the right thing to do."

Jasmine looked down at the crab cakes on her plate, no longer hungry. She inhaled a quick breath. "When … do you leave?" she hesitantly asked, while wiping her mouth with the cloth napkin from her lap.

Shawn couldn't possibly fail to hear the disappointment in her voice. His answer came slowly. "Um, I'm putting in my two weeks tomorrow." He looked down at the food in front of him.

"Tomorrow!" Jasmine blurted out. "Tomorrow? You aren't even going to be here for the marathon?" She questioned, staring at him. Even if he wasn't man enough to look her in the eye, her tone demanded an answer, an explanation.

"Well, my uncle really needs my help. He wants me to start on February 1st."

"Two weeks?" Jasmine questioned again. She was prepared to wait as long as it took to get an answer.

"I've been helping him on the side for about four months now, and his business has gotten out of hand. It's become too much for me to handle both jobs. He's hiring a marketer and a few other employees."

"*Sheila*?" Jasmine asked, changing the subject.

"She lives nearby. Everything worked out perfectly." Maybe he finally felt the tension between them. "I thought you'd be happy for me," he pouted.

Jasmine looked him in the eyes.

"You look upset," Shawn speculated.

"I'm honestly confused," Jasmine reacted.

"About what?"

"About why we're here, Shawn. At a romantic candlelit dinner ... at *Bygone's*!"

"I wanted to celebrate your birthday. And I wanted to thank you for your awesome friendship. I wanted to tell you goodbye." He looked clueless as to why she would be upset.

"'Awesome friendship,'" Jasmine repeated quietly. "Wow." She turned her face away, feeling silly and embarrassed. She felt tears coming and dabbed an eye with the napkin.

Guys are so stupid! How could he not know I've wanted him for seven years!

"I'm sorry, I don't know what's up with me today," she lied.

"You've just turned thirty! The big 3-0. That can be a scary thing," he alleged, completely clueless.

Jasmine raised her eyebrows in confusion and frustration, staring at him, unable to speak. *If you think for a second this is about me turning thirty, you have lost your dang mind, you idiot!* "If you'll excuse me," she seethed, pushing back her chair to step away.

⌒ FOUR ⌒

*J*asmine sat in her old beat-up Honda at the end of the grocery store parking lot, her head pressed back against the headrest of the driver's seat. She stared out the windshield, observing customers walking in and out, unable to process what had just happened, and waiting for her eyes to de-puff from crying.

She picked her head up when a shiny black Mercedes caught her attention. A young woman climbed out, talking on the phone. Her hair was blond and unkempt, and her drab-brown riding boots were a few seasons out of style.

Jasmine watched as she walked toward the storefront. "That should be me," she commented bitterly. "But no, I'm still in this old piece of crap and just got dumped by a guy who wasn't even my boyfriend." Her voice was getting louder and more bitter with every word.

She pressed her hands against her head, trying to ease the ache as she watched the woman reach the store's entrance.

She isn't even cute. At least show you have class if you're going to be driving around in a car like that. She rolled her eyes in disgust.

As the woman disappeared into the store, and just before Jasmine closed her eyes and rested her head again, her attention was caught by a young couple parking their car.

"Oh, don't you two look cute, all happy and in love," she sneered.

She watched the boy walk around to what she assumed was his girlfriend's side of the car and waited for her to get out. He pinched her backside as they began walking toward the store's entrance. Jasmine raised her upper lip in disgust and shook her head.

"It gets ugly," she warned, as if she was actually talking to the young girl. "Enjoy it while it lasts. Before you know it, one day you'll wake up and find out that he screwed another girl behind your cute little back, and that the last two years of your life will have been a complete waste."

She inhaled deeply as she dismissed the painful memories popping into her head.

The clueless girl kept walking, conversing with her boyfriend and lightly swinging their locked hands, ignoring Jasmine's advice.

She felt a lump forming in her throat as she continued to stare mindlessly out the window. *Why me?* she asked, as tears formed in her eyes.

Why me?

Why do bad things always *happen to me?*

Why can I never *seem to catch a break?!*

She closed her eyes as a fresh set of bitter tears streamed down her face.

I just want today to be over.

She couldn't help but think of Justin, her college boyfriend, while the bitter tears streamed down her face. She hadn't thought of him in a long time, but sitting here in the parking lot of a grocery store on a bitterly cold day, she brought all that pain back and more.

"Justin, you are such a pig!" Jasmine cried out loud. "I hate you! I hate that men like you exist!"

Tears continued to run down her face from her eyes to her cheekbones, then slowly trickling down and running under her chin. She didn't move a muscle. She was in too much emotional pain to even think about wiping them away. She just sat, staring into space, and ever so slightly shaking her head in disbelief as memories of catching Justin cheating flooded her consciousness.

"You looked me in the eye and lied straight to my doggone face, you piece of trash."

She continued staring straight ahead.

"And I believed you!"

She gritted her teeth.

"'I love you, dear,'" she said with mockery. "'Eyes only for you, babe.'"

Jasmine snorted.

"Thanks a lot. Now I'm frickin' thirty years old and can't trust a doggone rock if I want to."

She breathed heavily and squeezed her eyes shut, as if she were shutting Justin out of her life once again. Unable to ignore the tears any longer, she picked up her head and managed to reach for a napkin before placing her head in her hands and sobbing. Years of hurt and pain moved from her throat and streamed down her face.

Why does everyone hate me?

Why do I always get so used?

I feel so betrayed.

Justin, Eric, my own mother, and now Shawn.

"I have tried *so* hard!" she sobbed loudly, clenching her fists as one of them still held on to the napkin. Jasmine squeezed her eyes even tighter, then rocked back and forth in her car's driver's seat.

After a few moments, the tears stopped. She dabbed at her eyes with the napkin and said out loud, "You are a strong independent woman. You don't need a man. You don't need other people." She could literally feel her cold, icy, armored shell settle back into place. She felt strong again—at home.

Realizing she had let herself cry for the third time that day, Jasmine clenched her jaw and looked at the tear- and mascara-stained napkin. Her cold icy shell was working well already. She crumpled up the napkin and threw it on the floor next to the passenger seat, irritated with herself for giving in to tears and emotion again.

She popped her door open to quickly run into the store, but just as she did, she looked up and saw a mother carrying a toddler and holding the hand of a little girl who couldn't have been more than five years old. She paused for a moment to watch the small child skipping along, enjoying her own world. A slight smile started to creep onto Jasmine's face as she watched the innocent child.

Abruptly, the hand of the young girl was whipped into place, and Jasmine and the girl were jolted back into the mother's reality. Jasmine looked up at the child's mother and instantly saw her own mother. Instead of the short woman walking toward her own vehicle, Jasmine saw her tall, brown-haired, brown-eyed mother in her place. Jasmine turned to the happy girl, swinging her mother's hand, and wondered what she liked to do.

What are her hopes and dreams?

Jasmine wanted to get out of her car and go hug that girl so tightly. She wanted to look into her eyes and let her know what lay ahead—to prepare her for the disappointments of the future. She wanted to protect and warn her that one day the very mother that held her hand would despise her choices and actions, misunderstand her, and try to cage and hold her back.

As if she were talking to her own mother, Jasmine looked back to the mother who was strapping the toddler into a car seat, and asked out loud, "Why can't you just accept her? What are you so afraid of?"

The mother moved back to the grocery cart and began loading the groceries into the car's trunk. Jasmine kept talking to her as if she was actually having a conversation. "Why can't you just let her be? Why do you feel the need to control her and hold her back?"

Feeling ignored, she watched as the mother placed the cart in the cart return closest to the Chrysler minivan and returned to the driver's side door of the vehicle. The automatic sliding door shut. Jasmine winced in pain for the seemingly happy little girl who sat in the back seat.

The van backed out of the parking space and headed toward the stop light at the exit of the parking lot. "Goodbye," Jasmine said, feeling as if she had lost a friend. She waved her hand in the air weakly and kept watching as the van pulled out into the sea of moving vehicles.

After she lost sight of it, she turned back to look at the parking spot from which they had pulled out. Another vehicle already occupied the spot. A salt-and-pepper-haired man slowly left the vehicle as if he didn't have a care in the world. He looked to be about sixty years old and was wearing a tobacco-brown sweater that seemed to be as old as he was.

Fantastic, sneered Jasmine, *how comforting to know that this is what I have to look forward to: getting old and gray.*

"He's probably here buying himself a package of diapers," she assumed, out loud, in a sarcastic coldhearted tone.

The old man's hair blew slightly in the wind as he walked toward the store's entrance. His mustache crinkled as he peered over the top of his glasses, squinting his eyes ever so slightly to read whatever was written on a small piece of paper in his hand.

"It's just diapers, old man," ranted Jasmine, "Depends, Size L, fifty-two count."

He folded the paper and slid it into the front pocket of his loose navy-blue khaki pants and walked confidently but slowly toward the store. Jasmine noticed that he wasn't in a hurry.

I guess you run out of places to rush around to when you get old, thought Jasmine. *You're privileged to wander around slower.*

She watched him until he disappeared into the store.

Jasmine looked back at the old man's car. *Well, one thing I've already got is the crappy old car. Now all I need is some old clothes and a few more pounds.*

She took in a deep breath, trying to convince herself to leave her warm comfortable car to step out into the cold night air. She shivered just thinking about it and continued observing the people meandering in and out of the store. Couples, families, employees, young, old, male, and female. She sneered at the couple pretending to be happy and then, a few moments later, at the one that made no attempt to pretend.

Before she knew it, she saw the older man coming out of the store. Her attention was drawn to him again. As he pushed his cart toward his vehicle with his hair blowing in the wind, he appeared to be deep in thought. The cart held only a few paper bags, and Jasmine wondered what was in them.

What does an old man who has nothing to do buy at the grocery store? she thought sarcastically. Her mind continued to whirl, as if she was already preparing for her life thirty years down the road. *Definitely those diapers. Probably some Raisin Bran, because, you know, old folks need their fiber. Cream of Wheat because he's probably already started losing his teeth.*

Jasmine scrunched her eyes and paused for a moment, then returned to the list, *Prune juice, because, you know ....* She didn't actually know what prune juice was for, but she kept on going. *A few cans of fruit cocktail in heavy syrup, because you've got to get your fruit in. Jell-O, because what else can an old person ask for?*

Jasmine continued, stretching her imagination. *Bird seed for the squirrels, cat food, because he just looks like that kind of person.* She remembered a shopping trip she'd gone on with her grandma and felt confident she had named everything that must be in this man's grocery bags.

Oh, and Ensure, because—I don't know about that one either. I just know that Grandma and Grandpa always had Ensure in their cabinet. Jasmine shuddered at the thought of what it tasted like. She had snuck a sample one time, and only once, while visiting her grandparents. The lush satisfying picture of chocolate on the outside of the plastic bottle looked so much better than it actually was.

The man was putting his cart in the cart return now. As he rounded the back of his car and headed toward the driver's seat, he looked up just enough for Jasmine to notice that he had a slight smile on his face. He then disappeared into his car.

As he finished meticulously backing out of the parking space, she found herself wondering what secret he was hiding.

Oh my gosh. She slapped her cheeks and took a deep breath. *I need warm weather.* She groaned as she opened the door of her car.

Why does it get so dark and cold around here? She looked at the shopping list she held as she walked toward the supermarket's sliding doors. It read:

unsweetened almond milk

spinach

bananas

frozen peaches

frozen blueberries

chia seeds

fresh kiwis

oats

Greek yogurt

protein powder

coconut water

The list was long, and Jasmine ached, just thinking about all the bags she'd have to carry upstairs to her apartment. *I don't see how I can do all this right now.* And yet, she walked into the store, joining the sea of people feeling alone, uncared for, and unwanted.

She walked quickly through the store, grabbing what she needed for the immediate moment, stopping in the juice aisle on the way to the coconut water. She spotted the $8.99 bottle of organic acai berry juice—a luxury she usually passed up. Now, she stopped and picked it up.

I deserve this today, she decided. As she placed it in her basket, she felt a small smile curve across her lips.

∽ FIVE ∾

𝒥asmine turned on her blinker and waited in the turn lane for an opportunity to pull into her apartment complex.

"Come ON!" she complained with increasing frustration. It figured everyone decided to stretch out all across the road when she wanted to make a turn. As soon as she saw the slightest opening, she darted into the parking lot.

Once she pulled into her spot, she sat in her car for a minute, looking toward the stairs leading up to her apartment. She groaned into her hands; she was too exhausted and angry to move. *I should be with Shawn right now. We should be cuddling together on his couch watching a movie, stealing smiling glances at each other.*

Jasmine snorted to herself and rolled her eyes.

Not you, Jasmine. That's not for you, the voice replied.

She popped open her squeaky door and stepped out onto the cracked pavement. The cold night air streaming right through her thin nylons. A shiver went through her entire body.

"Why does it have to be so bone-chilling cold out here?" Jasmine mumbled under her breath, making her way to the car's trunk to retrieve her bags of groceries. Wobbling along the pavement, she was being careful where she stepped to keep her heels from falling in a crack. She then noticed a car parked a few spaces down, which belonged to an empty apartment. Jasmine moved her jaw with curiosity. *I could swear that's the old guy's car—the man from the supermarket. I guess he beats having a loud, obnoxious uni student for a neighbor,* she decided, as she clutched her belongings and shut the trunk.

She carefully walked across the old cracked pavement to the cement staircase.

I don't feel like walking up all these stairs right now. Not when my feet are killing me. Jasmine winced with each step she took.

Cute is about all these shoes have going for them.

As she neared the top of the third flight of stairs, her cell phone began to ring.

Is it Shawn? she wondered. *He changed his mind?* "I was just teasing about getting back with Sheila. It's you I want."

Who are you trying to kid? Jasmine smirked at the ridiculous thought.

Her phone continued ringing.

Who is calling me this time of night?

Maybe it's Brett? Maybe he's got some good news from the presentation?

Jasmine picked up her pace, trying to reach her door, unlock it, and set her groceries down inside, in time to reach for her phone before missing the call. She shifted all the heavy grocery bags into one arm, fumbling one-handedly through her purse for her key.

She reached her door at the end of the third ring. She knew there were only seconds between her and potential good news on the other end of the phone line, and she wanted to be able to answer to show her dedication to the new tasks she would be handling if a new position opened up for her.

Just as she managed to grab the key from her purse, one of the grocery bags started to slip out of her grasp.

Not now, she groaned.

Not knowing which one it was, Jasmine frantically tried to clench all the bags tighter as she turned the doorknob.

Yet, the bag slipped further.

Another ring ended.

She didn't have time to try to catch the falling bag, so she clenched her entire grip tighter, hoping she was grasping them all in the right places as she opened her apartment door.

Unfortunately, she wasn't. The slipping bag fell to the cement, and she heard something crack. Not having time to think about it, she practically dropped her other things onto the carpeted floor of her apartment to freely reach for her phone before it stopped ringing.

"Hello?" Jasmine answered frantically, relieved to be able to show her dedication.

"Happy birthday, Jasmine," said a woman's voice on the other end.

Jasmine lowered her head in disappointment and clawed at the back of her neck in frustration.

"Hi, Mom," she said quickly and emotionlessly, as she looked out the door of her apartment toward the groceries on the ground. Purple juice seeped from the white plastic bag.

"I hope you've had a good day," her mom quietly said.

Jasmine huffed. "It's … been wonderful," she fibbed.

"I'm sorry I didn't call sooner."

Jasmine pursed her lips and bit the inside of her cheek.

This gets more and more painful every year.

"Didn't bother me one way or the other."

There was a long pause on the other end of the line, then the silence was interrupted by her mother's voice. "I've been thinking about you all day." There was another pause, and what sounded like a shortness of breath. "I think about you a lot, Jasmine. How have you been?"

Jasmine shrugged her shoulders. "Busy."

"You're always so busy."

Yeah, so why don't we cut the crap and just hang up?

"Were you able to do anything special for your birthday?"

Jasmine examined the purple juice that was beginning to seep down the cement hallway. "Yes."

"Good."

More awkward silence. Again, Jasmine thought she heard a strain in her mother's breathing.

"I miss you ... I heard Megan had her baby."

What the heck do I care about Megan? I haven't seen her in years.

"Megan is such a sweet girl. I used to love watching you two play together. I remember when you girls met in kindergarten and ..."

"Yeah, well, that was a long time ago, Mom," Jasmine interrupted. "Thanks for calling. I have to get going." She was still peeking out the door and watching the purple juice making an even bigger mess.

"Is something bothering you, Jasmine?" her mother pestered.

"No, Mom, nothing is bothering me."

"Well, I do have one question to ask you before you get off the phone." Her mother's voice was timid.

Jasmine said nothing. She sat on the other end of the phone, oddly curious about what the question could be.

"I would like ..." her mother coughed, "for you to come for a visit."

"I'm busy, Mom," she blurted out.

"I know you're busy, Jasmine, but I haven't seen you in seven years."

Jasmine took a deep breath. "Christmas sales don't slow down once Christmas is over, you know. We're busy straight through to spring. I can't take off work right now."

Her mom was quiet for a moment. "I'm not asking you to come right this second. I'd like for all of us to get together the weekend of April 2nd."

Jasmine sighed out of relief. She knew she had a way out now, but she let her mother finish pleading her case anyway.

"That's almost three months away. I thought that would be enough time for you to plan to take a few days off."

"I can't, Mom."

"I thought we could all get together and clean out the attic," she continued. "You have some things in there, and I thought it would be fun to go through everything together, as a family."

"I can't, Mom," Jasmine asserted, "that's the day of my marathon. And there's no way I'm missing that."

"You didn't tell me you were running a marathon! Good for you. What about the week after?"

"It's not gonna work out. Just throw my stuff away. I don't want or need it anyway."

"Is there another day you'd like to come visit?"

"Mom, if I haven't made it clear, I really don't want to come home for a visit, okay? I don't want you, Dad, and Sara lecturing me on how I need to 'get married and settle down' again. Give me the speech over the phone. It's cheaper for everybody that way."

Her mother took a slow deep breath and let it out into the phone speaker. Apparently not wanting to let her daughter go just yet, she asked, "Did you take some time for yourself today?"

"I did, Mom," she answered, her irritation increasing.

"That's good. I'm praying for you, Jasmine."

"Praying for what exactly, Mom? Please enlighten me on exactly what you're praying for."

She heard her mother swallow. "I'm praying you'll let God use you, Jasmine."

"Use me?!" Her neck muscles strained. "You've got to be kidding me, Mom. When are you guys going to walk away from that nonsense? Do me a favor and stop praying for me. God. Hates. Me." There was both anger and bitterness in her voice.

Before she could continue, her mother cut in. "He doesn't hate you, Jasmine. Don't *say* that. He loves you. You know that."

"Loves me!" She laughed with an edge. "Loves me? And how exactly should I *know* that? Please, clue me in!"

"He loves you, Jasmine," was her mother's only response.

Jasmine couldn't hold back any longer. "You know what, Mom? I'm not sure what pill you swallowed and when, but I'll let you in on a little secret. God loves only a chosen few. And how to get into that group of chosen few is for only The Guy to know. For the rest of us unfortunate souls, He dangles us on a string and plays with our lives. It's about time you and Dad get your heads out of the sand."

"Are you reading your Bible, Jasmine? Are you praying?"

Jasmine could hardly contain herself. "Are you kidding me right now, Mom?" she asked in disbelief. "What exactly are you advising me to do? Go crawling to God on my hands and knees like you did, begging Him to allow me to be one of the 'chosen few'? Begging him to 'spare my life'?" With increasing bitter passion, Jasmine continued.

"You want me to sacrifice *everything* I have *ever* wanted and cared for, all my hopes and dreams, like you did? For what? So God can feel satisfied having squashed another human soul?"

Silence hung between them.

"Not *me*. Not *ever*. I *refuse*. I hate God. Don't threaten me with your God *ever again*." She found herself pointing at the phone with her forefinger. "If you ever so much as mention His name to me, I swear, I'll never speak to you again."

Jasmine heard a sniffle on the other end of the line. She knew she'd said too much, but she was unwilling to apologize. It felt freeing to finally put a voice to the way she'd felt about God all these years. She only wished the rest of her family were around to hear it as well.

"Goodbye, Jasmine," was all her mother said.

Jasmine hung up the phone.

She looked at the purple juice on the cement hallway outside. Instead of cleaning it up, she picked up the plastic bag that held the broken bottle and shut the door.

~ SIX ~

It was a crisp cold morning, typical for the middle of January in Maryland. Jasmine's hands fumbled numbly as she took out her key from the side pocket of her running tights and unlocked the door. She blew warm air on her hands as she walked over to the refrigerator and unhooked the pen from its spot. She marked an X through January 16.

"Eleven miles," she said, feeling proud of herself. She took a minute to look through the pages of the calendar.

"Five weeks in and already running long distances. I can't wait for it to get warmer."

Jasmine returned the pen and opened the freezer.

She growled. "I have got to get back to the grocery store. I literally have no ingredients left." She threw in what she could scrounge up, pushed the button on the Vitamix, and turned the dial to ten.

As she stood watching her fruit puree, she deeply inhaled. It had been exactly a full week since her birthday and the phone call with her mother, yet she still couldn't shake the last words she had fired to her mom. Bitterness from her childhood had wracked her brain all week. And, here it was, happening again. She stopped the Vitamix, poured the smoothie into a large clear glass, and sat down at the table.

How is it fair that You get so much control? she asked God bitterly.

You've managed to sabotage almost every single area of my life and there's nothing I can do about it.

"Some loving God *that* is," she fumed.

Jasmine took a gulp of her smoothie, as if taking out her anger on it. She glanced at her shelf, full of photography books, and slammed the glass on the table.

"Thanks, God," she said. "I bet You and Your angel minions are happy now, huh?"

She imagined God, sitting up in heaven. "Let's toy with Jasmine" He might be saying.

Oh, I have a good idea, she mimicked God. *Let's give that Jasmine girl a love for photography and then I'll allow it to cause a rift in her family because nobody understands her desire to be an optical engineer. I'll send her off to one of the best photography schools in the country, right there near her hometown. It will almost completely drain her of all her money, so she has to drive around in a piece-of-crap car.*

In her mind, Jasmine could hear the angels jeer. *Oh, good one!*

God chimed back in. *How about this one: I'll give her a killer offer twelve hours away from the school she graduates from in Arizona, then place her in housing that doesn't allow animals, so she'll have to choose between living her passion and re-homing her precious cat before she leaves.*

Yes! Yes! the angels chimed.

I'm not done yet, God continued. *When she gets to Maryland, the job won't be what she was promised, and it will fall through anyway. But she'll be stuck there, twelve hours away from everything and everybody she knows, and unable to get back home.*

The angels cheered and high-fived one another.

God went on. *I'll give her a sales job so she at least has a little something going for her, and then, as soon as she decides to trust someone again, I'll send Shawn back to his ex-girlfriend.*

Oh, perfect! exclaimed an angel. *And, what are the options if she comes crawling back to You on her hands and knees?*

I made her stubborn. She won't do it, God replied, with a victorious smile on His face.

Jasmine sat with her elbows on the small kitchen table, both her hands holding the glass tightly. She pursed her lips at the thought of God even having control of her stubbornness, yet, there she was, helpless and unable to do a thing about it.

We are right where God wants us to be. She heard the voice of her Sunday church teacher.

"Yes, I am, aren't I!" She laughed bitterly. "I am *exactly* where God wants me to be." Her nostrils flared and jaw tightened as she continued examining her situation. "I'm rotting away in this tiny apartment with no friends, no one to trust, not important or meaningful to anyone, and everything against me."

She finished the last swallow of her smoothie. "And, I'm too stubborn to do a single blasted thing about it."

Jasmine remained at the table, breathing heavily. When she finally stood up to rinse out her glass at the sink, a chill passed through her body. The sweat from her morning run had grown cold. She shivered, feeling more alone than ever.

Slowly, she angrily made her way to her bedroom. As she opened the closet to find something warm to wear, she caught a glimpse of herself in the mirror on the back of the door. She stepped over to it and stood there, bitterly examining herself in a way that she never had before.

Who are you? she questioned as she stared. *How is it that you can look yourself in the mirror every single day but never really see yourself?*

Jasmine examined her face critically. She let her hand run down her jawline, feeling her skin. She was looking at that complete stranger again—the one with cold, dark, bitter eyes. *Was that because she was so scared, so lost?* As she continued staring, she saw a young girl sitting in a cage. She looked more closely. To her surprise, she realized that the girl's face was the face of the one she'd seen in the grocery store parking lot.

As she lost herself in the image of that young girl, Jasmine saw her stand up and hold out her hand, as if she was asking for help. She watched the girl rattle the bars, then sit back down in defeat. The little girl curled up and placed her head in the pit of her arm.

Jasmine's eyes watered, and a tear ran down her cheek. She didn't budge, just stared at this poor lost girl who had the tiniest flicker of hope in her eyes. She wanted to reach out to rescue her. She wanted to hold her tight. She wanted to tell her that everything was going to be okay, but she couldn't open her mouth to speak. She could only stare without moving a muscle.

For as long as I can remember, I have been running from the big, scary, mean Man in the Clouds, Jasmine thought. *But I'm screwed. No matter how I go about it, I will NEVER be in control. I will NEVER have a say in how my life operates.*

More tears now trickled down her face.

Jasmine felt her jaw stiffen. She continued to stare, unwilling to break their gaze, not wanting to lose the girl.

How's that for fair?

God has you where He wants you, she recalled. Her jaw tightened even more, and her teeth clenched. She angrily squinted her eyes, still staring in the mirror. She began losing sight of the little girl. She pursed her lips in a last attempt to keep her from disappearing, but it was no use. Jasmine burst into miserable, defeated tears. She squeezed her eyes shut and let them flow.

I've been screwed from the get-go, she thought. *What a loving, caring, kind God You are.*

Jasmine stepped away from the mirror feeling even more helpless and hopeless than ever. "What's the point?" *Why bother when I'll just be met with whatever fate is destined for me, with or without my consent?*

Jasmine stepped back in front of her closet. None of her clothes looked worth wearing anymore. She lethargically pulled out a pair of jeans, a black T-shirt, and an oversized sweater. She took her scheduled runner's lunch, which she had prepared the night before, from the refrigerator, then headed out the door.

"Time to convince more people into buying luxurious wallpaper," she complained.

Jasmine stepped out of her door, locking it behind her. She picked up her foot to move down the hallway to the stairs. The bottom of her shoe stuck to the once-purple, now-brown sticky juice that had dried in a trail.

She shivered in the bone-chilling cold as she walked toward her car. The forecast had mentioned snow. She looked up into the sky. *It smells like it*, she noticed.

Pulling into the parking lot at work, she took her usual left turn to get to the back of the lot. As she drove down the lane, she spotted Shawn walking toward the building. There was no way to avoid him. What used to be a friendly wave and a full-faced smile was now a slight nod and a half smile. The past week had been awkward, to say the least. Every time she saw him, she imagined Sheila wrapped in his strong masculine arms. She imagined the sweet light kisses and giggles they would exchange. She imagined the secrets they'd have between them. She was jealous that Sheila could look forward to cuddling up with a man and feeling safe against the world, while she would be here, alone again.

She watched him disappear inside. It hurt.

Jasmine checked her makeup in the rearview mirror before she started the cold trek to the building. *At least he'll be in the elevator by the time I get inside*, she reasoned.

She walked through the sliding glass doors with her head down, in her own world.

"Good morning, Jasmine," she heard a quiet voice call out.

Startled, she looked up at Shawn with a surprised look on her face. "Oh, hi!" she said, with a questioning look in her eyes.

"I saw your car pull in, so I waited here for you." They walked toward the elevator without saying another word. The elevator door closed on just the two of them.

"What's going on, Jas?" he asked, with a puppy dog look on his face. "I don't like to see my best friend this way. You've been avoiding me ever since we went out to celebrate your big win last week."

Jasmine couldn't speak.

"Are you *that* upset that I'm leaving?"

If you only knew. "The world doesn't revolve around you, Shawn," she retorted.

She took a deep breath, trying to ignore the thoughts that were swirling in her head.

The elevator dinged and the doors opened. Jasmine faintly smiled at him before heading to her cubicle in the opposite direction of Shawn's.

He followed her, then suggested, "Want to grab lunch with me this afternoon? Please?"

Those darn puppy-dog eyes, thought Jasmine. "I'm busy."

"In the breakroom?" he pleaded.

She sighed. "Sure."

He gave her a big smile and a cheesy thumbs-up.

Her heart ached. She half-smiled back, heartbroken that in a week, even this would be coming to an end.

As she neared her cubicle, she saw Brett walking away from it. He caught a glimpse of her out of the corner of his eye and turned back. "I just left you a note," he pointed, "Garrett wants to talk this afternoon." He winked mischievously to assure Jasmine that it was something good.

Forgetting her rotten morning, and forgetting, at least for a moment, that Shawn was leaving, Jasmine's face lit up. "Really?" she asked eagerly, though she was afraid to inquire any further. She gave Brett a thumbs-up to show her appreciation and dedication as he straightened his tie and turned to walk away.

"Promotion, here we come!" she whispered excitedly, then she put her fists together and squeezed them.

❦

Jasmine finished her morning assignments and headed to the breakroom to join Shawn for lunch. She walked into the room and looked around for him. "Looking for me?" he asked from the doorway behind her. Her heart skipped a beat at the grin on his face. *I'm going to miss that smile*, she pined secretly.

"You look like you're in a better mood now," he commented, as he pointed his head in the direction of an available table.

"Brett stopped by my desk this morning. He said Garrett wants to talk."

"I hope you're not surprised!" Shawn commented.

Jasmine beamed, indicating her excitement.

"Still eating healthy, I see." He said, pointing to her runner's lunch.

"This is Week five."

"Out of sixteen, right?" asked Shawn.

Jasmine rolled her eyes. "Yes, you already know that. The race is on April 2nd, and you're leaving me high and dry, remember?" She tried to keep the disappointment out of her voice. "There won't be anyone to cheer me on," she added to mask it.

Shawn lowered his gaze to her. "You can handle yourself, you feisty woman." He encouraged, as he lightly punched her in the arm.

Jasmine shrugged her shoulders, grateful for the compliment, but feeling like her world was falling apart.

"Are you all packed up?"

"Oh definitely not," he responded. "I've got way more junk than I care to admit." He kept talking, but Jasmine didn't hear a word of what he was saying. She gazed into his eyes, half hoping he would notice how alone and scared she was.

As she did, she was suddenly startled when she opened her eyes only to see the young girl she'd seen that morning looking back at her from the mirror. That girl was still sitting in her cage, with an expression of animosity on her face. The hope that had been there earlier was gone, and in its place was hatred and disgust. With icy-cold eyes and pursed lips, the little girl firmly shook her head. Jasmine blinked, not sure what she had just seen.

Shawn gave her a funny look and touched her arm. "Are you okay, Jasmine?" There was concern in his voice.

"I'm fine," she said emotionlessly, half-staring off into space for a moment. "I'm fine," she again responded, nodding her head ever so slightly up and down. "I'm so happy for you, Shawn," she shared, knowing this was the end, acknowledging she had no chance. "We've talked about getting out of here and finding 'real' jobs for years, and now God has decided He's ready for you to leave."

"What's that supposed to mean?" Shawn asked, with a confused look on his face.

Jasmine looked down at the table. "Nothing. Never mind."

It was awkward between them again as they cleaned up their table.

"Jas, don't do this to me," he pleaded. He finally must have noticed the tears in her eyes. "You're going to be fine. You're always so busy and have so much going for you."

Jasmine inhaled sharply as Shawn continued talking.

"For eight years, you've shown everyone your amazing work ethic, and it's finally paying off. You're having a meeting with Garrett! Garrett, Jasmine! Do you know how many people are jealous of you right now?"

She accepted the compliment.

"You have so much going for you. You're climbing the ladder here. I'm betting that before you know it, you'll be the head of Corporate Client Sales. You single-handedly landed Johns Hopkins, Jas. Do you know how amazing that is?"

"Well, I didn't actually *land* them yet, I just got our foot in the door."

"Same thing. And, you're running a marathon!"

As she stood up from the table, she commented, "I'm happy for you, Shawn. I wish you the best."

She lightly punched his strong arm, then walked toward the door without looking back.

⌒ SEVEN ⌒

*J*asmine held her breath with a clenched jaw and hit Send. The screen went blank. Nervous excitement filled her body as she confirmed it; the email was there, with all the others she'd ever sent.

There it was. All done.

A make or break for my career, she thought to herself, as she crossed her fingers.

I can't wait till Garrett sees it. She was giddy with excitement.

She checked her watch, then started to pack her bag. *And, I'm done early!*

Brett rounded the corner. "Jasmine! The queen!" he emphasized, holding out his hand so she could high-five him. "You," his index finger pointing at her, "are on fire!"

"Thank you," she said, with a glowing appreciation on her face.

"From what I saw, the proposal you emailed us looks *fabuloso*. How are you celebrating tonight?"

She held up a piece of paper. "Grocery shopping."

Brett drew his eyebrows together. "Seriously, take some time to congratulate yourself. You're doing an amazing job, and we need you performing at your best."

"You know what?" she perked up, tilting her head, "I think I will. After I shop, I'll complete a bit of food prep and settle down in my recliner to watch the snow fall while I watch *Inside Job*."

"Ah, I love that show! But don't celebrate too long. We expect you back here bright and early tomorrow morning."

Jasmine raised her eyebrows, feeling controlled. "I'll be here."

"Atta girl!" Brett winked at her, then walked away.

❧

Jasmine turned up the radio in her car.

"We'll have high winds with temperatures in the low thirties for tonight. It would be a good idea to clear off the road as much as possible and enjoy the snow from inside."

"Finally some snow!" she exclaimed, using her shoulders to dance in her seat. "Today hasn't turned out so bad after all," she said with a grin.

As she left the supermarket, the wet chill in the air hit her. She stopped to pull her wooly belted coat tighter, holding her arms in close and putting her head down. She pushed her grocery cart faster and picked up her pace. The wind whipped fast and fierce. Snuggling with her special blanket and watching her favorite TV show tonight was sounding even more pleasant.

She finished packing the last of her groceries in the small trunk of her car and looked up at the sky. *That does not look friendly*, she noted, as she half ran to place her cart in the return.

It shouldn't take me but thirty minutes to get home, she thought as she calculated her odds of beating the storm. She couldn't spend another second on the thought, though, as another gust of wind hit her. She returned the cart as quickly as possible, then half walked and was half pushed by the wind back to her car.

As Jasmine pulled out of the store's lot, she recalled the last few episodes of *Inside Job*, wanting to catch herself up before watching more episodes. *Gosh, it's been weeks*, she thought to herself, remembering where she'd left off. The scenes started coming back to her. "Oh yeah," she said out loud, as she thought of Jones, a skilled and intelligent thief who had stolen a piece of art that was now being held hostage by his "friend," a fellow con man. She would've gone about the theft entirely differently.

Why didn't he think to do it that *way? It would have saved him so much trouble, and he wouldn't be held hostage right now.* She barreled down Highway 295, recalling details of the show.

Suddenly, she saw brake lights in front of her. Without warning, all the traffic, and Jasmine had to swerve, moving to the shoulder to miss hitting the car in front of her. She closed her eyes, waiting for the sound of a crunch. After a few seconds, she slowly opened her eyes and let out a deep sigh—no crunch.

When she maneuvered back onto the highway, traffic had gone from a crawl to a stop.

"Oh come on," Jasmine complained. "Seriously?" She craned her neck, trying to see what had caused the sudden stop. All she could see was a long line of brake lights. With her memories of the show totally disrupted, she turned on the radio to hear the news. She flipped through the stations, waiting to find out what had happened on the road. Yet, nothing but commercials played, so she turned down the volume and glanced at the clock.

"Come on!" she groaned with an increasing impatience in her voice. She slapped the steering wheel with the palm of her hand, twice, then peered out the windshield again to see if there was any sign of what was going on ahead of her. Still nothing except brake lights.

I've been sitting here for almost five minutes!

Jasmine flipped her radio to an AM station in hopes of figuring out what the holdup was.

"We have an accident on the 295 heading east between Calumet and Fifth. A tractor trailer is blocking all lanes, and traffic is at a standstill."

"Are you serious!" she shouted with irritation as the news came through. "What the heck! Why don't people know how to drive? Oh. My. Gosh. I do not have time for this!"

She pinched her lips together, knowing she was going to be stuck in her car for a while. She exhaled a loud frustrated sigh, leaned back on her seat's headrest, and lightly bounced her head against it.

Ten minutes passed, and Jasmine still had no idea how much longer she was going to have to sit here. She reached over to the passenger seat, deciding to attempt some research on the Hyatt project. With her computer half out of her bag, she changed her mind and replaced it. *I don't want to think about work right now. I want to be home, relaxing, and getting ready for the snowfall while I watch my favorite show!*

"Why does this stuff *always* happen to me?" Jasmine groaned out loud.

"Why *me* God?? Why can't You let me have just one evening of relaxation? Is that too much to ask?"

There was no response. Only a drop of water on her windshield, which interrupted her thoughts. "No!" Jasmine raised her voice, with increased annoyance. "Come on!!"

She looked at the time. It was 5:23. Almost thirty minutes had passed, and the sun had almost completely set.

So much for getting off of work early.

Jasmine strained her neck to look out the window in another attempt to see what was going on ahead of her. Nothing.

She slapped the palm of her hand against the steering wheel again in frustrated anger, thinking about the groceries sitting in the trunk of her car. A few more drops fell onto the windshield.

"That doesn't look like snow," Jasmine commented, aggravated. She sat forward to look up at the sky through the windshield. More drops descended. "This is NOT SNOW!" She screamed and pounded the steering wheel. "This is not snow!" she repeated through clenched teeth. "This was supposed to be snow. I'm *sick* of rain!"

Jasmine's complaints were interrupted by the ringing of her cell phone. She reached into her purse for the phone, then glanced at the caller.

She held the phone in confusion. "Sara?" she gasped, still letting it ring. *Why would* she *be calling me?*

Jasmine stared at the phone until the screen read "1 missed call." Then she threw it on the passenger seat, rolling her eyes disgustedly as she assumed she knew exactly why her sister was calling her.

"Did Mommy get her feelings hurt and tattle to perfect little Sara?" Jasmine mocked in disgust. She rolled her eyes again at how pathetic this was. "Grow up, you bunch of biddies."

The rain was coming down more steadily now, and it was completely dark when Jasmine finally saw the car in front of her inch forward.

"It's about time," she declared and breathed deeply. "Now move, people!"

She inched her way forward as three lanes of traffic and a merging highway were being channeled into one lane. She stayed inches from the bumper in front of her to ensure that no one could squeeze in between.

Finally, an entire hour after she left the grocery store, Jasmine passed the scene of the accident. The rain was coming down even harder now, making it difficult to see what had actually happened. Still, she squinted and gawked out the window. There were police, several emergency vehicles, and some people about, and she saw a vehicle turned on its side in a ditch. "That's what you get when you don't know how to drive," she muttered angrily as she drove past. "Take some lessons before you get on the road."

When she had passed the wreck and was driving at normal speed, the rain was coming down harder and heavier, making it even more difficult to see. It had begun to sleet, and Jasmine felt the wind grow increasingly stronger. She tried to turn up her wipers, but they were already on full blast.

"This is so freakin' aggravating! I should be inside my warm apartment, in my pajamas, with my groceries put away, food prep finished, a hot chocolate and remote in hand, getting ready to push 'Play' on Season Two, Episode Four. But no, not Jasmine! That would be too much of a treat, wouldn't it, God? Apparently, Jasmine doesn't deserve a treat today, does she?"

As she pulled into the apartment parking lot, the rain and sleet were coming down so hard that it was virtually impossible to see where she was going. She managed to make it to her parking spot and now sat in her car, staring up at her third-floor window where she could just see the faintest light from a small table lamp. Jasmine wondered what the heck she should do.

Do I stay here till the downpour stops? With my luck, it will rain all night, she complained, as her neck muscles tensed.

She sat for a few more minutes, staring out at the hostile rain, not wanting to go out in the storm. Her mind drifted to the last time she had experienced weather like this. She was on her pink bike, riding as fast as she could, looking for her mother who had been out taking a walk and was caught in the sudden downpour. Her head was down to keep the rain from getting into her eyes. Off in the distance, she spotted her mom, walking as fast as she could to get home. Jasmine was only twelve years old and wanted to rescue her mom. She smiled when she saw her and pedaled even harder, feeling every bit like Superwoman. Jasmine decided she would ride to her mom, give her the bike, and walk home in her place. This act of selfless love was sure to show her mother how much she loved her. When Jasmine reached her mom, however, she was met with a harsh tone she couldn't quite make out due to the pounding of the rain.

"What?" Jasmine shouted through the downpour.

"Go home! What in the world are you doing?" her mother shouted at her.

"I brought you the bike so you could get home faster," Jasmine yelled, suddenly realizing the absurdity of the idea.

"Go home right now, Jasmine!" Her mom pointed her finger toward the house. "Does Dad know you're out here?"

"No." Jasmine shook her head slowly, looking at her mother in a way she never had before. She turned her bike around toward home. She'd never been so crushed and humiliated in all her life.

Tears streamed down her face. *What did I do wrong? I was just trying to help! Why does Mom hate me so much?*

Jasmine felt a cry that originated from deep inside her. It hurt. All at once, she wasn't in a hurry to get home. She slowly pedaled up the small hill feeling alone, uncared for, and unwanted. "I've always been in the way," she yelled out to the rain. "I've always been Stupid Jasmine. Why did I think this was a good idea?"

Back in the present, Jasmine didn't want to remember any more of that story. She decided that getting out of the car and facing the freezing rain would be more pleasurable than reliving that stupid idea to rescue her mom. Eighteen years later, it still cut deep, as if it had just happened yesterday. She sniffed, then dabbed each eye with a coat sleeve.

The rain was pelting the car so loudly that Jasmine could hardly hear herself think. Reaching over to the passenger seat, she zipped up her purse to at least keep the contents inside it dry and pulled her leather computer bag closer. She counted to five, then popped open her car door, hurried out, and ran to the trunk with her head down. Too bad her coat didn't have a hood. She muttered something not worth repeating under her breath while she fought to insert the key and unlock the trunk.

Thrusting her work bags behind her, she fumbled through the trunk, frantically loading as many of the plastic-handled supermarket bags onto her arm as she could. There wasn't any way to avoid getting soaking wet.

It figures, she grumbled, *the one freakin' day I decide to buy an insane amount of groceries it has to dump buckets of rain.*

Feeling immense frustration, Jasmine stubbornly insisted to herself that she was going to get every single one of these groceries upstairs in one trip.

As she grabbed the last bag and tried to straighten up, she seemed to be leaning to one side. Quickly, she decided to balance herself by grabbing the milk, the laundry detergent, and the toilet paper with her other hand. For a second, she considered leaving the toilet paper in the trunk, but that would be letting the rain beat her. Everything was going inside, in one trip. As she leaned down to punch a finger-size hole in the plastic of the toilet paper package, her leather bag slipped from her shoulder and hit the mass of grocery bags she'd looped on her right arm. She swore at the top of her lungs to the rain.

She managed to pick up the toilet paper package with one finger and stood up, balancing her shoulder bag and lifting everything up and out of the trunk at once. The sleet and rain pelted her face. Her arms were so full now that she couldn't shut the trunk. Thinking quickly despite the downpour, Jasmine maneuvered the bags and lifted her shoulders, desperately using her body and the weight of the grocery bags to pull down the trunk to a point where she could grab and finish shutting it. Somehow it worked, though it shifted about twenty pounds of groceries down to her wrist.

Jasmine proceeded to trek across the parking lot. At this point, her only goal was to get to the stairway and out of the frigid rain. Yet, on her first step, the heavy bags began to slip even further down her wrist.

She realized almost immediately her plan wasn't a good idea. Her only hope was to walk faster and hope that she made it to the stairwell so she could at least escape the rain and sleet. She picked up her pace, leaning forward, splashing through deep puddles filled with water all over the parking lot.

"This is absolutely ridiculous!" she yelled loudly, looking up to the sky as the rain pelted her face.

"I hate You!" she screamed. Jasmine was losing her grip on the bags as well as her sanity. She picked up her pace, splashing and half running for shelter.

"Can I help you, ma'am?" a voice called out to her.

Without knowing who was talking to her, she allowed someone to prop up the mass of grocery bags that were sliding off the soaking-wet wrist of her coat, and the two of them finished the dash to the stairs together.

Once they were under the shelter of the stair roofing, the man began untangling the bags from Jasmine's arm. As he neared the last one, he said kindly, "That was quite impressive! How in the world did you manage it?" Then he chuckled.

I don't find this at all amusing, and I'm in no mood for small talk, she thought. She barely managed a polite smile.

"Why don't we rearrange the bags so we're both carrying half of them?"

Still Jasmine said nothing, but this time she managed to nod her head.

"What apartment are you headed to?"

"Three B," she answered, trying to hide her immense embarrassment.

"All the way on the top? Nice!"

They headed up the stairs without saying another word. As Jasmine reached the first landing and turned to start up the second flight of stairs, she caught a better look at the man who was helping her, then did a double take.

I feel like I've seen this guy before. She wracked her brain, trying to figure out where. As she rounded the second landing, she got a better glimpse of him.

Yes! she deciphered. *I knew I recognized him. It's that old man I saw at the grocery store parking lot.* That *was* his car she'd seen in the recently used spot. He still had a contented smile on his face and walked up the stairs carrying half her groceries as if he hadn't a care in the world.

As they reached the third landing and headed toward Jasmine's door, the man spoke again. "It must be nice to live on the top floor."

Confused, Jasmine blurted out, "What in the world could possibly be nice about living on the third floor?"

"Well, other than not having to hear anyone living above you," he chuckled again, "the exercise! Stair climbing is arguably one of the healthiest and most beneficial things you can do to exercise your brain."

Jasmine laughed, but she was afraid the laugh sounded more nasty than amused.

"Stair climbing is the safest and most efficient way to exercise multiple muscle groups at the same time," he added, still exhibiting that same smile.

"I *run* for exercise," defended Jasmine. She didn't mean to be rude exactly, but she was still just as annoyed as she'd been since she drove away from the supermarket. She set down her bags of groceries so she could unzip her wet purse and reach in for her key.

"Good for you!" he said. "Running is a stellar form of exercise, too." He waited as she opened her door. "But stair climbing engages more muscles than either walking or running. Running is great for *leg* exercise, but stair climbing strengthens your leg muscles, while simultaneously providing a thorough workout for your glutes, quads, and hamstrings."

He didn't look like he was the exercise type, so Jasmine felt safe in responding, "You've watched too many TV commercials, old man." She turned her back to him before she rolled her eyes, then pushed open the door.

"When you climb stairs," he continued, ignoring her snide remark, "your heart rate goes up, and when your heart rate goes up, your heart pumps more blood to your whole body. Hence the reason it's one of the healthiest and most beneficial things you can do for that precious brain of yours." As he finished that last sentence, he winked at her, just the way her grandpa used to when he was proud of her for some reason.

Jasmine raised a brow at this clearly crazy old man.

"You can leave the groceries there," she instructed, pointing to the cement outside her door.

"Climbing stairs is good for your balance too," he concluded as he lowered the bags to the ground.

"Exercise or no exercise, there's nothing good about having to lug my entire existence up to the third floor every day. This is the worst place I've ever lived."

"You get *exactly* what you focus on" was his reply to her complaining.

Jasmine raised an eyebrow, informing him that she didn't care about his opinion and had no idea why he'd said what he had.

"Your brain is an amazing piece of technology, and it focuses exactly on what you tell it to. It goes and finds all the evidence you need to support that thing, that belief. If you believe there's nothing good about living on the third floor, your brain will find all the evidence it needs to support that belief."

You clearly have nothing to do with yourself, thought Jasmine, still standing in her doorway but wanting to get her things inside and say goodbye.

"Thank you for your help," she said, donning an artificial smile and letting him know it was time for him to go.

"Can I help you with anything else?" the old man asked kindly.

"No, thank you," she said snarkily, closing the door behind her.

Jasmine was completely exhausted by the time she had gotten everything into her apartment. She looked at the pile of wet plastic bags that surrounded her kitchen table. It was already late into the evening. She now had to get out of her wet clothes and shower, as well as dry off her purse and leather computer bag, on top of everything else she had planned on doing. Discouraged and sad, she decided there would be no food prepping tonight, nor any snuggling down with her blanket, hot chocolate, snow, and her favorite show. A lump was caught in her throat. She wasn't sure whether to break down and cry, or try to ignore the situation.

As she put away the groceries, she found herself thinking about the old man. It seemed strange that he was still around. She wondered who he was, and why he was out in the rain.

Something felt different about him. He seemed like an intelligent, kind person, but that didn't fit the persona of someone who lived in this part of town. She was grateful for his help and felt bad now that she wasn't more friendly to him.

Jasmine finished putting away the last of the groceries and picked up her purse to dry it off. As she stood at the sink, she looked out the window at the nasty weather, imagining how pretty snow would look right now. She inhaled deeply, then headed to her bedroom to change out of her wet cold clothes and take a shower.

By the time Jasmine was finished showering, she had lost her appetite along with her desire to watch TV. She needed to get up early to go on her morning run before work anyway. She looked at her comfy chair and decided she would have to wait for another day.

⌒ EIGHT ⌒

*J*asmine laced up her running shoes and placed her key in the small pocket of her tights. As she walked down the stairs, she popped in her headphones and began flipping through the music in her phone.

What do I feel like listening to today? she thought as she scrolled through her playlists.

"*Rocky?* Yes," she said with a smile. "I could use some motivation today."

Jasmine walked to the back of the parking lot, where she carefully stepped through the wet bushes and tall grass that buffered the busy four-lane road separating the apartments from an alluring 700-acre park. She stepped over the guardrail and waited for a chance to dart across the traffic.

Once on the other side, she walked up the steep grassy hill to reach the sidewalk that circled the lake. *I wonder if this counts as stair climbing*, she mused, still slightly offended that the old man didn't think running was good enough exercise. She pushed the Play button and the loud rhythm of the song sounded in her ears. She turned the volume all the way up and began running, pumping her arms with confidence as she ran. Songs from the *Rocky* soundtrack always had a way of bringing her mojo back.

⁊⎯⎯⎯⎯⎯⎯⎯⎯◦

On her way to work, she couldn't help but think of Shawn. This was his last day of work at Nuevo Design. It had been hectic around work the last couple of days with his replacement arriving and settling in. Jasmine didn't like her. She sighed and turned on her blinker to change lanes.

As she pulled her car into the building lot, she spotted Scott, carrying in balloons for Shawn's going-away party. Instantly, she felt sad.

How in the world am I going to survive this place without him?

Upstairs, as she got off the elevator, she was greeted by Corbin, the administrative assistant, who called out her name so loudly it frightened her.

"I've got good news and bad news," he claimed, obviously feeling important. Without waiting for a reply, he continued, "The good news is, I found out what Karen was talking to Brett about the day of your big meeting ...." His voice trailed off.

Jasmine instantly stopped and squinted her eyes. "Tell me."

"The bad news is, it's not good."

"It's never good when it involves Karen."

"You're not going to believe this," he taunted, "She's asked to be part of the Johns Hopkins project with you," he said cautiously.

He must have been waiting for the explosion he got.

"Oh. My. Gosh. Are you freakin' kidding me? I knew that snake was up to no good. That's *my* project. She's not going to touch it!"

"What else do you know? What did Brett say? Why hasn't he said anything to me? I hope that little weasel doesn't think she's going to steal this promotion out from under me. Why can't she find her own projects? I am so sick of her piggybacking her success off *my* hard work. The race sponsorship was *my* idea. The artist outreach project was *my* idea. The Johns Hopkins project was *my* idea, and if she thinks for a single *second* she's going to pop in and try to take the reins for this, too, she has another thing coming." Jasmine hardly had taken a breath and was now practically panting.

Corbin shrugged. As Jasmine walked away from his cubicle, she muttered under her breath to herself on the way to her desk. "I'm sick of it. She's no different from Sara. Willing to cheat her way to success by riding on someone else's coattails."

Jasmine turned on her computer and went straight to her email as she did every morning. There was an email from Brett. She opened it and skimmed through it quickly, looking for anything about Karen. Nothing was mentioned exactly, but there was a meeting scheduled for February 5th, and Karen was cc'd on the email. So, what Corbin had told her was most likely true.

"That blasted snake," she whispered, as she opened her agenda book to begin her day. Then she glanced at the time and groaned. *I absolutely must finish all the showroom emails with the updated sample books before the end of today.* She felt swamped.

⟿

"Hey! Look who made it!" Shawn announced as Jasmine stepped into the breakroom.

"Wow, a lot of people are going to miss you," she commented as she looked around the room.

"Either that, or they want some cake."

"What's *she* doing here?" Jasmine questioned when she spotted Karen.

Shawn gave her a sad smile, then asked, "What's got you all worked up?"

"Her!" she pointed in disgust.

"Karen?"

"Do you even have to ask?"

Shawn sympathetically shifted his attention toward her. "Don't let her get into your head, Jas. You're too good for that."

"She's been in my head since the day she showed up here," she retorted, rolling her eyes. "I mean, seriously, of all the thousands of places in Baltimore where that woman could have chosen to work, she shows up *here*! It's just ... so infuriating."

"What is it with you two anyway?" he asked, stepping closer to her. "What *actually* happened?"

Jasmine gave him a look as if he should already know.

"Was it the Christmas party?"

"Yes, that too."

"When you overheard her talking about you in the bathroom?"

"Yes, but honestly, I knew from the first day I saw her that she was a snake. There's just something about her." Jasmine paused. "I could see right through her. She's had an eye on my position from the day she walked in the door."

"You have nothing to worry about, Jasmine. You're talented at what you do. Karen doesn't have a chance."

"She does, though! That's the thing! She's so sneaky. She's been piggybacking off my success from the very beginning. She's been a nightmare. And now, somehow, she got herself invited to the meeting Brett and I are having with Garrett about the Johns Hopkins project on the 5th! I'm telling you, she's awful!"

Shawn reached out and pulled Jasmine in close, while he jiggled her shoulder up and down.

"It's gonna be okay, Jas. I told you, she doesn't stand a chance."

"But what if she gets on the project *with me*?"

"She won't. But *if* she does, just assign her all the dirty work. Have her do all the MSDS sheets for every single product you show. Have her do every single measurement and price calculation. Have her look up and provide the fire ratings for every single product."

"That's for my team to do, though."

"Well, if she works her way onto your team, it's for Karen to do."

"I knew I liked you," she teased, feeling only slightly better.

"And, you'll have Brooke here," encouraged Shawn, referring to the new hire who was his replacement.

"I don't like her, either" Jasmine said coldly.

"Of course you don't!" Shawn teased, lightly backhanding her on the arm. "That's the Jasmine I know and love."

Jasmine shot him a side-eye, knowing it was the truth.

"What could possibly be wrong with Brooke? She seems nice," Shawn politely asked.

She shrugged her shoulders. "She's arrogant and thinks she knows everything."

"That's why they hired her, you nut!"

Jasmine didn't respond.

"You gonna have some cake?"

"I'll take it to my desk. I have a ton of work to get done today."

"Another reason why Karen doesn't stand a chance," he said with a grin.

Scott approached them. "We need to have going-away parties more often," he said to Shawn. "This cake is delicious!"

Jasmine felt a lump in her throat when she tried to laugh at Scott's lame joke. She felt tears coming on but managed to swallow them down. "I'm gonna head to my desk," she said, walking to the door.

Back at her desk, she opened her email draft for the New York City showroom, but she couldn't concentrate.

"Not another blasted headache," she mumbled as she reached into her drawer for two Excedrin.

⁓

"I knew you'd still be here."

Happy to hear Shawn's voice, Jasmine stopped typing and turned around to give him a sad smile as he slowly approached with his hands in his pockets.

"So, I guess this is goodbye?" she asked, standing up.

Shawn pulled her in close and gave her a side hug.

"You know I'm a little jealous, right?" she asked, stepping away from him.

"You don't need little ol' Shawn anymore," he reminded her. "You're one of the big dogs now, remember?"

Jasmine's smile was faint. "I know, Shawn, but I'm not even sure this is where I want to be. I want to be in camera design."

"Then go do camera design! Do what makes you happy, Jas."

"It doesn't work like that, Shawn. Not everybody has an uncle who'll provide them with their dream job."

"Yes, but everybody has a choice."

"Actually, no, they don't."

"What are you talking about? Everybody has choices, Jasmine."

"You may think you do, but God is in control of everything and everybody."

"What about the people who don't believe in God?"

"Doesn't matter. He still controls everything. We're all *exactly* where He wants us to be. He sees everything and knows everything."

"Sounds like you need a different religion," Shawn commented.

"I wish that was how it worked."

"Come here, girl," Shawn said, pulling her close. "I sure am going to miss you."

She heard his voice quiver and looked into his eyes. "You *are* going to miss me!" she said, noticing a drop of moisture in his eyes. "That tear is for me, right?"

"It is," he agreed, as he pulled her close one more time and squeezed her arm.

When he let go, she just looked at him, feeling sad, unable to say anything else. All she could do was take a deep breath and try to smile.

"I'm moving on, you're moving up," he said. "I'm happy for you, Jasmine. You've worked hard for this."

"So have you Shawn. I wish you all the best, and I'll miss you." *And I hope you and Sheila break up.*

"I'll miss you, too," Shawn responded, with a bittersweet smile on his face.

She watched him walk away. That lump was back in her throat and she shook her head while she watched him board the elevator. She waited until the elevator doors closed, then she sat down in her desk chair, placed her head on her arms, and wept.

∽ NINE ∾

It had been almost two weeks since Shawn left, and Jasmine's days were filled with research, scheduling presentations, and meetings that were focused on bringing Brooke up to speed on the finalization of the spring marketing plan.

Brooke was proving to be exactly the headache that Jasmine had envisioned her to be. Previously, she'd been the marketing specialist at two other design firms, so Brooke thought she knew everything about the industry. Yet, she was hesitant to go through with what the marketing team had already set in place, pitching ideas that were not only different from where Shawn and his team were going but in the opposite direction. She particularly expressed concern about being a presenting sponsor for the marathon.

That was the topic of today's meeting with Brooke and her marketing team. Jasmine was ready to review all the reasons why it was such a good idea. She and Shawn's team had worked long and hard on this project, and she was bound and determined not to let it go to waste.

As Brooke began the meeting, Jasmine's animosity toward her grew.

"We've already spent $13,000 on a campaign I see going nowhere," Brooke explained, as she pointed the cursor toward the diagrams on the Smart screen. "And, we'll have to spend a significant amount of money to complete the project. It seems to me this is a waste of an idea, and we ought to cut off the funding immediately so that we can focus our dollars on something we're positive will give us a return on our investment. I'll be meeting with Brett soon to discuss possible new ideas. Would anyone like to go first?"

"I would," Jasmine admitted, raising her hand, "but I have a question first. Have you ever actually run a race?"

"No, I haven't," Brooke replied, maintaining her composure.

"I have." Jasmine paused before continuing to make her point. "Plenty of prominent people attend packet pickup expos, and plenty of them are participants in marathons. This is an opportunity for Nuevo Design to gain exposure in a place that has virtually no competition."

Brooke blankly blinked at Jasmine. She had no rebuttal prepared, so Jasmine continued. "Our company will be on all of the event paraphernalia. The event shirts, the signage, the race bibs, the awards, everything. We will be able to include promotional items in the athlete packages. We will be in the press releases with all of the local media. The opportunities are endless. I have seen several presenting sponsors, and never have I seen a design company in attendance."

Brooke smirked. "There's a reason you've never seen one. Don't you think that if it was that good of an idea, some design company would have already figured it out? It's an expo center for people who run," she responded with a disparaging look on her face. "We're in the design space. We aren't selling T-shirts. Does anyone have any actual ideas?"

After the meeting ended, Jasmine returned to her desk, infuriated. *That arrogant woman has no idea what it takes to run a marathon, let alone how to market for a design company.*

She stared down at all her sticky notes and to-do list. *This is getting to be beyond what I can handle.* Jasmine had other things to do: contacting several more designers to review their work to decide whether they were good fits for Nuevo's brand, reaching out to corporate design firms, scheduling manufacture tours for the new hires, and more. In addition, tomorrow was the fifth, the day of the unusually scheduled meeting with Garrett, Brett, and a few others, including Karen.

I could use a drink right now, she thought, as she pressed her fingers to her head.

You're in Week eight, Jasmine, said the voice in her mind. *You absolutely are NOT having a drink.*

When she got home, she pulled out the alcohol she'd locked up when she started her marathon training. *It'll be just one night,* she tried justifying to herself. *One drink won't ruin my training.*

The next morning Jasmine woke up with a dizzy headache. *Why did I do this to myself? Can I afford to skip one day?* She walked painfully into the kitchen and looked at her running schedule. "Five miles today. You can do it, Jasmine," she said out loud, trying to psych herself up for it.

She took a deep breath, then changed into her running clothes right that second, before she could talk herself out of it.

Later, as she drove to work, she continued thinking about what that day's meeting would be about. Somehow, without even realizing it, Jasmine felt as if she was headed to the principal's office, like she had in high school. She remembered that like it was yesterday. She had been in ninth grade when she found a slip of paper in her locker about seeing the principal.

Pulling her car into the parking lot, she was brought back to her current situation.

Why do I feel so nervous? Am I afraid Garrett is going to pull this project from me? She backed into her usual space at the end of the lot, took a deep breath, and closed her eyes for a moment before gathering her things to exit the car. *Keep it together, Jasmine,* she coached herself as she walked to the entrance. *You've got this. You're good at what you do, and there's no reason Garrett would have anything negative to say about you.*

But even as she thought it, she didn't believe it. Something felt *off*.

Jasmine couldn't focus on her work. She had to wait until two o'clock for the meeting. No matter how much she tried to convince herself otherwise, she was extremely nervous.

"Jasmine?" Anna, her team member, was standing next to her desk.

"Yes, Anna, what is it? I'm very busy right now," she snapped.

"Here are the MSDS sheets."

"Take them to Sylvia, please. I won't be able to review them today. I have a lot on my plate right now, including a meeting with Garrett about the Johns Hopkins project."

As Anna walked away, Jasmine put her head in her hands. *What's wrong with me? Why am I so nervous?!*

Her mind continued wandering. *I've done everything in my power to research exactly what I need to*, she thought. *I've talked to Madelynn*, the design director for Johns Hopkins, *on the phone several times, and I've prepared the most amazing gift for her. I've dotted my i's and crossed my t's.*

And then, it was 2 p.m.

Jasmine walked down the hall feeling alone and scared. She hated not being able to hear a pep talk from Shawn, her only cheerleader. She walked into the conference room trying to act as cool as possible. She was thankful that the other big names who'd been there for the original presentation weren't going to be there now. Today, it was only Garrett, Brett, Derek, and Sylvia.

And Karen.

"Hi, Jasmine," Karen said with a didn't-think-you-were-going-to-get-ahead-of-me-did-you? smile.

Jasmine wanted to slap that smile off her face. Instead, she simply responded, "Hi. Karen," and gave her the most superficial, if-you-think-for-a-second-you're-going-to-take-this-from-me, you've-lost-your-dang-mind smile. She said what she needed to say to Karen with her eyes and energy.

"I'm so happy I was chosen to be part of this incredible opportunity with you," Karen replied, loudly enough for Garrett to hear.

"It's my pleasure," said Jasmine, flashing a more cunning smile, knowing what she had in mind for Karen.

Garrett didn't waste any time, and got right down to business. Looking down at the papers in front of him, he began, "Jasmine, your presentation last month was epic. You have a very thorough understanding of the products we offer. You spoke intelligently about each one in great detail. You've done an outstanding job researching this client. You know the ins and outs of the design team at Johns Hopkins. It seems you've studied everything you possibly could. You presented a full exposition to Madelynn, the design director for Johns Hopkins, and you've mapped out every possible question the team might ask, even the most tedious ones. You've done an outstanding job presenting the information, and we appreciate that. However ..."

I knew it! I knew there was going to be a "however." Instantly, Jasmine began breathing faster.

"There's something missing. Upon further examination, we observed there wasn't enough of the correct emotion in your pitch ..."

Garrett kept talking, but Jasmine felt a pit growing in her stomach. *Not enough emotion?* she thought, trying to pay attention but almost jumping up to speak. *We're putting ridiculously overpriced paper on a wall! How does that need more emotion?*

Instead, she forced herself to listen as Garrett continued. "We understand this is new territory for your team; we aren't familiar with cold-pitching large companies, but when cold-pitching a client who isn't actively seeking our services, it's vital to sell to the correct emotions."

Clearly not understanding what he was getting at, Jasmine continued to defend herself in her head.

"So," Garrett went on, smiling as he extended a welcoming gesture with his hand to Karen, "we've decided to bring Karen in on the project with you, and the two of you will pitch together on the Johns Hopkins campus. We feel that Karen can provide the emotional attachment to the products we offer that's needed. She has experience in understanding the emotional components in renovations."

Jasmine raised her eyebrows in disbelief, unable to say a word, then blinked her eyes several times, as she tried to wrap her head around what she'd just heard come out of Garrett's mouth.

Then, Garrett turned to speak to Karen.

For the moment, there was nothing Jasmine could do; all she knew was that Karen wasn't going to speak a word at her presentation. Not one solitary word.

Jasmine sat quietly in her chair at the conference table, looking calm as a cucumber on the outside, and knowing *exactly* what had happened. *She put the idea into Brett's head, saying who knew what, and Brett conveyed it to Garrett. Garrett has a right to be nervous*, thought Jasmine defensively. *His name and reputation are on the line here.*

After thanking Garrett and shaking his hand, illustrating with her artificial smile that implied she agreed with the plan, Jasmine stormed off down the hallway, completely ignoring Karen and the others in the room. *How did I know this was going to happen?*

How come this has never come up before? she questioned herself, fuming at her desk. *I'm really good at what I do, and no one has ever complained about me not speaking to the 'correct emotions' of the client. That is, until now.*

In a fit of desperation, she decided she was going to clear off everything on her agenda for the rest of the day, and however many other days she needed to, in order to figure out what encompassed speaking and selling to the "correct emotions."

Before she realized it, it was 8 p.m. *How is that possible? How is it 8 p.m. already?* Jasmine packed up her bags and headed out to her car, tired and hungry. *I guess it's drive-thru pizza*, she thought as she pulled out of the parking lot.

Later, as she sat alone and exhausted at her kitchen table, eating a pizza she knew she shouldn't be eating, the first tear rolled down her cheek. The lump in her throat had grown so big she could hardly chew, let alone swallow, and her jaw began quivering.

Her mind wandered back to her childhood. She was nine again, sitting at the family dinner table, looking up at her father as he angrily said to her in an inconvenienced tone, "How stupid can you be, Jasmine? Don't you have any brains? Why in the world would you do that?"

He was referring to the sticker she had put on the toaster. Right now in the present, however, it was about a presentation her career depended on. In her mind, she heard Garrett saying to her, "How stupid can you be? Don't you have any brains?"

She looked at the rest of the pizza on her plate, and realized that she didn't have the appetite to finish it. She picked up her plate and slid the last slice into the trash. Then she walked to the locked cabinet, turned the key, and pulled out the alcohol. She hated herself as she poured, but somehow, she couldn't stop herself.

"You have no brains," she said to herself out loud, her tone just as angry as her father's had been. "You're so stupid. God gave you no brains, so no matter how hard you try, THERE

IS NOTHING YOU CAN DO!" Her tone was bitter and sarcastic, and she kicked the cheap chair across the kitchen as she shouted. She broke down in tears and poured herself another drink.

Leaning on the counter, she stared out the window at the lights in the buildings surrounding her own. Her voice was dangerously quiet now, mimicking her father's. "You're stupid, Jasmine. Don't you ever think things through properly?

"I guess I don't, do I, Dad? Good ol' stupid Jasmine. Always in everybody's way."

In the kitchen, Jasmine relived every time she could remember feeling stupid, in someone's way, or not important enough to be heard and understood. She could hardly take in the immensity of the memories and emotions that flooded her mind.

Fingers were pointing at her and mouths were moving, but she heard nothing.

Jasmine poured another drink to drown herself, to avoid thinking anymore.

❧

Jasmine's alarm clock went off at five in the morning. Her hand reached out to the small nightstand and firmly smashed the Stop button, then she pulled the covers over her throbbing head. For the first time in eight weeks, there would be no running.

∽ TEN ∾

*J*asmine spent her whole morning searching for a way to connect with the emotions of the university that Nuevo Design was soliciting, asking them to renovate and modernize the floors and walls of their buildings.

As she stepped into the office's bathroom, she couldn't avoid noticing herself in the mirror. She stopped and looked for a moment. She was a vision of tiredness and exhaustion, complete with dark circles under her eyes. Jasmine needed help. She needed help at work; she needed help in her personal life; she needed help everywhere. And, she knew it, but she didn't know where to get it. She didn't know what to do except to, somehow, keep trying.

She lightly slapped her cheeks, trying to snap out of her current state. She was far too busy for this. She took a deep breath and returned to her desk.

Jasmine focused her attention to several notes written down on paper. She began rereading them to remember exactly where she was in her process.

You have a huge variety of decorating options.

You can choose from hundreds of prints, textures, and colors.

It's easy to clean.

Easy to clean? Really? Who am I kidding? thought Jasmine. *I have no idea what I'm doing. I really* am *stupid. Why did I think I could pull this off? Everything I've ever tried has failed.*

As she continued her internal dialogue, she picked up a pen and crossed a huge X through the entire page. She crumpled it up, threw it in the garbage, and leaned back in her chair.

Jasmine's thoughts were interrupted by a text coming through on her phone. As she looked at the screen, wondering who it could be from, she read, "You have a package."

A package, she thought. *What could it possibly be?* She thought back over her recent online browsing. *I know for a fact I haven't purchased anything recently.*

<hr />

Upon returning home from work, Jasmine went straight to the room that held the apartment parcel lockers. As she began to turn the dial on her locker door, she heard someone say to her, "Hi there, young lady. I see you've dried off."

She knew exactly who it was.

Her nose wrinkled as she questioned him without looking. "What are *you* doing here?"

"I suppose I'm doing the same thing you are. Retrieving my package."

"You *live* here?" she asked, surprised, now turning to look at him.

"Why yes, I do." He extended a hand to Jasmine. "Victor Laubenstein."

Jasmine was not a shaker of strangers' hands, but she felt obligated to oblige because he had helped her out a few weeks earlier. "Jasmine Stone," she echoed, returning the favor.

"It's nice to formally meet you, Jasmine. What a pretty name you have."

Unfamiliar with properly accepting a compliment, Jasmine's eyes glanced at him for a second and then swept the floor while they shook hands.

"I'd never seen you before a few weeks ago," she said, turning the dial on her locker.

"Oh, I just moved in at the beginning of January. I live in 1B."

"Yeah," she said, then whispered under her breath, loud enough for Victor to hear, "A creepy old man living in my apartment complex. How comforting."

Victor ignored the comment. "Flowers!" he exclaimed, looking at the outside of the box as Jasmine pulled it from the locker. "Someone loves you," he commented, giving her the same wink she remembered him giving her during the storm.

Jasmine's forehead scrunched and a quick frown covered her face in surprise. "No one loves me," she asserted, looking him in the eye to make her point very clear.

Victor's shoulders dropped. Surely, he felt her animosity. "If you ever need anything, feel free to let me know."

"I'll be sure to ring you up if I do." Her response was obviously sarcastic. "Maybe you can run up the stairs, pumping blood to your brain to get some *real* exercise."

"You know, Jasmine," Victor broke in, moving a step closer, "things are not always as we perceive them to be."

Jasmine took a step back and squinted her eyes while she spoke. "Old man, things are *exactly* as we perceive them to be."

Victor tipped his head to her. "Enjoy your flowers, Jasmine," he replied, as he turned to walk to his own locker.

Jasmine left the room, justifying her rudeness by thinking, *I'm not taking advice from some bored washed-up nobody who has nothing important to talk about.*

On her way to her apartment, she wondered who in the world the flowers could be from. She couldn't imagine they would be from Shawn. Why would he be sending her flowers? That didn't make sense when he'd made it very clear that he and Sheila had worked things out and were back together again. *My birthday was almost a month ago*, she thought. *And even if I were to randomly get flowers for Valentine's Day, that's still over a week away.*

Are the flowers from Garrett?? Is this what the company does when someone is promoted? A bit strange, but okay, maybe. She finally reached her building and found herself running up the steps so fast she was skipping a few stairs at a time. Curiosity had gotten the best of her, and she couldn't wait to tear open the box to see who the flowers were from.

Jasmine was thankful there was a pull tab to make the box easier to open. She was more excited than she had expected she would be. Her curiosity was killing her.

Inhaling deeply, she pulled the tab all the way down the long cardboard box. As she opened the first flap, she noticed a quote in white font printed on the box. In large letters, it read: *"Someone thinks you're pretty special!"*

She quickly exhaled and rolled her eyes. "Don't get excited, Jasmine. You know all about marketing ploys. No one *actually* thinks you're special."

She kept going, opening the second flap and looking inside. A thin piece of cardboard kept the flowers protected and hidden from view. The air filled with a hypnotic smell, and she closed her eyes and sniffed the fresh-cut scent. *I haven't smelled flowers in a long time.*

Attached to the second flap was a gold-foiled envelope with something inside. Jasmine stared at the envelope, unable to pull out the note she knew was in there. She was afraid to reveal the sender. She had no idea what to expect. She didn't want to get her hopes up only to be disappointed.

She froze for a few seconds more, unable to decide which she wanted to do first: Remove the layer of cardboard to reveal the flowers or read the note.

Finally, she chose the note.

Reluctantly, she pulled the paper from the envelope. On a beautiful, glossy, thick card were the words:

My Dear Jasmine,
I'm sorry I haven't sent you more flowers.
I know they were one of your favorite things to photograph.
I love you so much,
Mom.

Jasmine's knees buckled, and she instantly broke down in tears. Years of pent-up emotion erupted all at once. She melted into the black kitchen chair, placed her head in her hands and sobbed, still clutching the note.

She sat back in her chair and stared into space as the final lingering memory that had flooded her mind faded away.

She then looked back at the box on the table and stood to remove the cardboard lining that hid the flowers. The smell had already filled the entire small living area. Jasmine picked up the plastic surrounding the bouquet and the glass vase that accompanied it. She removed the bubble wrapping from the vase and began removing the plastic from the stunning bouquet of flowers containing lilies, roses, carnations, cushion poms, and greenery.

Giddy with excitement, Jasmine immediately grabbed her scissors and began trimming the stems. A smile appeared on her face. She felt like a little child again, doing something she loved. She laid out all the flowers on her counter, grouping each with their own kind. First, she grouped the peach roses, then the pink lilies, then the lavender cushion poms, then the bright pink carnations; lastly, she laid down the greenery. Then she stepped back and looked at exactly what she had to work with. She chose three flowers for the base of her bouquet—a lily and two roses. She plucked off their excess leaves to keep them from spoiling the water, inserted some greenery, and pulled the arrangement back, looking at it from all angles to see how she was doing.

Jasmine was in heaven. She spent almost a full hour arranging the bouquet, making sure there was depth and interest to it. Then she placed the entire bouquet in the vase and stepped back, once again, to look it over. The soft pink lilies made her eyes dance across the perfectly balanced design. The lilies were surrounded by the gorgeous orange-peach roses, lavender cushion poms, and lush greenery, which added brilliant color and a simple sophistication. Finally, the hot pink carnations brought the whole thing to life. It was breathtaking.

Jasmine glanced at her bookshelf. A large box sat on the bottom shelf that hadn't been opened in over three years. Hesitantly, she walked over, opened the box, and peered inside. She closed her eyes at the sight of it, automatically reliving a memory.

⟅⟆

It was Christmas morning, and Jasmine was twelve years old, almost thirteen. Her family took turns opening their presents one at a time, so that each one could be enjoyed. It was now Jasmine's turn. With a look of excitement on her face, her mother handed her a medium-sized box that weighed about three pounds. Jasmine was curious. She pulled the Christmas teddy bear wrapping from the box, and her mouth fell open.

"What!" she exclaimed in total shock. "Thank you, Mom!"

Inside the box was a Sigma SD9 camera. Jasmine couldn't believe her eyes. She wasn't expecting it at all. She got up from the floor and hugged her mom tighter than she ever had before. "Thank you, thank you, thank you," she said, jumping up and down with excitement as she admired the box. She hugged her mom again and looked up at her. "How did you know?" she asked.

Jasmine's mom smiled that knowing mother's smile and lightly hugged her back.

"You're welcome" was all she said, patting Jasmine on the back.

❧

Jasmine's mind then drifted to the first picture she'd ever taken with the camera. She smiled as she remembered telling her mom and Sara to "Scoot close!" before snapping the photo. She looked at the camera, smiling, as she recalled all the places it had been and all the photos she had taken. She even remembered getting into trouble when she took it all apart, and her dad thought she had broken it. Her parents were shocked when she was able to put it back together.

Jasmine sniffed back a few painful tears, not wanting to start crying again. She sat down on the floor, staring into the box. This very camera, which had brought her so much joy, had eventually become the source of conflict and contempt between she and her mother. She finally reached in and pulled it out of the box to admire it. It felt strange to be holding it again.

Tears began welling up in her eyes again. However, these were different tears—tears of sadness and regret and loneliness. "Mom," she called out gently, "I need you ... I miss you. I ..."

There, on the floor with the camera in hand, Jasmine placed her head in her hands and sobbed uncontrollably.

⌒ ELEVEN ⌒

Jasmine reviewed her schedule. Today was chest and back day. She spent five minutes warming up for her forty-five-minute workout. She was feeling good. After warming up her muscles, she rushed into the kitchen to grab some water. She caught a glimpse of the voluminous bouquet of flowers on the table, now even more in bloom. She slowed and involuntarily closed her eyes as her nostrils widened to take in the scent. *Thank you, Mom*, she smiled.

Feeling a new zest for life after pulling out her camera and photographing the beautiful bouquet, Jasmine had decided that today, because it was Saturday, she would run the five miles she had missed earlier in the week. She'd been beating herself up over it but decided she would make up for it today and put the mistake behind her. She also renewed the promise to herself that she wasn't going to drink again. *I'm going to finish this training without skipping another run and without alcohol.* As she worked out, adrenaline from her renewed decision pumped her up and got her even more excited to be back on track.

She slid her apartment key into her pocket and walked to the door, taking in a big whiff of the scent of the flowers before going outside.

It was a gorgeous winter day. The perfect day for a run. With a pep in her step, Jasmine jogged down the stairs, went quickly to the back of the parking lot, crossed the four-lane highway, and headed up the hill to the wide sidewalk. There seemed to be an unusually large number of people at the park today. She quickly stretched, turned up the volume on her phone, and started her five-mile run. She chose *Rocky* again— her go-to for motivation.

Seemingly quicker than usual, her five miles was up, but her favorite song had just started. Not wanting to interrupt it, she sat down on the nearby bench, leaned her head back slightly, and closed her eyes while she sang quietly, along with the loud voice in her ears.

As the song played, Jasmine got lost, imagining herself running that last stretch and crossing the marathon finish line. She visualized all her hard work paying off, and imagined how proud she would be of herself. Without expecting to, she felt emotional. *I've been dreaming about this day since I was a little girl!* She had always believed that one day she would be crossing a finish line—that someone would be draping a 26.2 medal around her neck.

The song kept playing, but Jasmine was too choked up to keep singing.

Her day was less than two months away.

With her eyes still closed, she hummed softly, enjoying the sunshine on her face and the vision of finishing her marathon in her mind. As the song came to a close, Jasmine slowly opened her eyes to bring herself back to reality. When she did, she jumped, spooked; someone was now sitting on the other end of the bench.

"I'm sorry," he apologized, putting up his hand. "I didn't mean to startle you." He pointed to the other benches. "All the other seats are taken."

Jasmine smiled a faint embarrassed smile without speaking and got up to leave.

"You like *Rocky*," he commented.

"Yes."

"I'm assuming you're a runner!" he said enthusiastically.

"Yes." Noticing the way he was dressed, she inquired, "You're a runner, too?"

"I like to consider myself one, yes. I'm training for the Marathon in a couple of months," he said excitedly.

"Me too!" She paused now, willing to engage in conversation.

"Is this your first one?" he asked.

"It is! It's something I've been wanting to do for quite a while, and this year it worked out. What about you?"

"This will be my second. I ran it about five years ago and thought I'd give it another go now."

"Oh nice! Maybe you can give me some tips. Are you using a training plan?"

"Not this time around, but I'm second guessing myself. It gets hard about halfway through. What about you? Are you using one?"

"I am. I'm using the SheRuns schedule."

"I've heard that one is really good. How do you like it?"

"It seems to be working pleasantly so far. I love it because it has speedwork, interval training, and a meal schedule."

"That is definitely a plus. Do you run here often?"

"I do, actually. I live in those apartments over there," Jasmine gestured, "so I walk over here."

His dropped his jaw. "You cross that road?" he pointed.

She laughed. "I've only been honked at a few times."

"Well, I promise, it wasn't me," he said, putting his hands up innocently. "I don't believe I asked you your name."

"Jasmine Stone."

"It's nice to meet you, Jasmine," he said, putting out his hand. "I'm Bradley Copeland. So, what do you do, Jasmine?"

"Oh," she said with a nervous laugh, "my job isn't important."

He looked at her with question in his eyes. "Everybody's job is important. Lay it on me: What do you do?"

What I would like to say is, "I save lives. I help cure cancer. I'm important."

"Well, basically, I convince a lot of rich people and wealthy businesses to buy overpriced products they don't really need." She lowered her head, feeling uncomfortable with where the conversation was going.

"What do you sell?" he asked, with a curious expression on his face.

"Umm, wallpaper," Jasmine admitted, feeling embarrassed even saying it.

"Wallpaper is very important," he encouraged.

She raised an eyebrow at his enthusiasm.

"It's wallpaper. It's not important," she restated. "It doesn't mean anything. It doesn't matter."

She was sure that he could hear the cynicism in her voice. He was probably analyzing what the best way to answer her would be.

Jasmine kept going. "We chop down trees to make walls look better."

"What you do is important," he insisted.

"I sell *wallpaper*," Jasmine said more forcefully to ensure that he heard her correctly. "We make and sell pretty things. I'm not saving lives, feeding the hungry, or solving crimes."

"*You* may not be," Bradley replied, "but is it possible the people who do save lives, and feed the hungry, and solve crimes need pretty things in their life?"

She didn't have an answer ready because she'd never thought of it that way before.

Bradley added, "You're servicing somebody who thinks that ten thousand dollars' worth of luxury wallpaper is a good deal."

Jasmine shrugged her shoulders and bit the side of her cheek. She was uncomfortable not having a response.

Bradley kept talking. "Listen, we all need one another. The firm that buys the wallpaper from you needs you. You're important to them. Your company, which sells wallpaper, needs the printer to produce them. Your employer, who brings in designs from artists, needs you. We all need one another, and without each one of us, humanity wouldn't be able to thrive."

He could probably tell by the look on her face that she wasn't convinced yet. "Think about it this way," he said. "You represent a luxury brand, right?"

"Yes, I do. An overpriced brand," she said, still feeling cynical.

"What about if there was no fashion? What if no one designed those artful Calderas you're wearing?"

Jasmine looked down at her shoes and instantly remembered walking into the shoe store to get fitted for running shoes and seeing this specific pair on a shelf. They were perfect.

"Do you know the specific person who designed those shoes?" he questioned.

Jasmine thought a second and replied, "No, of course I don't."

"But is that person important to you?"

Jasmine paused before answering. "Yes. I suppose so."

"What if all you had were white shoes and black shirts and brown pants? How boring would that be? What if we had no movies? What if we had no music? What if we had no books?" He paused before continuing. "Life would be *nothing* without art and pretty things, Jasmine. Life would be *nothing* without the imaginations, skills, and talents of everyone on the planet. Every one of us, even the most minimalistic, needs art and 'pretty things.'"

"Jasmine," he said, in a voice so caring and passionate that it startled her, "*you* are astronomically important."

Jasmine shook her head as he spoke, refusing to believe what he said could possibly be true.

But he wouldn't give up. "Without you, the owner of your apartment wouldn't be able to put food on the table for his family. Neither would your employer. The saver of lives couldn't come home from a long day at work and smile at the choice of wallpaper that she and her husband had picked out. Everyone needs you, and you need everyone."

It didn't make sense. How could she, Jasmine, be so important if someone else was in control of her life? Wasn't God in control of everything she did? Doesn't God always have her right where He wants her? Didn't God pull the strings and decide who was and was not important?

"Yes," she said, half agreeing with his point of view but disagreeing with the other half. "But I can sell eight million dollars' worth of wallpaper and no one will care. No one will notice. No one in my industry notices. The homeowner who bought the paper has no idea who I am or what I do. I'm invisible. The wallpaper designer gets mentioned in the design magazine, the homeowner gets to live with it and enjoy the pretty thing, the company makes the money, and I'm just an invisible worker, living in a tiny apartment. I do *so* much and no one knows."

Bradley was quiet for a moment and then said, "Jasmine, do *you* think you're important?"

Surprised by the question, she answered without thinking. "No, I *know* I'm not important. Nothing you say will convince me otherwise."

Bradley hesitantly but confidently continued. "Then it wouldn't matter if you did save lives. If your *fundamental* belief about yourself is that you are not important, you'll unconsciously find a way to minimize whatever you do, no matter what it is. And you'll fight hard to keep that belief alive. Can I share with you my perspective?"

Jasmine shrugged her shoulders. "Sure."

"What you just described to me tells me you're the linchpin that keeps all those people moving. You're extremely important. Everyone knows what you do, whether they want to or not. Without you, Jasmine, the designer of that pretty wallpaper someone so painstakingly chose wouldn't have been connected to the firm you're selling it to. The consumers of the wallpaper, whoever they are, would have nothing but white, boring, or outdated walls without you. Your company wouldn't exist without you and your co-workers."

Jasmine could feel passion rising inside Bradley as he spoke.

"It takes all of us. Human beings live in different parts of the ecosystem, and that's okay. It's necessary. Our lifestyles may be far apart, but that doesn't matter. What matters is that you serve people to the best of your ability, and the only way you can do that is if you believe you're important."

But feeling important is arrogant, Jasmine thought, even though she didn't say it out loud.

Without replying to anything Bradley actually said, Jasmine asked his question back to him. "What do *you* do for a living?"

Bradley raised his eyebrows and smiled, which showed his dimples. "I'm a high school guidance counselor."

"That explains it," said Jasmine sarcastically.

"Sorry. I get passionate about things like this," he said in return.

"It's okay. Honestly, you gave me some things to consider. I've got a promotion at work that's hinging on an important project I need to pull off, and this helped tremendously." It was uncharacteristic for her to admit something like this, but she felt good doing.

"It was incredible to meet you, Jasmine," said Bradley with a big smile on his face. "I thoroughly enjoyed our conversation."

There was a pause.

"Do you happen to be looking for a running partner?"

Jasmine snickered. "Is that a cheesy way of asking for my phone number?"

His dimples showed again. "You caught me," he chuckled, putting his head down and his hands in the air.

"I've never actually had a running buddy. That might be fun."

"Next Saturday?" questioned Bradley. "Same time, same place?" He waited for her answer.

"Sure," said Jasmine, realizing she was going to have to rearrange her schedule because she didn't usually run on Saturdays.

❦

As she walked home, she had a bounce in her step and a smile on her face. Things were looking up.

She unlocked and opened her door, and was welcomed home by the smell of the flowers. Without even showering or changing her clothes, she sat right down to her presentation script and wrote out, word for word, the correct emotional reasons why using Nuevo Design's services was imperative.

That evening, after finishing the week's food prep, Jasmine sat in her recliner with her special blanket and a cup of hot chocolate in her hand. She lit her winter candle and cozied up to finally watch her favorite TV show. When she got up, after two episodes, to refill her mug and get a snack, something outside caught her attention. Little white specks were glistening against the streetlight. She squealed in delight. *SNOW!* She'd been waiting for snow for a long time. And it hadn't even been in the forecast. She stood in her kitchen, gazing out the window at the tiny specks of snow, remembering the snow in Arizona that had looked exactly like this.

She could only remember one time in all her eighteen years there when it had snowed. Her mind went back to the sun-faded blue recliner that sat in front of the living room window of her parents' house. She was fourteen, and she'd looked in amazement out at the snow, which was blowing more than falling. Everyone else in town was worried about the wind and electricity, but Jasmine wasn't. She stared out into the night, contemplating her future, and wishing she was one of those little specks that could just blow away.

↝ TWELVE ↜

*I*t snowed on and off for the next two weeks. The plows were busy clearing roads, and Jasmine couldn't help but think of Bradley's words about importance while she drove to work. These people were just plow drivers, but for her, and everyone else on the road, they were lifesavers.

Two weeks had passed since Jasmine met Bradley, and the two of them started a friendship that Jasmine did not see coming. Bradley talked to Jasmine about concepts and ideas she had never thought of before. She had even gone out to lunch with him after one of their Saturday runs. She didn't particularly like meeting new people, but Bradley was different. She hadn't talked to anyone this much in her entire life. They talked about their childhoods, their jobs, Bradley's whittling hobby. She had even managed to tell him about Karen.

She had a newfound enthusiasm at work after meeting and talking with Bradley, and everyone noticed, including Brett. She was bringing in clients and artists and closing deals left and right. Brett assigned several more projects and tasks to her and her team. Finally, she was receiving the recognition she'd always wanted. She finally felt important. People were finally recognizing what she was worth.

Today was Tuesday, the day of the Johns Hopkins presentation. Jasmine stood at her desk, packing her bags and her rolling suitcase. *I can't believe today is the day!* she thought with excitement. Out of the corner of her eye, she saw Karen approaching.

"I'm ready to deliver the emotional aspect and really make the sale happen," Karen said with what Jasmine saw as a pathetic smile. "I'm so excited to be a part of this company and the good leadership we have here."

Jasmine wanted to throw up, but instead she smiled until she turned around to zip up her bag. Karen had no idea what was coming. "We're going to be phenomenal," Jasmine said with a sly smile. "Are you ready to go?"

Jasmine led the way, and the two of them awkwardly rode the elevator downstairs and walked out to the company vehicle.

I can't wait until this is mine! No more squeaky doors. No more having to park in the back of the lot. No more rolling the windows down by hand. She smiled with excitement despite having her worst nightmare in the passenger seat next to her.

"I am so tired," Karen said with a yawn. "My youngest is teething, so I was up until almost two in the morning rocking her. Then my five-year-old daughter, who's a wild sleeper, was scared of a monster under her bed and crawled into mine at around four. Her feet were in my face after about ten minutes. Of course, my husband didn't help with anything. He just wakes up and expects breakfast. I had to dress everyone and make them all breakfast, then get the kids' backpacks ready."

Karen kept chattering. *Don't you ever shut up? Do I look like someone who cares about your kids' sleeping habits?* Jasmine wondered to herself. She was glad it was only a twenty-minute drive to the university.

When they arrived, everything was set up and ready to go. The samples were out, the food was set up, and Jasmine, who was nervous but still confident, began her speech. She glanced at her watch and began exactly at the top of the hour.

"Thank you all very much for being here," she said with a big smile on her face. "My name is Jasmine Stone, and this is my assistant, Karen Boggs. If any of you need anything, such as a refill or garbage that needs to be thrown out, I'm sure she would be happy to assist you." She turned to Karen with the most insidious smile she could muster.

"I want to let you know what to expect over the course of the next hour. After I take some time to introduce myself, we'll look at each product in detail, then I'll answer any questions that you may have."

Jasmine could feel Karen watching her as she pulled up each product, one by one, and spoke thoroughly and intelligently about them in excellent detail. She began with the floor pieces and moved through the paint and finally to the wall coverings.

As she finished speaking about the last product, Karen stood to take over. "But listen," Jasmine said with conviction. Karen's mouth dropped open as she tilted her head at Jasmine, clearly asking her what she was doing without actually speaking. Jasmine smiled slyly, winked at her, then continued on. "The truth is, we aren't here to talk only about how wonderful our products are. The real reason we've gathered here today is to talk about your dreams, your emotions, and your passions." Jasmine's voice dropped to enable everyone to pay closer attention.

"I invite you to think about something for a few minutes. What if there was no fashion? What if there was no art? No differences? No emotions? Where would we be as humans?" Jasmine paused to allow the participants to contemplate her questions.

"I invite you to look at this plain white wall to my right." She motioned toward the white wall with her hand. "What do you *feel* when you look at that wall? Are your emotions stirred? Does it make you feel calm or excited, peaceful or inspired?" She paused again to allow the question to marinate among the participants.

They were nearly finished eating their food and she knew she had their attention. She kept on speaking, with even more passion. "The true value of a wall covering isn't that you own a piece of art, or that this conference room can be an example of the wealth on this campus. The true value of putting a pattern, a color, or a texture on a wall is that, when you walk into the room, there is a subconscious emotional shift."

Jasmine spoke with a passion she didn't even know she possessed. She held up a sample. "When you walk into a space with light blue floral on the walls, you feel calm. When you walk into one covered with bright yellow zebras, you feel excited, ready to have fun." The crowd mused, displaying their attention as she held up the zebra sample. She then reached for a different wall covering sample and held it up. "When you walk into a space covered with diagonals, you feel a little jolt. There's some movement, some momentum, some curiosity." She paused for effect, then put the samples down on the table and stepped closer to the small crowd, looking in the direction of Madelynn.

"What it's about is the emotional response. How do you want your *students* to feel when they enter their classrooms? How do you want your *faculty* to feel when they walk into their breakrooms? How do *you* want to feel when you walk into the library? Which spaces do you want to feel cozy? Which do you want to feel vibrant? Which do you want to feel sophisticated, peaceful, or optimistic? What do you want your spaces to *feel* like?"

Jasmine stepped back to her place behind the podium that she was using.

"In closing, aside from the fact that our products are the best on the market, what's most important is that we carry the work of some of the best designers and artists in the world. We have a wide variety of wall coverings and floor designs that can go with any style or emotional qualities and tonalities you want to feel when you enter your spaces. I want to thank each and every one of you for being here today. It was my pleasure to share my expertise with you, and we look forward to providing excellent service for you in the future. Are there any questions?"

Jasmine finished her presentation and looked at Karen, who was sitting with her mouth agape, as were some of the others in the room. Karen hadn't seen this coming, and neither had the audience.

As Jasmine packed up her things, she was the one who did the talking, while Karen sat silently, perturbed. "You were right, Karen. I'm so excited to be a part of this company and the good leadership we have here."

"That was my job," she said with irritation.

"Oops," Jasmine replied, her smile vaguely insulting. She turned away, yanking her fist down, knowing she'd completely nailed the presentation. Karen knew she'd nailed it, too. Jasmine was ready to return to the office to celebrate.

As they walked toward the building's exit, she noticed Karen had stepped into the bathroom without saying a word. Jasmine smiled to herself, feeling like she'd finally won.

As she sat waiting on a couch in the lobby, she flipped through a campus magazine that she found on a nearby table, remembering her own college experiences from so long ago. When she returned the magazine to the table, something else caught her eye: a book sitting on the ledge beneath the glass table. The author's name captured her attention, and Jasmine leaned forward to ensure that she was seeing it correctly.

"Victor Laubenstein?" Jasmine gasped. "Victor Laubenstein?" she repeated, with the book now in her hands. She turned it over, and sure enough, her neighbor's picture was right there on the book's back cover, flashing the same contented smile he always wore on his face. She gasped again, putting her hand over her mouth and looking around to see if anyone had heard her.

What the heck is this? She flipped the book back to the front to read the title. *The Brain and You*, she read, completely surprised.

As she cracked open the book to see what it was about, Karen plodded around the corner with an aggravated frown on her face. Jasmine was afraid Karen would notice that she looked as if she'd seen a ghost. She slowly stood up to walk out the door.

They rode in silence back to the office. All the insulting and cynical comments Jasmine had been considering unleashing no longer seemed appropriate. They both had a lot on their mind, and when they arrived back in the office, they were equally glad to remove themselves from each other's company.

Jasmine couldn't wait to get to her desk to look up Victor Laubenstein, but when the elevator doors opened, her team member, Anna, was standing there waiting for her.

"Jasmine! I'm so glad you're back. The manufacturer called to say the sample book is delayed. They want to know if we can pick it up on Friday instead of Tuesday."

"Absolutely not. I just promised Madelynn at Johns Hopkins that we'd have it delivered to them on Friday afternoon. Call them right away and make sure we're their top priority. We need it by Wednesday; Thursday at the absolute latest."

Brett was standing at Jasmine's desk when she arrived. He had an excited look on his face but sounded nervous when he said, "Okay, I can't wait a single minute longer. How did it go?"

"I nailed it," Jasmine said confidently, excitement in her own voice.

Brett squealed. "I knew you would," he replied, moving his hand up to high-five her.

Jasmine smiled and high-fived him.

Brett then fired a million questions at her about Madelynn, the questions that were asked, her follow-up, and everything else in between. As he walked away, he called over his shoulder, "We love you, Jasmine!"

"Thank you," she responded, feeling important.

Still standing, Jasmine leaned over the top of her chair and was about to type Victor's name into the search engine.

"Oh," Brett said, turning around again. "Sylvia's waiting for you. She has a couple of questions about the showroom for April."

"Fantastic," she replied, giving Brett a thumbs-up. "I'm on my way."

As soon as she could, Jasmine clocked out and sped home. Noticing Victor's car wasn't in the spot for 1B, Jasmine ran up the stairs, unlocked her door, pulled out her computer, and hurriedly looked up Victor Laubenstein. Her mouth fell open again. She couldn't believe her eyes.

Victor Laubenstein is a cognitive and behavioral neuroscientist and best-selling author. Jasmine placed her head in her hands and squeezed her temples. She closed her eyes and racked her brain, attempting to remember everything she'd said to him. All she could come up with was that she was unfriendly and rude. With her hands now pressed against her cheeks, Jasmine read on. *Cognitive neuroscience addresses questions of how psychological functions are produced by neural circuitry. The emergence of powerful new measurement techniques such as neuroimaging, electrophysiology, optogenetics, and human genetic analysis combined with sophisticated experimental techniques from cognitive psychology enables neuroscientists and psychologists to address abstract questions such as how cognition and emotion are mapped to specific neural substrates.*

Jasmine didn't understand what she'd just read. All she knew was that she had made a colossal mistake.

He is best known for his work in biological psychology, developmental mechanisms of behavior, and brain plasticity. Beyond his 50+ academic publications, he has published many popular books, including his best-selling books The Brain and You, Neural Functions, *and* Where Does Perspective Come From?

Her forehead crinkled in disbelief.

Laubenstein is the winner of the George B. Millon Prize in Cognitive Neuroscience, a member of the Federation of Global Societies for Neuroscience and Behavior, a research fellow in the Institute for Ethics of Stress and Behavior, and ....

The article went on further, mentioning several textbooks he'd contributed to, his other academic contributions, other awards he'd received, and the study groups and societies of which he was a member. She was both flabbergasted and confused. After she finished reading, she stepped away from her chair and walked carefully down the steps to see if he had returned home. His parking spot was vacant.

Jasmine sat down on the bottom step of the stairs in somewhat of a daze. Again, she attempted to recall the conversations they had so briefly exchanged. She felt awful about the way she'd treated him, embarrassed that she had been snarky with such a prominent person. She tried to remember what he'd said to her. Looking back, she realized his words were intellectual but also kind. Clearly, he knew Jasmine was not in his league, but he never looked down on her.

Jasmine spotted someone taking their garbage to the dumpster. *So, who is he?* she asked herself sarcastically, *some kind of a world-renowned mathematician?*

Victor was right. Things truly weren't as she perceived them to be. Jasmine sat on the bottom step, determined to wait for Victor to come home. Her wheels were turning. *What exactly do I say to him?*

I'm sorry?

I didn't know you were so important?

Why didn't you tell me who you were?

Why were you so nice to me?

Why are you living here?

Do you have a Doppelganger with the same name, and this isn't really you?

Jasmine sat on the steps for almost an hour, thinking and watching people as she waited for Victor, but he didn't show.

Finally, she slowly and tiredly walked up the stairs, returning to her apartment. *Maybe it was a good thing I didn't see him?* she thought. *What would I have actually said anyway?* In her apartment, she sat at her computer looking at the article, still in disbelief. As she stared at Victor's internet picture, a vibration from her phone brought her out of her trance. *Hi Jasmine, I hope you enjoyed the flowers. I miss you. Hope to see you soon. I love you.*

Sitting with her phone in her hand, Jasmine felt a touch of guilt that she hadn't thanked her mother for the flowers. Now, she stared at her phone instead of the computer. After a few minutes, she began her reply:

Hi Mom, thank you ...

There was a long pause as the cursor blinked. Jasmine found herself at a loss for words. She erased the reply and started over.

Hi Mom, I miss you, too ...

That didn't feel right. *Do I actually miss her?* wondered Jasmine, feeling a pang of guilt, if she'd admitted the answer was no. She erased that reply as well, and began typing again.

I've been busy at work ...

That didn't feel right either. She stared at her phone again. *It shouldn't be this hard to write a simple text.*

Jasmine moved to the sink to get a drink of water, while she tried to figure out exactly what she wanted to say to her mom. Through the window, a glare of headlights caught her attention, and she strained to see if it was Victor returning home. It wasn't. She stayed put at the window so she'd see when he finally arrived. She began her text to her mother over again.

Thanks for the flowers. I pulled out my old camera for the first time in three years.

Jasmine again found herself staring at the phone, unsure of what else to say. She decided she didn't really want to say anything about the camera.

"Why *did* Mom send me those flowers anyway?" Jasmine asked herself out loud. "She never even liked me taking pictures." She recalled the argument between her and her parents when they found out she'd applied to photography school. After heated words were exchanged, Jasmine's mom stated with disdain and disappointment in her voice, "We are NOT paying the bill for this mistake of yours. I should never have bought you that camera." Those words still hurt, even after ten years.

Jasmine looked down at the blank screen on her phone. The cursor blinked.

Thank you.

Jasmine hit Send.

The glare of headlights once again brought Jasmine's attention outside. At last, it was Victor's car. She watched him park, open his door, and walk toward his apartment with a small bag in his hand. His hair was blowing in the light wind, and he looked as if something was on his mind. Jasmine watched him until he disappeared under the stairwell.

∽ THIRTEEN ∽

*H*er alarm went off: 5 a.m. Jasmine was mentally and physically exhausted. It had been a week since the presentation at Johns Hopkins, and she anxiously awaited the results. She groaned and closed her eyes after taking a look at her running clothes. She had an unusually long run planned for this morning—one that she wasn't particularly looking forward to. The distances were starting to pick up as Jasmine entered Week eleven of her sixteen-week training. Her phone buzzed. She knew exactly who it was, and she picked up her phone with a smile on her face.

Hey beautiful lady! Time to get up and smell that fresh running air :)

It was Bradley, checking in to ensure she was awake and preparing to run. Jasmine focused her gaze toward the ceiling while she pondered. She was so thankful that she had met him when she did. They'd decided to keep each other accountable for fulfilling their commitment to run the marathon. She wasn't sure where their friendship was headed, but scrunched her eyes shut in pain as she was sure it was too good to be true and wouldn't last. He seemed so settled, so wise, and so kind, and she was all over the place. Yet, there was no time to dwell on that right now. She glanced at her phone one more time and smiled. She texted him back.

Up and headed out the door now :)

Me too :)

She laced up her running shoes, grabbed her key, and jogged down the stairs. As she reached the bottom of the stairs, she spotted Victor's car. She still was in shock about her bizarre discovery about him the week before. However, she hadn't yet bumped into him accidentally.

Jasmine started toward the back of the parking lot. She walked through the dirty plowed snow covering the path to the grass, making sure to step carefully. A chill journeyed down her spine. The snow had almost completely melted, and all that was left was the plowed piles of dirt and garbage.

❦

Shortly after Jasmine had reached her cubicle at work, Brett walked toward her. He had a huge smile on his face and was lightly clapping his hands. Jasmine was relieved. It could only mean good news.

"What is it, what is it?" she asked excitedly.

"It's a go!" Brett said, pumping his fist in the air. "I taught you well."

"Oh. What. Ever!" she retorted, not accepting his arrogance.

They high-fived each other, knowing what it meant for both of them.

"Garrett will be back here to speak with you later this week about some super-exciting news," he said, purposely teasing her.

"What's the news?"

"Changes. That's all I know right now." He winked.

"A promotion?" she asked, trying to eke out all the information she could.

"I'd say yes," Brett hinted with a grin.

Jasmine clapped her hands together, quietly whispering, "EEK!" It was finally happening. She picked up her phone, too excited not to share the news with Bradley.

Good news! she texted him, hoping he would be curious enough to respond right away.

Feeling relieved, she started a texting conversation with Bradley that lasted most of the entire day.

⁂

A few days later, Jasmine was sitting in the conference room with Garrett again, though this time with a totally different energy. He didn't look worried or even concerned, as he had in the previous meetings that she'd attended. He never wasted time; and as usual, he got right down to business. Looking down at the papers in front of him, he acknowledged,

"Jasmine and Karen! I honestly have to say, I can't believe you two pulled it off. Exceptional job! You both have shown extraordinary commitment and dedication to Nuevo Design."

Jasmine was grinning from ear to ear, thinking, *I could've done without Karen being acknowledged alongside me, but right now, that doesn't matter.*

"Jasmine," Garrett said, addressing her directly first, "you have an amazing and thorough understanding of the products, and your confidence is what helped sell them. You know how to speak intelligently about the details and features, and we appreciate that detail—that level of commitment. Thank you."

"And Karen," he said, turning to her, "you were able to help in gaining this client with your ability to speak intelligently about the emotional qualities necessary to provide the benefits of this product ..."

"Actually, sir," Karen interrupted, "Jasmine didn't allow me to speak at the meeting at all. I'm sorry to say she went against your instructions and tried to sell the correct emotions herself, while referring to me as her 'assistant.'"

Garrett looked at Jasmine, as if asking for an explanation.

Jasmine smiled; she'd had time to prepare herself for this. "I had a fit of inspiration, sir, and didn't want to chance messing things up. I hope you'll forgive me," she said, confident she would be forgiven.

Garrett didn't seem to care. "So," he continued, "we're running your new title through the board of directors. Right now, we'll be charging the expenses to the product development budget ..."

Garrett went on, but Jasmine missed a few sentences at that point.

The board of directors! thought Jasmine, hardly able to control her excitement, but trying to remain professional. *It's true! I really am important now!*

She brought her mind back to the conversation.

"Here's what's going to happen," Garrett stated with professionalism in his evenly toned voice, "Jasmine, I've created a temporary position for you. I see moving promise in your work, and I'll be reporting on your progress to the board so they can vote to make the position permanent. I'll know by the end of the quarter what their decision will be. If the vote is a yes, you'll be presented with a job offer, and we'll go through the proper procedures to officially fill the position."

She could hardly believe what she was hearing. She'd waited so long for this moment, and it was finally happening.

"In the meantime," Garrett went on, "you'll continue to reach out to corporate businesses and get more presentations lined up, doing exactly what you did this time. We'll start with local businesses first, then branch out, and your team can help you as necessary. Karen, you'll assist Jasmine and learn alongside her, so you'll be able to step in immediately in the event it's ever necessary."

Garrett looked down at the notes he had in front of him.

Jasmine glanced at Karen and noted that she was fuming.

I knew it! I can see it in her eyes. I knew all along Karen was trying to steal this new position out from under me.

"I'm going out on a limb with you, Jasmine," Garrett said, "but I'm willing to take a gamble on you. You'll have a company car for your travel to presentations until we make the full transition, then we'll set up your budget to provide you with a personal car. You'll have a company credit card to handle your expenses, as well as all the benefits of the Head of Corporate Sales position. If all goes well, we'll officially announce your new title after our quarterly meeting on April 12th." Garrett paused. "Do you have any questions?"

Any questions! thought Jasmine. *No, I don't!* "No, none that I can think of right now," she replied, hardly able to contain herself. *And I know exactly what I'm going to do as soon as this meeting is over.*

"If there are no further questions, let's get back to work."

Back at her desk, Jasmine moved aside the documents and sample designs she was working on before the meeting. She took a deep breath, suddenly thinking of everything that had just been dropped on her plate. But she didn't care because it would be worth it. *I'm finally making it! I'm finally important. The board of directors of Nuevo Design will be talking about me! I can't wait to tell Bradley the good news.*

With her day packed full of things to do, she decided to put everything else aside for a few minutes and went straight to the Mercedes website. *Style, here I come!* she thought excitedly as she scoured the site, deciding which car she wanted.

That evening at dinner, Jasmine couldn't stop talking. She and Bradley had chosen to eat at a small café and ordered a simple meal of egg salad sandwiches, pickles, and homemade chips.

"I can literally *feel* your excitement, Jasmine," Bradley commented with a smile.

She'd told him all about the presentation; that when sales were slipping, she had the idea of using the designs of small single-story artists who were struggling to make it into the big leagues, and to cold-pitch to businesses to get them to upgrade their current facilities. And about how Garrett had taken a gamble on her, allowing her to try this out, and it worked! She talked about her disdain for Karen and how she'd finally screwed her over by assigning her all the dirty work.

Bradley could hardly keep up with how fast she was talking.

"And, listen to this," Jasmine continued, hardly taking a breath, "I receive a company car that I get to choose! I already found the one I think I want. I also receive a bigger office, away from all the 'little people.' And, I get an expense account, a gas card, and a pay raise! It turns out you were right after all, Bradley. I *am* important! Now, all I need is for time to pass faster."

Bradley cocked his head, while he listened to Jasmine speak, surprised by how she referred to her co-workers as the "little people." He twitched his nose before he spoke. "I'm happy for you, Jasmine, I really am. I've very much enjoyed getting to know you, and I really appreciate you sharing all this with me."

"Thank you!" Jasmine accepted, finally stopping to take another bite.

"May I ask you a question?"

"Of course!" she gushed, prepared for more praise.

He calmly leaned back in his chair and inquired, "If all these things were taken away from you, would you still feel important?"

Jasmine was taken aback. She looked at him in disbelief, not knowing what to say. He waited quietly, giving her space to think through her answer. After a few seconds, she squinted her eyes and announced, "You have no idea how hard I've worked for this."

"I don't," agreed Bradley, "but that doesn't answer my question."

Jasmine couldn't believe her ears. She glared at him, unsure of what to say. "This is what I've wanted for a long time!" trying to convince herself that this was the truth.

"Why is that?" he asked, not letting her off the hook.

Jasmine hadn't really thought of that before, and she certainly didn't want to think of the answer right this second. This was supposed to be a celebratory conversation, not a let's-make-Jasmine-answer-uncomfortable-questions moment.

He was still waiting for her answer.

"How dare you?" was all she could say. "You waltz into my life thinking you know me and start asking personal questions that are none of your business. Let me make myself very clear, Bradley Copeland: You have no idea who I am or what I have been through."

He didn't seem to let what she'd said offend him. He remained quiet as Jasmine continued releasing her emotions at him.

"I thought you were my friend. I thought you actually cared about me," she accused, then she got up from the table and slapped down $20 in front of him. He tipped his head toward her as she stormed out.

Jasmine couldn't believe what had just happened. She knew their friendship was too good to be true. *I can't trust anyone*, she affirmed, pounding her fist on the steering wheel. *I'm always going to be alone in the world. No one will ever truly care about me.* She sat in the café parking lot, staring through the windshield, contemplating her promotion. Finally, she reached down to grab her car keys, which she'd thrown in the passenger seat, and noticed she had a missed call and a voice mail on her phone, both from her mom.

"What does she want now?" Jasmine questioned out loud, with irritation in her voice, as she reached over to pick up the phone. "Why is she communicating all of a sudden?"

She pressed the button to listen to the recording. *Hi Jasmine, it's Mom.* Her voice was hesitant and unusually weak. *How are you?* There was a pause. *I miss you.* Then came a heavy sigh. *I know you have your marathon on April 2nd, but is there any way you could come home soon?* There was a pleading in her voice, followed by a weak breath. *Dad and I would like to talk with you.*

"Oh you would, would you?" Jasmine retorted, with mockery in her voice. "And what exactly are you going to say, Mom? Huh? Are you going to say, 'I'm sorry for toying with your life, Jasmine. I'm sorry for despising every choice you ever made. I'm sorry for calling you stupid. I'm sorry for loving your brother and sister more than I love you. I'm sorry your father and I didn't care enough about you to actually have a relationship with you. I'm sorry I never took the time to understand you?' Is that what you're going to say?"

"Or how about, 'We're proud of you, Jasmine, for pursuing your passion. We're proud of you for working hard even though we sabotaged your dreams.' Maybe you'll tell me how thankful you are that I'm so unique and special, and that you can't imagine not having me as a daughter. Huh? Is that what you're going to say, Mother dear?"

She was yelling louder as she picked up speed, heading toward home.

"Oh, what did you say?" Jasmine continued talking to herself, pretending to have a conversation with her mom. "That's not exactly what you had in mind? No worries, Mom, it was a joke. I didn't think any of that would ever actually come out of your mouth. But sure! I'd love to come home. I'll drive across the entire country if necessary to prove to you what it's like to chase your dreams and continually be sabotaged along the way with that silly God of yours. Oh, and guess what? I made it without having to go crawling on my hands and knees to beg for it. I did it myself—my way. Sure, Mom, I'd be more than willing to spend half my vacation time going home so you and Dad can 'tell me something.' I'll show up," she declared bitterly as she sped down the highway.

When Jasmine arrived home, she stomped straight into the kitchen where she had some of the flowers from her mother drying. She snatched them up and threw them into the trash.

"Flowers don't cut it, Mom," she uttered, as the lid slammed shut.

⌒ FOURTEEN ⌒

The next work week was nightmarish for Jasmine. She hadn't been this busy since cramming to finish up her final projects in college. The only difference was that in university, she wasn't training for a marathon at the same time. She certainly hadn't expected to have this much work dumped on her all at once, but she kept trudging forward, counting down the days until she could sign the paper stating that she'd accepted the new position. It was only twenty-eight days away. She was positive she could perform the work being piled on her, to show that she could perform at the level expected of her now that she permanently had the position. It might take a few extra Excedrin, but she could do it.

Jasmine was increasingly frustrated with her team's lack of cooperation, especially Karen's. As Jasmine's temporary assistant, Karen seemed to be at her heels 24/7, just waiting to snatch her promotion away.

Today, because Jasmine was late to work due to her long run, she was extra agitated and snappy.

She picked up her phone and dialed Anna's extension. "Anna," she snapped, "who was the one who took the sample book to Johns Hopkins? I just got an email from Madelynn saying she hasn't seen it."

"I believe it was Pat. Would you like me to send him to your desk?"

"Yes, and hurry, please."

Jasmine slammed the phone into the receiver.

Pat showed up a few minutes later. "Where's the book?" Jasmine insisted. "I just got an email from Madelynn, and she said she hasn't seen the book. Who did you give it to at Hopkins?"

"I, uh, forgot to pick it up on Friday," he stammered nervously.

"Forgot to pick it up on Friday!" Jasmine repeated, moving her head forward in disbelief.

"Yes, ma'am."

"Are you kidding me? That book was supposed to be picked up from the plant on Thursday, to be delivered to the university on Friday, Pat!"

He was staring at Jasmine, clearly unsure of what to say.

"My. Gosh!" Jasmine exclaimed. "Can't you people do *anything* right? Do I have to do *everything* myself? Please, tell me you're kidding!"

Pat wrung his hands together and shook his head.

"Get away from my desk!" Jasmine instructed, with her teeth clenched. "Get away! Please, just go away. I'll take care of it myself!"

Jasmine regretted the words as soon as she'd uttered them. She knew she didn't have time to go all the way to the manufacturer's plant to pick up the sample book *and* deliver it to Madelynn at the university. She thumbed through her agenda, and quickly decided her lunch break would be the best time to go.

Jasmine snatched her purse and ran to the stairwell rather than wait for the elevator. *I should be sending Karen to do this right now,* was all she could think. She threw the purse into the passenger seat of the compact company Focus and backed out of the spot without even looking behind her.

"I don't have time for this," she mumbled angrily, speeding out of the lot. "I hate this drive. And, this is the worst possible time that I could be on the road. It's horrible during lunch hour." She sped to the highway's entrance ramp, trying to get in front of as many drivers as she could, while she had the chance.

If I can make good time, she reasoned, *it should only take me forty-five minutes to get there, and I could have the book delivered and be back at the office by two o'clock.* She then quickly cut in front of a few more cars.

As she'd predicted, the 295 was packed. Traffic was crawling at thirty-five miles an hour, leaving Jasmine's Focus inches away from the bumper in front of her.

"Come on!" she seethed. "Don't you people know how to drive in traffic!" She whipped over into the middle lane as she saw that it was moving slightly faster than her lane. After a few seconds, she moved back into the right lane when it seemed to have sped up a bit.

Someone honked.

"Shut up!" Jasmine yelled harshly, tailing the vehicle's bumper in front of her so no one else could merge.

⌁

When she'd picked up the sample book, she'd checked the time. *Unbelievable*, she grumbled as she whipped out of the lot, *I'm not even going to get to Hopkins until almost 2 p.m.*

The pressure of her headache was growing intensely. "I'm so sick of these headaches!" Jasmine cried out in anger.

Again, she sped up as fast as she could to merge back onto the highway, where she continued cutting in and out of lanes. *Now, I won't even have time to eat lunch, which is just going to make this headache worse.*

Traffic had sped up to approximately fifty miles an hour now, and the right lane was moving significantly faster than the others. Jasmine felt like she was winning.

"See ya, suckers," she said arrogantly, passing the drivers in the middle lane. She rode the car's bumper in front of her, making sure that no one could squeeze in front of her. Unable to take the pain any longer, she reached over to grab her purse to retrieve more Excedrin. Just then, the car in front of her slammed on its breaks, causing her to slam on hers.

"You have got to be kidding me!" she yelled belligerently. "Can you people not just drive down the road?"

The cars in the middle lane began passing her yet again. "Oh, heck no!" she exclaimed, whipping her car over to the left lane, cutting off a pickup truck driver who flashed his lights at her in irritation.

"You don't scare me, truck," she muttered under her breath. When she was able to speed back up to forty-five miles an hour, she reached over to grab her purse again.

Just as she grabbed the Excedrin, she heard the sound of an explosion with a crunch. It was the loudest sound that she'd ever heard in her entire life, and she was suddenly crumpled into the dashboard experiencing excruciating pain. She struggled to breathe as her body went limp. "Help!" she cried weakly, as tears burst from her eyes, and as her wails trailed off, "NO! NO ...."

In a panic, Jasmine tried desperately to get out of the car. She attempted to open her car door and get out, to get away from the impact, but the door wouldn't budge. When she tried to move, she felt another surge of excruciating pain sear through her body.

"OW!" she yelped out in pain, breathing heavily.

Jasmine was trapped, as if an extremely heavy weight was laying on top of her. She blinked her eyes in shock, as if trying to wake up from a bad dream. When she opened them again, she saw people walking around outside the vehicle, almost in slow motion. She began to weep, still unsure about what was happening. Jasmine wasn't sure how badly she was hurt, but she knew something definitely wasn't right.

As she cried out in extreme pain, she heard the sound of sirens in the distance. Fire trucks, ambulances, police cars, and other emergency vehicles she didn't even recognize continued appearing on the scene. Flashing lights were everywhere. She tried to look around to see what was going on, but she couldn't tolerate the pain buzzing through her body the instant she tried to move her head.

Swiftly, someone in a uniform leaned down next to her broken window and began talking to her in a loud rushed voice. "Ma'am, I'm Captain Seymour of the Baltimore Fire Department. We're here to help you. I am going to cut this airbag out of the way so I can get closer to you, okay?"

"Okay." Jasmine couldn't stop her tears.

He finished cutting the airbag out of the way so he could examine her.

"It hurts! It hurts!" was all she could say, as tears streamed down her bloodied face. "Help me, please! I can't get out!"

"Where are you hurting?" he asked patiently.

"My legs. I can't move them!" Jasmine replied through her tears. "And my face hurts."

He reached through the broken window and felt her legs as a few more pieces of glass fell from the window. He noticed that the front engine compartment had enclosed on the gas pedal and seemingly crushed her ankle.

"We are going to get you out of there, okay?" he stated, then he spoke into his radio. "She's conscious, alert, and moving all extremities. Some contusions to the face. A black eye, broken glass wounds, a lip wound, and a broken nose. We're going to have to cut her out."

He leaned back down to her window. "Ma'am, we are going to use some tools to cut that side of the car and then we are going to move you out on a board, okay?" He waited, likely so Jasmine could show a sign of awareness.

She barely shook her head through her tears and sniffing. "I can't have a black eye," she whimpered, thinking of herself standing in front of a group of people, giving a presentation. "How broken is my nose?"

"We will get you out, ma'am," was his only response before he began shouting instructions.

He leaned back to her, again. "In a moment, you'll hear a very loud noise. That just means we are getting you out, okay?" He proceeded to speak into his radio. Instantly, other uniformed emergency personnel were standing around her vehicle, as Jasmine heard the painfully loud sound of the Jaws of Life, as it began prying her car apart. The jarring made her neck hurt, and the process seemed to be taking forever. She just wanted to be out. She wanted to go back to work, where she could send Pat to get the sample book and take it to Johns Hopkins, like he was supposed to. She was breathing heavily now and called out for help again in words that were made completely inaudible due to the loud roaring of the Jaws. The rescuers continued cutting away at the company car with the Jaws of Life, while Jasmine waited to get out. The machine sounded like it was going to crush and break her bones as it helped her rescuers rip the doors away from the vehicle.

Seeing the look of terror on her face, the captain leaned in again, asking, "Ma'am, are you okay?"

"I'm scared!" Jasmine feebly said, as a fresh set of tears streamed down her face.

The firefighters pulled both doors from the driver's side of the car and threw them onto the side of the road. Jasmine suddenly felt pain in her neck and realized that someone had reached in and put a cervical collar around her neck to stabilize it. Then she heard another person loudly speaking to her.

"Listen, ma'am, we are doing our best to get you out quickly, okay? This isn't going to be comfortable. We are going to put this here," he said, pointing, "and then we'll slide a board underneath you. When we pull you out, keep your hands across your chest right here, okay?" He wasn't quite as patient or calm as the captain.

The man placed her hands across her chest, and she tried bracing herself for the pain. "One, two, three ...," he counted, then he moved her up.

"OUCH!" Jasmine screamed.

"It's gonna hurt, ma'am. One, two, three ...," he repeated, as she was tugged backward toward the board.

Jasmine screamed again in pain.

"We've got you," he assured, patting her lightly on the shoulder. "This is the last pull. One, two, three ...," he called again, for the final time, as they rescued her from the wrecked car.

"AH!" Jasmine cried out after she caught a glimpse of the crunched company car from which she'd been pulled. The pain seemed to hurt even worse once she glimpsed it.

Once she was placed on top of the board and on the stretcher, she was quickly rolled to the waiting ambulance. Someone reached out and placed a white sheet over her legs and panicking, she called out, "What's that for! Did I lose my leg? Am I going to be able to walk again? I have to walk again!"

"We are going to take you to the local trauma center," she heard someone in a different uniform say to her, as they lifted her into the back of the ambulance.

Jasmine looked up at the ceiling of the ambulance. She was in indescribable pain. *This isn't what I had planned for today!* Suddenly, she whimpered, "The book! I need the sample book!"

"Ma'am, you are in the back of an ambulance. We are taking you to a trauma center."

"I know that, but I must have my book of samples," Jasmine explained in frustration. "It has to be delivered today!"

No one answered her this time. The paramedics were busy placing her ankle in an air cast to keep it from moving, so they could get her to the hospital as quickly and painlessly as possible. As soon as they secured the stretcher, they inserted her with an IV filled with pain medicine and began firing questions at her.

"Ma'am, do you know your name?"

"Jasmine Stone," she responded.

"Do you know your birthday?"

"January 9."

"Are you allergic to anything?"

"I don't know!" Jasmine irritably responded.

"Can you take a deep breath?" they asked, pushing lightly on her chest.

"Can you see this object?"

She panicked as she watched the paramedics working quickly to hook her up to cables and wires. She heard beeping noises as a mess of red, green, white, and clear wires were placed all over her. Someone placed a strap on her arm and began squeezing it tight to attain her blood pressure. Another asked her to inhale deeply. One paramedic pulled something large out of the compartment next to her, while the other pressed buttons on a monitor. One of them was also patting her on her shoulder, telling her everything was going to be okay, while simultaneously radioing to the trauma center to notify them of her condition.

Everyone was working so quickly and routinely. Jasmine tried to glance over at the monitor she was attached to for some answers, but all she saw was a mess of lines and graphs that she didn't understand.

When the racing ambulance hit a bump, she cried out in pain. "When will the medication kick in?" Jasmine groaned. "How much longer until we get to the hospital?"

"We are doing the best we can, ma'am," a paramedic gently responded.

After her vitals were taken, Jasmine felt a paramedic move down to address her leg wound, but she couldn't see what was going on due to the white sheet placed over the lower half of her body. She only could imagine what the problem was. "What happened?" she cried out in more pain. "IT HURTS! Will I ever be able to walk again?" Thinking about the possibility that she might not, she burst into a new set of tears. "The marathon!" she wailed.

Again, someone lightly patted her shoulder, trying to calm her down. "Ma'am," their voice said calmly, "try to concentrate on breathing slowly. We've got you. You are going to be alright."

As Jasmine lay in the back of the ambulance, with EMTs surrounding her as she cried tears of pain, she closed her eyes and imagined herself being pushed around in a wheelchair for the rest of her life.

⌐ FIFTEEN ⌐

$\mathcal{J}$asmine lay in her hospital bed, staring up at the ceiling. A beeping noise was coming from the monitor, and an oxygen mask covered her face. She was in a different room now than before. She looked around, trying to orient herself and figure out where she was. Looking down, she noticed that she was wrapped in a very large white bandage from her toes all the way up to the bottom of her knee.

She inhaled deeply, laid her head back on her pillow, and tried to remember what had happened. The last thing she remembered was nurses and medical personnel frantically buzzing about her stretcher, as she was being transferred from the stretcher into a hospital bed, then being asked more questions. She remembered someone cutting off her pant leg and being hooked up to an IV machine. She'd slept all night, and in the morning she was informed that she needed surgery. She then was asked a few more questions before a mask was placed over her face. After that, she wasn't sure of anything up until now.

Jasmine still felt some pain and was groggy. A nurse stood right beside her, waiting for her to wake up. When she saw Jasmine's eyes flutter, she bent closer to speak to her.

"Hi," she said, with a sweet smile. "My name is Brittany, and I'm here to help you with your recovery from surgery. I'll be monitoring your incision site, and I'll make sure you're comfortable. Don't be afraid to ask for anything you need, including pain medicine, if you're still having any pain."

Brittany lightly patted the wound and continued talking. "I'll be monitoring your pain as well as your heart rate and breathing. Your oxygen mask must remain on for another thirty minutes, and if everything goes smoothly, you'll only need to stay in the recovery room for an hour, okay?"

Oh, I'm in the recovery room, Jasmine remembered. Suddenly, everything started to make sense. She nodded her head slightly, indicating to the nurse that she understood.

"Do you have any questions for me?" the nurse inquired kindly.

It took Jasmine a minute to speak, but when she had the strength, she asked weakly, "What happened to me?"

"You were in a car accident, and you were brought here in an ambulance. You have broken several bones in your foot and ankle and now you're in the recovery room, following your trip to the operating room. The doctor will speak with you when you're brought to your room. He'll answer all your questions about your injury."

Jasmine said nothing. She closed her eyes again, then took a deep breath. Brittany must have noticed she was shivering because she covered her with a warm blanket.

Before long, Jasmine's gurney was wheeled to a room. As a nurse settled her into her bed, Jasmine noticed a clear bin that contained her belongings sitting on a small table. Tears started to form in her eyes. She sniffed them back and winced in pain; she'd forgotten she'd broken her nose and wounded her lip.

The nurse checked her vitals, gave Jasmine a few instructions, then walked out of the room.

Jasmine sat alone in the room, unsure of what to think. She breathed heavily and quickly, trying to keep more tears from falling, but she couldn't hold them back any longer. A floodgate opened as she thought about her marathon and her promotion.

What in the world am I supposed to do now?

There was an ache in her chest. She knew she needed to call Brett, but she couldn't bring herself to do it. Not right now. The pain medication was making her drowsy, and she drifted off to sleep.

Jasmine woke up a bit later to another nurse taking her vitals. "Hi," she said, not quite as kindly as Brittany. "My name is Katelyn. I'll be taking care of you today. Is there anything you need?"

"I'm very thirsty," said Jasmine, exhaustion reverberating in her voice.

The nurse quickly returned with a cup filled with ice chips. Jasmine had never been so happy to see ice in all her life. She felt so hot and thirsty.

"The doctor will be in shortly," Katelyn stated matter-of-factly, as she walked toward the door. "If you need anything, don't hesitate to push the call button."

A few minutes later, there was a knock on the door, and a doctor slowly walked in. "Hi, Jasmine," he said brightly. "I'm Dr. Peltos. How are you feeling?" He was an older gentleman and reminded her of Victor.

"I've been better," she said sarcastically, with a slight smirk on her face.

"You did very well during surgery, and there were no complications," he shared, before breaking the discouraging news to Jasmine. He turned to the monitor that displayed the X-rays of her broken ankle. "If you look here, you can see you suffered a severe Trimalleolar fracture, which is a combination of your fibula, your tibia, and your talus all cracking," he explained, as he pointed to bones Jasmine didn't even know existed. "You also broke some of your metatarsal bones," he showed, displaying additional X-rays on the screen. Jasmine felt more pain just looking at her shattered bones. Dr. Peltos pulled up some more images on the screen, then went on.

"Now, I'll show you what we were able to do with the surgery," he said with a smile, displaying his obvious love for his profession. "We put your ankle bone fragments back where they belong and stabilized them with plates and screws."

Again, he pointed to an X-ray of Jasmine's ankle. "These plates and screws will hold the pieces together while they're healing. Once they've healed, we can remove them while we rehabilitate the ankle." Dr. Peltos spoke as if it was wonderful news. "Do you have any immediate questions?" he asked her.

"How long will it take me to recover?" she pressed, worried about work and her promotion.

"I'm very familiar with this question," he asserted, "especially when this surgery is due to a car accident. Your leg will be numb for the first twelve hours or so. After that, you'll start to feel some tingling and pain. You'll wear a splint, which is hard in the back and soft in the front to give your ankle room to swell. A period of immobilization and non-weight-bearing will be necessary, and once that is completed, you'll have physical therapy to work toward gaining mobility back in your foot and ankle. During that time, you'll use crutches, a wheelchair, or a knee walker, whichever you choose, and once you're fully able to bear weight on your ankle, it will be protected by a boot. After that period, you'll start working on strength and stability training of the foot and ankle."

He patted Jasmine's arm before continuing. "But there's no need to worry. All of this will be supervised by your physical therapist, and you'll be given exercises to perform at home as well. After foot and ankle surgery, it usually takes between six to eight weeks before you can start bearing weight. That's how long it takes for the bones to heal. You should be good as new in less than four months." He finished up his speech as if he said the very same thing often enough to have it memorized.

Four months! She gasped, *I can't be like this for four months!*

Dr. Peltos had told her how her bones were shattered and put back together, but all she heard was that her world had shattered. There was no quick remedy or physical therapy for that.

❧

Jasmine woke up again to the sound of the nurse moving about her room. She was checking her vitals again. "Hi there," Katelyn acknowledged. "How are you feeling?"

Jasmine responded to the nurse with frustration. "I was training for a marathon."

"Oh, I'm so sorry, dear," Katelyn said, sounding genuinely disappointed for Jasmine.

"And, I travel for work."

"Listen, you're being well taken care of here. You'll be back to normal in no time at all."

"Do you know when I can go home?" Jasmine asked.

The nurse spoke in a soft voice, placing a hand on her arm to comfort her. "Dr. Peltos is one of the best orthopedic surgeons in the city. He did an excellent job repairing your foot and ankle, and he'll take excellent care of you. You couldn't have asked for a better doctor."

Jasmine slightly smiled at the nurse and tried to appear happy. Yet, all she could think of was her shattered dream of crossing the finish line at 26.2 miles, and her hope of being promoted to the new position. This wasn't the way it was supposed to go. Jasmine wiped an angry tear from her eye.

"Is there anything I can do for you?" Katelyn asked with compassion.

"I need the bin," Jasmine said, pointing to her belongings.

"Is there something specific I can get for you?"

"I need my phone and my agenda," Jasmine answered, with worry in her voice.

It was late afternoon, and Jasmine knew she couldn't delay calling Brett any longer.

She finally looked at her cell phone. There were several missed calls from him, missed calls from Karen, and a few texts from Bradley. She'd been dreading this moment for hours. She inhaled deeply and closed her eyes as she dialed Brett's number.

She listened to the first ring, and then the second.

"Jasmine! Where are you?! Are you okay? I've been trying to get hold of you for hours. You never dropped off the sample book."

Jasmine sat in silence for a bit as she tried to figure out exactly what to say.

"Hi, Brett," she said carefully. "I'm in the R. Adams Cowley Shock Trauma Center. I was involved in a serious accident yesterday while taking the sample book from the plant to Johns Hopkins. I'm okay, but my ankle is broken in several places, and I have a severe crush injury to my right foot."

"Oh no," stated Brett. She thought she could detect some slight compassion along with the questions in his voice. "Were you driving the company car?"

"I was."

Another pause. "But you're okay?"

"Well, I'm alive, if that's what you're asking."

Yet another awkward pause.

"What will this mean for me, Brett?" Jasmine inquired hesitantly.

"Listen," Brett advised, clearly not sure what to say. "You take it easy for the next week. We can keep covering things here in the office for that time, and if we need anything, we'll be in touch through phone and email."

Despite his calming words, Jasmine could hear the uneasiness in his tone. She knew things really weren't under control in the office at all.

"I'll send Karen over to the hospital to pick up the sample book and have her deliver it to the university. You do still have the book, right, Jasmine?"

"I do."

"I'm sorry this happened to you. When you get a chance, today or tomorrow, can you email over whatever you know about your work schedule? I'll have Karen review it, and we'll transfer those tasks to Karen and your team."

Jasmine closed her eyes and said nothing, knowing exactly what this meant.

Brett finished, "Right now, you rest and recover, and we'll talk later, okay?"

"Yes," was all Jasmine could manage around the lump in her throat, as Brett hung up the phone.

Jasmine opened her agenda. It was packed with presentation appointments and several things to do. Yet, here she lay in her hospital bed, unable to walk and hardly able to move more than her fingers without feeling pain. Her phone rang again. She looked down at it and commented bitterly, "If Karen thinks for a second I'm going to talk to her, she's lost her mind."

Filled with sudden rage, Jasmine weakly threw her cell phone as far as she could. It landed on the ground and bounced to the wall. The agenda soon followed it, and she began to cry. Today was Recovery Day One, and she was already tired of the pain.

She pushed the button to call the nurse to up her pain dosage. While she waited, she landed her head on the pillow and tucked her face in the crook of her arm. Her shoulders shook as she erupted into angry defeated tears.

By the time Katelyn entered the room, Jasmine was already fast asleep. She saw the phone in the corner and the agenda sprawled all over the floor. She could guess from the look of things what must have happened. Katelyn lightly placed her hand on Jasmine's arm and whispered, "It's going to be okay." Before she left, she picked up Jasmine's phone and the agenda book and placed them on the side table next to the bed.

The next morning, Jasmine awoke to a text from Bradley, which said, *Wake up beautiful girl, time to get up and smell that fresh running air :)*

Instantly, she was reminded of her current situation. She tried to reach for the light on her bed, but in the process she strained her ankle, and the pain caused her to blurt out angry words under her breath. Instead of turning on the light, she responded to his text: *Don't ever text me again. Ever.*

It seemed harsh, but Jasmine had known he was too good to be true from the beginning. If she got rid of him now, she wouldn't have to deal with more disappointment down the road. She deleted all their texts and then his contact information from her phone.

She plopped the phone next to her on the bed and attempted to go back to sleep. She drifted in and out for almost an hour, then jolted up in her bed, again wincing in pain. She sat up and called for the nurse. Jasmine was sweating and having hot flashes. She'd forgotten for a moment that it was the following day, and a different shift, when another nurse arrived.

"Hi Jasmine," the nurse said kindly. "My name is Bethany. I'll be taking care of you this morning. Did you need something?"

"I'm sweating," Jasmine said, panting for breath.

Bethany asked her a series of questions while taking her vitals. She suggested that Jasmine's pain medication was up too high and that she was having a reaction to that.

"Did you have any dreams?" the nurse asked.

Jasmine laid her head back on her pillow. "I did," she said, confused as to why this would be a question.

"Were you panting heavily in your dream?"

Jasmine thought this was a strange question, but it was true; she was still panting heavily. "Yes." She nodded.

"That can happen when pain medication isn't correctly accepted by your system," Bethany explained. "Why don't you get more rest now? We'll get this straightened out, then we'll give the crutches a go-around."

Jasmine awoke again to the nurse taking her vitals and checking her breathing again. Several hours had passed, and for the first time since the accident, Jasmine felt as if the pain had let up enough for her to be somewhat comfortable.

"Did someone come to retrieve the sample book?" she asked Bethany.

"Yes, ma'am. We handed it to a lady named Karen."

Jasmine grimaced at the mention of her name. "Thank you, I appreciate it."

"Would you like to give the crutches a try?" Bethany asked enthusiastically.

"Sure," Jasmine replied, knowing that the faster she was stable on crutches, the faster she could leave the hospital.

e⟶೨

It took Jasmine three rounds of crutch therapy to show that she could manage to get herself from one place to another without the aid or assistance of a nurse. She was ready to be in the comfort of her own home. Three days was too long to be cooped up in a hospital bed.

Jasmine received her discharge papers and was helped into the back of an ambulance to return home. When they arrived, medical personnel carried Jasmine up the stairs and into her apartment. She felt so helpless and embarrassed, imagining everyone who happened to be around was watching the scene. The team helped her to her room, dropped off her belongings, asked her to sign a few papers for the pain medication, instructed her to closely follow her doctor's written guidelines, and they left.

So, this is it, she thought to herself as she was once again all alone. *Off to get the next helpless individual who can't walk up a flight of stairs if their life depended on it.*

Jasmine took in a deep heavy breath. She grabbed her pain pills and the large water container that was left on the bedside table, then started to read through the care instructions that she'd been given.

"Resting the ankle involves avoiding putting weight on it and limiting movement. Icing will help alleviate pain and reduce swelling.

"Compression will further help reduce swelling and inflammation. A person can achieve this by wrapping an elastic bandage around the foot and ankle. Elevating the ankle will help reduce swelling and inflammation, which will help reduce pain.

"Talk to your doctor about taking an oral anti-inflammatory medication, which will also help reduce pain.

"When lying down, place pillows under your leg to keep it raised above your heart, which will cut swelling and help the wound heal ...."

Jasmine could read no further. She was exhausted, and her eyes were drifting off the page. An incoming call from Brett appeared on her cell phone. She could only stare at it, unable to pick it up. She propped up her leg with pillows, lay back, and fell asleep.

⌁ SIXTEEN ⌁

*J*asmine woke from her nap covered in a cold sweat, feeling groggy and even more tired than before. She was panting heavily as she looked around, at last reminded that she was in her own bed with a shattered ankle.

She'd never felt this way before. She was cold and hot at the same time, and extremely hungry. She painfully reached for her medication and her bottle of water. As she swallowed the pill, she looked at the time: four p.m. *Oh gosh, I've been asleep for over three hours,* she realized, feeling frustrated as she rubbed her eyes and reached for her phone.

There were three missed calls and a voice mail from Brett. Jasmine groaned as she remembered that he had called her just as she had fallen asleep.

She listened to his voice mail. "Hi Jasmine, it's Brett. I need you to check your email at your earliest convenience. Thanks."

Her heart sank, as she sadly thought, *I know* exactly *what the email will be about.* She indignantly reached for her crutches, then hobbled into the kitchen to find some food before checking her email. It took her several minutes to maneuver herself out of her bed and into an upright position so she could stand on one leg, then wobble into the kitchen.

When Jasmine opened the cupboard, she cursed out loud, remembering she hadn't yet gone to the grocery store before the accident. Instantly, her heart started beating faster and she quickly sat down at her kitchen table. She continued breathing heavy and felt dizzy, as her head rolled from side to side. She let go of the crutches to put her hand to her head, becoming more and more nervous about what was going on. The loud crash of the crutches, which had fallen to the floor, startled her. She wanted to cry out for help and scream in anger at the same time, but she didn't have the energy for either. Heat began rising through her body as she sat. She felt sick to her stomach, as if she might throw up. Breathing deeper and deeper, her head began spinning.

The next thing she knew, she woke up on the floor in a puddle of sweat. An instant fear came over her body, as she remembered a dream she'd had while she was passed out. It was the same one she'd had several times in the hospital. In it, a driverless black Mercedes pulled up to a curb to pick her up. Each time, she was dressed in different clothing and standing in a different place. Yet, in every dream, just before she was about to climb into the car, it quickly pulled away, as if it was poking fun at her. She could hear inaudible words being spoken as it sped away. This particular time, the sideview mirrors mockingly waved goodbye.

"NO!" Jasmine cried out as she laid in a heap on the floor. She wanted to rip off her cast and throw it out the kitchen window. She wanted this all to just be a bad dream, but her pain told her otherwise. "Why?" Jasmine clamored. "Why me?" Slowly, she began pulling herself back up onto the kitchen chair, hoping to escape the pain in her ankle.

Her breathing finally regulated after she drank some water, and she was finally able to open her computer. She glanced at the time. It felt as if hours had passed since she'd fainted, but the clock on the screen showed it was only 4:19. She reluctantly opened her email.

There it was—Brett's email. Afraid of what she would see, her heart pounded, and Jasmine hesitated before opening it. Finally, she clicked it open. *Hi Jasmine*, it began.

I'm happy to hear you have made it home to begin your recovery. We're hoping you have a quick one and can rejoin us in the office very soon. Please see the attached document from the Human Resources Department. You can contact them regarding time off, insurance, etc.

In the interim, we've temporarily delegated your work responsibilities to Karen Boggs. Please send her the account reports at your earliest convenience, as well as giving her access to your calendar. You might keep in contact with her to ensure that the current projects stay on track and move forward.

Please get back with me at your earliest convenience to discuss moving onward from here. We're looking forward to having you back soon.

Best regards,

Brett

Jasmine felt sick to her stomach. She sat numbly, staring at the screen, knowing this was what was coming but unable to process what she'd just read. A document was attached. Her curiosity got the better of her, and she clicked on it.

If you've been seriously hurt in an accident and are unable to work because of associated injuries, you are entitled to recover all your missed income, money for your medical bills, and more.

After reading that first sentence, Jasmine instantly regretted opening it, as she scrolled down through four pages of text. She was exhausted and discouraged just thinking about it. Knowing she could delay no longer, Jasmine picked up her phone and called Brett. She inhaled a few calming breaths while waiting for him to answer.

"Hi Jasmine!" he answered enthusiastically. "It's good to hear from you. Were you able to send Karen the reports and a link to your calendar?"

Jasmine couldn't speak.

"Jasmine? Hello?"

She hung up the phone and stared out into space. Maybe Bradley was right. Jasmine was being replaced already, after only three days of being gone from work. She reread his email and called him back.

"Hello?" Brett answered.

"Hi. I'm sorry; not sure what happened there." She paused, then Jasmine spoke up for herself. "Brett," she said in a determined voice, "I can *do* this. I can do this from home."

She heard Brett sigh. "I'm afraid it's not up to me, Jasmine," he responded weakly.

Jasmine narrowed her jaw and answered back. "If you had the balls of a man, Brett, you would fight for me. You know I can do this, and you know I'm the only one who can carry the sales department to where it needs to go."

She softened her voice, realizing that she might have seemed too harsh with her intensity. "I need this, Brett, please, I need this," she pleaded.

"How long are you going to be out?" he asked, a slight irritation in his voice. She could tell this wasn't the conversation he'd expected to have.

"I go back to see the doctor in six days, so they can check my healing progress."

There was a long pause, then Brett inquired, "How long is the whole recovery process?"

In a cast for six or eight weeks, in a walking boot for six more weeks, then a brace for six or eight weeks after that, she thought. "I'll be back as soon as possible," Jasmine promised him.

"Read that document and fill out the paperwork, Jasmine," Brett rebutted. It was clear that he wasn't going to stand up for her. "And please send Karen the reports. She needs them ASAP."

Jasmine woke up the next morning to more pain. Before she was fully awake, she groggily attempted to sit up. She was almost halfway there before she was forced back down again. She landed on her pillow and tossed her arm over her face, reminding herself, again, that this wasn't a dream. It was her new reality. "You have a shattered ankle that's being held together by screws, Jasmine," she said out loud. "You can't just hop out of bed anymore."

She then reached for her medication, trying not to strain on her ankle further. She swallowed a pain pill and angrily laid back down on her pillow, looking up at the ceiling in the half-sunlight room, reliving the moments leading up to the crash. Her mind began racing.

Why were you following so close?

Why didn't you take an Excedrin at the office? Or when you stopped at the plant?

Why did you tell that lazy good-for-nothing Pat that you would go get that stupid book? You knew you didn't have the time! And, you hate going to the plant!

And why does there always have to be so much stinking traffic on that road?

Jasmine closed her eyes in frustration at herself and smacked her pillow over her face.

Feeling better once the pain meds kicked in, she decided to attempt a shower.

She very quickly realized that taking a shower wearing a molded cast was extremely difficult. As much as she tried to keep the cast clean and dry, per the doctor's instruction, some water had seeped down into it. Not knowing what to do, she tried to shove a corner of her towel as far down as she could into it, but it was simply too tight, and water continued to trickle down her leg.

She hobbled on one leg, leaning first on the bathroom counter, then the doorframe, then the wall, and finally the closet, to pull out some clothing. Getting dressed was an even harder battle. Her sweatpants got stuck on the damp cast wrap fabric and being wet inside had caused her skin inside it to itch. She became increasingly frustrated as the morning wore on. Over an hour had passed, and all she had accomplished was half a shower and barely getting dressed.

Feeling hungry, she retrieved her crutches and headed toward the kitchen. On her way down the hallway, her right crutch slipped out from under her just enough to almost toss her to the floor.

"This is so stupid!" Jasmine growled out loud, wanting to send the crutch hurling down the hall. She hadn't even moved around that much and already the crutches were creating sores under her arms. Halfway down the hall, she stopped to catch her breath. Pain was beginning to return. She finally made her way to her small kitchen to find something to eat. As she stood at the counter cutting up an apple to dip in cream cheese, she lost her balance and fell against the refrigerator. Trying to catch herself without putting pressure on her leg, she stuck out her hand for balance, just happening to hit her race calendar that was stuck to the fridge. She now stood face-to-face with it. Today was Saturday, and the last X she'd marked was Tuesday. She read the little note in the corner of today's date: Run with Bradley :).

In a fit of frustration, Jasmine ripped the calendar from the refrigerator and threw it across the room toward the garbage can, whimpering in defeat. She leaned both her hands against the countertop, closing her eyes as a surge of pain shot through her ankle. Tears began to flood her eyes, but she quickly blinked them away, while continuing to cut the apple. She could hardly chew, and she didn't even have an appetite. Her nose began to run, so she turned toward the box of tissues set on the table, just far enough away that she couldn't reach it without an effort. She closed her eyes as the tears began to plop. "I can't even wipe my nose," Jasmine whimpered slowly and quietly, feeling utterly defeated.

"Why, God?" Jasmine whispered, sliding down the wall onto the floor. "*Why?*"

She wept into the long sleeve of her shirt for several seconds before continuing her questioning monologue.

"Why do You hate me so much?" she whispered softly. "What have I ever done to You? What have I done to deserve this?" She could hardly speak through her tears. She sat there, on her kitchen floor, and bawled like a baby. She was lost; her spirit broken.

"You know what, God? You win." She sniveled, wiping her nose with her forefinger. "Here I am. Alone and defeated. But I want you to know that this wasn't a fair fight. You're a Bully."

SEVENTEEN

*J*asmine reclined in her chair to keep her leg elevated, staring at her computer, finishing up the form for HR. Her patience ran thinner as the hours went by, but it had to get done. Today marked her fifth day home after her hospital stay, and she hadn't so much as stepped outside since she'd been carried up to her apartment.

She looked out the window, noticing it appeared to be a nice day outside. Putting aside her work, she opened her phone and checked the weather: fifty-four degrees and the sun was shining. As she held her phone, she received a text. She opened it right away, thinking it must be from work.

You have a package, it read.

Jasmine all but jumped out of her chair. "Yeah!" she exclaimed. "I know exactly what this is!" She squinted her eyes from the door to her crutches. "Yes," she decided. "I'll attempt it. I need some fresh air anyway."

Excited at the idea of getting outside, she closed her computer, carefully put down the recliner footrest, and picked up her crutches.

Thirty minutes later, all Jasmine had managed to do was go to the bathroom, put on her shoe, and find her key. She was exhausted by the time she reached the top step. She stared down at the rest of the stairs. *Okay, maybe this wasn't a good idea. Never thought I'd ever be trying to figure out how to make it down three flights of stairs on crutches, but here we are.* "How wonderful it is to live on the third floor," she mocked.

"Okay, seriously, do I hold on to the railing, or do I just rely on the crutches?"

She put the crutches out in front of her, then brought them back in. She put her right stiff leg out in front of her and brought that back in as well. *Please tell me no one will see this,* she thought, looking around. *Surely it can't be that hard to figure this out.*

Finally, Jasmine placed both of the crutches on the step below her and jumped to it with her good foot. Her cast hit the step as she jumped down, and she opened her mouth in pain, but nothing came out.

Suddenly, she heard voices at the bottom of the stairwell. She froze, hoping no one would see her. She heard them walk up the first flight, then the second. She held her breath. She then heard keys jingle and breathed a sigh of relief.

She attempted the next stair. It didn't take Jasmine long to figure out how to get down them all, but by the time she reached the bottom, her armpits were searing in pain, and she was regretting leaving her apartment at all. She leaned on her crutches for a few minutes, hoping the pain would pass before continuing on. As she closed her eyes to rest, a cool spring breeze blew her unclean hair.

Okay, the goal here is to get to the mailroom as quickly and invisibly as possible.

The parking lot was starting to fill up with more and more people returning home from work. She watched as person after person mindlessly moved to and from their cars without a care or thought in the world about being able to quickly and easily place one foot in front of the other. She was jealous. It wasn't fair.

She took a deep breath and continued to the parcel-locker room. When she arrived, she had to move aside to let someone out before entering. *So much for being invisible*, she sighed, keeping her head down to avoid any eye contact. By the time she reached her box, she realized she hadn't given any thought to how she was going to bend down and enter the code.

Why can't this just be easy?

Trying to be subtle, she glanced around to see if anyone was watching as she struggled to figure things out, but no one seemed to care. Finally, she leaned her crutches against the wall and awkwardly angled herself down to her box, her leg sticking out in front of her.

Of course, my locker has to be the second from the bottom.

The package was small, but it was too big for Jasmine to hold along with her crutch handles. She tried several times to balance the package in her hands, eventually deciding the only thing she could do was to embarrassingly tuck it under her chin and head for the exit. She clicked her way down the sidewalk and across the parking lot, squeezing her neck harder and harder as she felt the box beginning to slip out from under her chin. About halfway to her apartment block, she stopped to adjust the box, then kept going—this time trying to move faster.

Jasmine felt the box slipping again but decided, with determination, to make it to her stairwell before stopping again to adjust. Just as she reached the stairwell, she lost her grip on the box, which slipped down and bounced a few feet away from her. "Dang it!" Jasmine yelled. "This was *not* a good idea. Why did I not think to bring a backpack?"

Jasmine heard keys jangling not far away, and she peeked up as she bent down to retrieve the package, catching sight of Victor Laubenstein walking away from his door and toward her. She mumbled under her breath and quickly pulled her upper body back.

Victor bent down to retrieve the package. As he stood up with it, he gasped in surprise. "Oh my goodness! Whatever has happened to you, my dear?" Both curiosity and empathy were apparent in his voice.

Wanting to disappear into the cement, she stared at him, feeling humiliated, unable to speak.

"Here, let me take this upstairs for you," he offered, and he headed toward the flight of stairs.

Jasmine followed behind him, but as soon as she attempted the first step, she realized she had no idea how to walk upstairs with crutches.

What worked on the way down, clearly won't work on the way up, she mused.

"May I help you?" Victor asked, noticing that she was frozen in place.

"I've got it," Jasmine insisted, scratching her neck, while her face spread into an artificial smile as she felt even more embarrassed. Frantically attempting to pretend she had everything together, she started up the steps. Accidentally, she put more pressure than she meant to on her right foot and silently winced in pain, hoping not to alert Victor. With only a few more painful bumps, she figured out that when going up the stairs, she needed to lean her body weight on the crutches, hop up to the next stair with her less hurt foot, then bring the crutches up to that stair.

Victor was waiting at her door when she finally reached the top. Jasmine badly wanted to take a quick break and catch her breath, but she chose to keep going down the hall to her door, as if everything was just fine.

"Would you like me to unlock your door for you?" he asked, obviously seeing the pain on her face. He reached out for her key and then asked, "What happened?" with genuine concern for her as he unlocked the door.

"I was in a car accident on the 295; crunched between two vehicles," Jasmine explained, "and it crushed my ankle."

"Oh, I'm so sorry to hear that," Victor replied, scrunching his head between his shoulders as if he felt her pain. Catching a glimpse inside of Jasmine's disheveled apartment, Victor inquired, "Are you up here all alone?"

Jasmine was baffled by Victor's continual kindness. "Yes, but I'm fine," she stammered, knowing full well she wasn't fine but not wanting to argue with this prominent educated person.

Victor, however, reacted to the truth Jasmine was sure was written on her face. "You shouldn't be up here all alone, my dear," he said as he invited himself into her apartment and helped her get settled into a chair.

As he dawdled backwards toward the door, Jasmine suddenly burst out, "Who are you?"

She must have surprised him with the question, as he responded, "I'm Victor Laubenstein."

Jasmine narrowed her eyes and asked the question again. "No, who *are* you, Victor Laubenstein?"

"Oh, I'm a cognitive behavioral neuroscientist," Victor answered modestly. "What makes you ask?"

"I saw your book in a lobby at Johns Hopkins University."

"Interesting," he said with surprise. "Well then, who are *you*, Jasmine Stone?" he asked with genuine curiosity.

"You mean who *was* I," Jasmine complained with agitation, still trying to get comfortable in her chair. "I work for a company called Nuevo Design. I was a sales rep, but now

I'm just a cripple in a chair." She paused for a moment before finishing her thought. "And, there's nothing I can do about it," she said, shaking her head in disbelief.

"What exactly do you mean by that?"

"You know, God and His little puppet strings up there, yanking us around," she explained, while her hands danced invisible strings.

Victor couldn't possibly miss the anger and bitterness oozing from her voice and present in her eyes. He observed her with compassion when he spoke. "May I share something with you, Jasmine?"

She shrugged her shoulders and answered defeatedly. "Sure."

"I've come to realize that one of the most important decisions you can make in your entire life is whether or not you live in a friendly or a hostile universe."

She scoffed and her head tilted to the side. "Well, let me tell you: I live in a hostile one."

An awkward silence seeped into the room. Then, Victor commented, "Be careful, Jasmine. What you choose to believe about life is very important."

"Why does it matter what I believe?" Jasmine asked disdainfully.

"Because your beliefs predict and produce your future."

She wrinkled her forehead, alerting Victor that she didn't quite comprehend what he was saying.

"What proof do you have that you live in a hostile universe?" he asked.

Jasmine laughed scornfully. "My *entire life* is proof that I live in a hostile universe."

"Like what?"

"Oh geez, where do I even begin?" she asked, throwing her hands up in the air. "Let's just start at the very beginning, shall we? I'm the youngest child of three, and my mom and dad didn't even want me. True story," she said, trying to convince Victor that it was. "I heard them say once that they wanted another boy. I've been a nuisance to them since the day I was born."

Victor continued listening.

"My sister is the one who always does everything right, and I'm the black sheep of the family. Jasmine never does anything right. She's just too stupid."

"What else?" she said, becoming increasingly more flustered the longer she went on. "I went to photography school and was supposed to have a job waiting for me here in Maryland right after graduation. The week I arrived, the job fell through. I can't keep a boyfriend to save my life. My only friend just moved across the country. I've broken my ankle. I've probably lost my job. I can't run the marathon that I've been dreaming about my entire life. Anything else you want to know? Any more 'proof' you need?" Jasmine leaned her head on the back of the chair, completely exhausted.

"So yes, Victor," she said, picking her head back up. "I'd say that I have proof that I live in a hostile universe. Everything is against me, and no matter how hard I try, no matter what I do, I can't catch a break. Bad stuff *always* happens to me."

"You know, Jasmine, humans fascinate me. I've dedicated my life to studying how we operate, and what I've come to realize is that our brains are the most amazing technology that's ever been created. Your brain is your superpower, and your mind is the controller of your brain. Your mind tells your brain what to think, how to feel, and how to act, on a day-to-day, minute-by-minute basis. Your brain loves instruction. If you instruct your brain to focus on the fact that you can't catch a break, that's all it will do for you. That's all it will notice. Every single thing you do in life will be filtered through the lens of that belief you have, which is 'I can't catch a break.'

"Contrary to what most people believe, there are no outside forces controlling how you choose to think. What you choose to focus on is what you create. If you focus on the fact that you've had all these terrible things happen to you, that's exactly what you'll see, and that's *all* you'll see. More and more 'bad' circumstances and things will continue to *happen* to you. And, you're absolutely correct—no matter how hard you try, no matter what you do, bad things will *always* happen to you."

Jasmine remained silent while Victor continued to speak about a concept that seemed foreign to her.

"The way an individual views life is about perception and perspective. Those are based on our belief system—in our neurosynaptic connections. For me, personally, I've decided to believe that I live in a friendly universe—an empowering universe—where everything that happens, whether I perceive it to be good or bad, is working *for* me rather than against me. I believe there are no mistakes, only learning experiences. I believe that every human being is a powerful creator who gets to choose their destiny."

"No mistakes?" Jasmine questioned skeptically. "I can't just stick my head in the sand and pretend that everything is okay. I'd love to live in your friendly universe, but I live in a reality where life stinks and we're all screwed."

Victor inhaled deeply and seated himself on her floor before responding. "Who decided that for you?"

"Decided what?" Jasmine questioned.

"Who decided you live in a reality where life stinks and we're all screwed?"

Jasmine hesitated. Then replied, "God did."

"How do you know that?"

Jasmine stared at him, unsure of how to respond.

Victor continued on. "The truth is, *you* decided that. Jasmine decided a long time ago that the world was against her, and that somehow, no matter what she did, she was screwed. And so, you've been repeatedly living out that belief over and over and over again, making those neural connections attached to that belief stronger and stronger, until it's become a way of life for you. That belief is guiding your thoughts, guiding how you feel, guiding your actions, and it has become your reality. It has brought you here, to this very moment in your life, where everything continues to be against you. And, it will continue to guide your future. God is not creating your reality; *you* are, Jasmine, through your thoughts."

Jasmine had no words. She simply couldn't respond.

"Jasmine," Victor said passionately, "if you believe God is angry and mean, you'll find evidence and proof for that belief. And if you believe God is friendly and loving, you'll find evidence and proof for that belief as well. You get to choose. With our free will, we all get to choose what beliefs we decide to develop. By choosing this belief you've enrolled your reticular activating system to focus on the fact that God is mean and is out to get you."

"What's a reticular activating system?" Jasmine asked with curiosity.

"The reticular activating system is a set of interlacing nuclei in the brain that plays a critical role in a person's behavior and habits, and it acts as a filter, instructing your brain on what to focus on. On any given day, a human brain takes in approximately 35 gigabytes of information. Think about it, do you remember every single person that you passed on your way to the mail locker?"

"No," Jasmine shook her head.

"And you also don't remember every car that passes you on your way to and from work, correct?"

"Definitely not."

"Can you tell me every single color that is in this room without looking around first?" Victor quizzed.

"Purple, brown, um … green …" Jasmine's eyes moved around trying to recall the colors. "I can't remember all of them," she admitted.

"There is red on the binding of that book," Victor reminded her, pointing to her bookshelf. "Have you ever seen that book before?"

Jasmine chuckled. "Of course. I probably see it every day."

"But it's not necessary to your survival, so you don't need to remember that. It's not important to you. You've chosen not to focus on it."

Jasmine tilted her head, intrigued with the practical science.

"So you can see, we don't need all of that information that our brains take in every day. In order to conserve the most amount of energy, you have the ability to tell your brain what it needs to focus on and retain. Each individual has the ability to choose what they would like to make a behavioral habit."

Victor was interrupted by the sound of his cell phone, ringing on his hip. As soon as he picked it up, his countenance changed. "I'm sorry, Jasmine, I've got to take this," Victor said, with a gleam in his eye. "It's my wife."

Quickly pulling a pen from his shirt pocket, he scribbled something down on Jasmine's package. "If you need *anything*, please don't hesitate to ask me," he instructed her with a smile. He half dropped the box on Jasmine's lap, waved goodbye, and sweetly answered his phone. When he was gone, she looked down at the package to his scribble. It was Victor's phone number.

"My *wife*," Jasmine repeated out loud to herself. "His wife?"

Jasmine sat staring at the empty space in front of her with her jaw dropped. For the first time ever, Jasmine was beginning to understand that things might not be as she'd always perceived them to be. Her mind went back to the day she'd accused Victor of being an old man—a washed-up nobody who had nothing to talk about. She looked down at his phone number written on the box. She certainly needed help with a few things: a ride to the hospital and food, for starters. However, there was no way she was asking this important not washed-up old nobody of a scientist who suddenly had a wife to help her.

I'll call a nurse service, Jasmine decided, as she ripped open the package. She pulled out the waterproof cast cover and smiled to herself. Everything else may be wrong in the world, but at least now Jasmine could take a real shower and keep her cast dry.

⤳ EIGHTEEN ⤳

*J*asmine hung up her phone and pounded her fist on the table. It had been ten days since her accident, and her work tasks were being ripped from her grasp one by one. She hadn't liked Brooke from the beginning and, once again, she was proving to be arrogant and snobbish, acting as if she knew everything there was to know about marketing. Without Jasmine there to push the race sponsorship, Brooke had managed to pull the plug on the event, moving the marketing money somewhere else.

Her phone rang again. She closed her eyes in frustration and leaned her hands on her head before answering. "I don't even care anymore, Brooke," she muttered under her breath as she picked up the call.

"Hello," Jasmine snapped.

"Hi!" came the cheery voice of Victor Laubenstein on the other end of the line. "I'll meet you down at the car. I've pulled it up to the stairs for you."

"Oh!" Jasmine blurted out, pleasantly surprised that it was him but also nervous about returning to the hospital. "I'll be right down."

"You take your time now. There's no rush."

She took a deep breath. She was happy to be able to walk away from her computer for a few hours, but she wasn't looking forward to the doctor's appointment. She scrambled around for a few minutes, making sure she had everything that she needed. Ensuring that she had all her paperwork and documentation, Jasmine placed her purse over her shoulder, reached for her crutches, and walked out the door.

As she reached the bottom step, Victor was waiting there to help her into the car that he'd practically parked on the sidewalk for her.

"I don't know how to thank you, Victor," Jasmine said with humility in her voice. "I really appreciate this."

"No problem!" he said, grinning as he opened the passenger door of his black Volkswagen Jetta for her. "Thank you for asking."

"I'm sorry, I meant to be down here before you arrived because I need to grab my mail, but I got stuck on the phone. It's been over a week since I've checked it."

"No worries," he said kindly. "I can get your mail. You just make yourself comfortable." He gently helped her sit down on the passenger seat.

Jasmine's heart started pounding as she sat sideways in the car, with her legs still resting on the sidewalk. She couldn't pick her feet up to put them inside.

"You take your time," Victor said sweetly, taking Jasmine's key and walking to the mailboxes.

Images of her ankle crushed in pain raced through Jasmine's mind and paralyzed her legs. She swallowed hard and pursed her lips. She wanted so badly to pick up her legs and stick them into the vehicle, but each time she attempted to do it, she felt the crushing impact of the car's engine on her leg.

When Victor returned with a large stack of mail, he exclaimed, "My child!"

Jasmine's face had gone deathly pale, and she still sat in the same position she was before he'd left. She felt silly and embarrassed.

Victor placed her mail on the car's roof and knelt down next to her. He gently picked up Jasmine's left foot by her heel and carefully placed it inside the car. She turned her upper body as he repeated the action with the foot in the cast. He then retrieved the mail from the roof and handed it to Jasmine.

"Wow, that's a lot of junk," she commented after thanking Victor for his help. She stuffed the mail into her purse and held on tightly to the seat as he slowly drove to the parking lot's exit. He looked in both directions, then pulled out onto the road.

"Look out, Victor!" Jasmine squealed, panicking, while clutching the armrest and the doorframe.

Victor quickly tapped his brakes, heeding Jasmine's warning. But there wasn't anything except one car in the far distance moving toward them. "I'll drive as carefully as I can," he reassured her as he kept moving down the road.

"I'm sorry," she apologized, taking deep breaths, and trying to calm herself down.

Spotting the photo on his dashboard, she changed the subject. "Your wife is beautiful."

"She sure is," Victor replied. "My sweet, Clarissa." His eyes crinkled. "We've been married for thirty-seven years," he said thoughtfully. "She's in Europe visiting her mother."

"Oh!" Jasmine said, trying not to act totally surprised but now even more curious.

Again, she frantically grabbed the armrest and braced herself stiffly as she yelled, "Victor, STOP!" She closed her eyes and cringed as she saw the brake lights in front of her. Her heart felt as if it was going to pound straight out of her chest. She was trembling with fear, and her knuckles had turned white. She breathed heavily as she reached for her bottle of water. "I'm sorry," she apologized again, a quiver in her voice.

Victor checked his speed and tapped his brakes to reassure Jasmine.

"No apologies necessary," he gently replied. "You live in a friendly universe, remember?" he quizzed, as he moved his brows upward, curious if she remembered their previous conversation.

"Unfortunately, I can't agree with that. Even if I wanted to believe it, I couldn't. How can I possibly believe I live in a friendly universe when I now can't run the marathon I've been dreaming about my whole life? How can everything be working out for my good when all I've worked for over the last ten years is slowly but surely being ripped away from me? I can't even ride in the front passenger seat of a car without panicking." She rolled her eyes at how pathetic her life was.

Victor nodded his head ever so slightly, understanding her perspective. "You trust, Jasmine. All beliefs, whether positive or negative, are built on trust and faith. Would you say you have faith and trust that life is working *against* you?"

Jasmine could only nod her head in affirmation.

"Your faith in that belief carries you throughout your days. Your faith in the belief that 'life stinks and there's nothing you can do about it' is creating synchronicities and opportunities for that belief to carry itself out, and that has become your reality."

"Where does the trust part come in?" Jasmine prodded.

"Trust is established through the evidence that you provide to your brain, which thickens the myelin sheathing that reinforces the synaptic connection," Victor responded. "Is it possible that you could decide to have faith and trust that life is always working *for* you rather than against you?"

Jasmine sat dumbfounded, without an answer.

"What I've found in my behavioral study is that most people don't realize we have subconsciously adapted our beliefs as children. Were you born believing you were screwed?" Victor asked.

"I guess not."

"That means then, that somewhere along the way, something happened, and you adapted the belief that God controls you and there's nothing you can do about it. Somewhere you decided to believe that everything is working against you, and that your God likes to punish you. May I ask you a question, Jasmine?" Victor inquired.

Curious, Jasmine nodded her head and obliged.

"How do you know when something negative or bad happens to you?"

"Seriously?" she asked, perturbed by the question. "I mean, not to state the obvious, but it's when something bad happens to you."

"Like what?" Victor asked. "Can you give me an example of something bad that's happened to you?"

"Like crushing my ankle in the company car and losing my entire future?" Jasmine responded, pointing to her ankle.

"Who told you that crushing your ankle was a bad thing?" Victor asked, pressing her to examine her thoughts.

"Excuse me?" Jasmine looked in his direction, irritated.

"Your accident was a circumstance, right? Something that was out of your control?"

"Yes."

"Who told you that it was bad?"

"I did!" Jasmine blurted out.

Victor continued driving, slightly nodding his head up and down in agreement with Jasmine. "Yes, Jasmine, *you* did—*you* decided," he affirmed, as he pulled into the hospital's entrance. "Jasmine Stone decided the circumstance that was out of her control is a negative thing. It's something that has happened *to* her, not *for* her. In all honesty, you could have chosen to decide that this was a good thing, right?" he asked, looking at her. "I mean, the way I've chosen to see it is, I met a new friend. We may have never had this conversation had you not broken your ankle."

Jasmine bit at the inside of her cheek as she gathered her things to get out of the car, contemplating what Victor had said.

"Our job as humans isn't to control life's circumstances. Our job is to control how we choose to react to them. The psychological suffering is optional." Victor then parked the car and walked around to the passenger door to help her into the hospital. "You take your time. There's no rush. I brought plenty of things to work on to keep me occupied," he said smiling, with his thinned hair blowing in the light breeze.

"Thank you, Victor," Jasmine replied. "I'll call you when I'm done." She reached into her purse to pull out her phone, but she couldn't find it. She crutched back to Victor's vehicle and motioned for him to roll down the window. "I think I left my phone in there," she said.

Victor looked around for a few minutes, then called her phone to see if they could find it. Yet, only silence was heard.

"I know for a fact the ringer was on," she commented, disappointed. "I must have left it at home on the table."

"No worries," Victor said, unmoved by the situation. "I'll watch for you."

Jasmine sat nervously in the waiting room. It smelled warm, a little antiseptic and sterile, and was stuffy, which made her feel even more anxious. The chair she sat on was hard and uncomfortable, and she found herself continually glancing at the clock. Slowly but surely, seconds ticked by. She began to breathe deeply. She wasn't quite sure what to expect, and she nervously tapped her left foot lightly on the tile floor. She reached into her purse, pulling out her lip balm, and remembered she'd stuck the stack of mail in it in the car. Relieved to have something to do to pass the time, she began riffling through the stack. *Garbage*, she thought, setting the grocery store advertisement aside. *Insurance company*, as she put that envelope on top of the grocery ad. The new Kia Sportage. *No thanks. I was going for the Mercedes, but thank you for reminding me that I won't have that either.* She placed the car brochure on the junk pile.

She continued thumbing through the mail, making two stacks. *Junk, junk, bill, junk, random catalog from a company I've never heard of. How did that even get here? How do they know my name and address?* Jasmine placed the catalog in the garbage pile.

A small envelope fell from the stack that was still in her hands onto the floor, and Jasmine uncomfortably bent down to pick it up. She recognized her mother's handwriting on the front and stared at it for a few seconds. It had been a very long time since she'd seen her mother's handwriting. She curiously opened the envelope, not sure what she would read inside. She snickered slightly when she pulled out the small card that had a big "E" on the front in a calligraphic design. *Oh Mom, these are so outdated.* She sniffed the card. It smelled like the closet in her mom and dad's bedroom, and instantly, her mind was transported back to the time when she and her sister dug through it, looking for hidden candy.

Jasmine opened the small card.

Dear Jasmine, she read, in her mother's distinct handwriting. *I need some time with you.*

Jasmine wrinkled her forehead and looked more closely at the card to be sure she'd read it correctly.

I know I don't deserve it, and I know I'm the last person you would want to be alone with, or spend any time with, because I've given you so many reasons to not want to do so. But I am asking you—begging you—for a little bit of your time. I want my baby to come home. I want to see your face, my sweet Jasmine. I want to hear your voice. I want to hold your hand. I want to tell you that I'm sorry.

Jasmine deeply breathed. She couldn't see the words through the tears that had instantly welled up in her eyes, and she had to wipe her eyes with her sleeve to continue reading.

Jasmine, I want to be able to touch every area I can think of where I've hurt you. I want to ask your forgiveness. I want to hug you and hold you tight.

A tear dropped onto the card as she again wiped her eyes with her sleeve and sniffed.

My heart is aching. My dear Jasmine, I love you more than you will ever know.

Mom.

Jasmine could do nothing but stare at the card in complete surprise. This didn't feel right, and it was certainly the last thing she'd expected. There was a desperation—a genuineness to the writing that took Jasmine by surprise. She read the card again.

"Oh, Mom," Jasmine whispered through her tears, not knowing what to think. She sniffed and yet again used her sleeve to dab her eyes. She reached into her purse to pull out her phone and text her mom, only to remember that she'd left it at home.

She tried to finish going through the rest of her mail, but it felt irrelevant now. She put everything back into her purse but held on to the outdated note card. Something felt off.

"Jasmine Stone," the nurse called from the doorway. Jasmine's thoughts were interrupted, and she placed the card carefully into her purse, reached for her crutches, and followed the nurse down the hallway.

Jasmine sat upright on the exam table with her right leg elevated, and her left dangling off the side of the table. The nurse had sliced through the soft cast and was opening layer after layer. Jasmine was fascinated by the intricacy of the cast. She'd had no idea there were layers of cotton and tape, plaster, then more cotton. The nurse continued peeling away the layers until, finally, her ankle appeared under a compression bandage that still needed unwrapped. On the outside of it, there was spotting. Jasmine took in a sharp breath. *Oh no*, she said quietly in her head. *That can't be good.* She began imagining having to go through more surgery and more pain. She could hardly breathe when the nurse began unwrapping the bandage.

The more the nurse unwrapped, the more blood spotting Jasmine saw. *What happened?* she thought. *Why is this healing so wrongly?* She wracked her brain, trying to remember everything she had done over the past week. *Did I walk around too much? Did I bump it too much?*

Finally, the bandage was off. Jasmine stared at her leg in disbelief. Her ankle was still somewhat swollen, and there was a long curved incision scar, approximately seven inches long, covered with tape. The nurse tapped gently at the tape and smiled at Jasmine just as Dr. Peltos walked into the room.

"Jasmine!" he said, cheerfully. "How are you? How are you feeling?"

"I'm here," she said with a nervous smile, not feeling the need to say anymore to answer his question.

Dr. Peltos carefully began pulling the medical tape from the incision site. Jasmine felt sick to her stomach. Black and blue bruises surrounded the entire wound. She panicked and her heart sank. Her breathing became shallow, and her eyes felt as if they bugged out when she saw there were actual staples in her leg.

"Are you all right?" Dr. Peltos asked, clearly sensing her tension.

"I didn't know there were real staples," she said squeamishly.

Dr. Peltos chuckled as he lightly touched the wound and the stitches. "Congratulations, Jasmine!" he admonished. "Your recovery is moving along very well. This is healing up remarkably." He moved to the computer screen.

"But there's blood spotting," she replied, confused.

"That's totally normal," the nurse responded.

Jasmine couldn't believe her ears. She smiled with relief. *Maybe I do live in a friendly universe.* Startled by her own thought, she began to wonder if what Victor had said was actually a possibility.

Dr. Peltos showed Jasmine the progress of the plate and screws in her ankle and had nothing but praise for her recovery. "You are in excellent physical health, Jasmine, and that's speeding up your recovery. We'll take your staples out today and get you fitted in your hard cast. We still don't want to put pressure on your foot, but you're healing beautifully. Do you have any questions for me?"

Jasmine shook her head, still surprised.

"All righty, then I'll see you in a few weeks!" he confirmed, and walked out of the room.

Jasmine was all smiles when she walked out the hospital doors. She was excited to be in a hard cast. Already, it was easier to get around. She sat down on the bench, looking around for Victor's black car, flustered that she'd forgotten her phone. After only a few minutes, the car appeared in the entrance circle. Jasmine waved happily as she stood to work her way toward the car.

"I'd say it's a possibility that I live in a friendly universe," she exclaimed happily, holding up her leg to show him the new cast.

Victor beamed as he helped Jasmine into the car.

⌒ NINETEEN ⌒

$\mathcal{J}$asmine thanked Victor for the ride to the hospital and for the kindness he had shown to her. She started up the stairs to her apartment, careful not to bump her new cast. She was exhausted and in a lot of pain. The doctor and nurse had touched her wound, agitating it. Now, she was looking forward to taking some pain medication and getting into bed to rest.

As soon as she opened her apartment door, she spotted her phone and immediately remembered that she needed to call her mother. Jasmine took a pain pill, got herself comfortable, and picked up the phone. There were seven missed calls.

"What do these people want?" she said to herself, unlocking the phone. Instantly, her heart sank. There was one call from Victor, one from Karen, and five from her dad. Without listening to the voice mails and without pausing to think, Jasmine immediately called her dad.

"Come on, pick up," she voiced urgently.

"Hi, Jasmine," a worried voice answered.

"Dad, what's wrong!"

There was a pause on the other end of the phone, as he sniffed. "It's your mother." Another long pause and a sniff. "She's in the hospital, Jasmine." His voice quivered.

Jasmine's stomach dropped. "What happened?"

Another awkward pause. "She … has cancer, Jasmine."

"Cancer!" she exclaimed in shock. "Cancer?"

"Stage four. We aren't sure how much longer she has left," her father whispered in a broken voice.

"What do I do?" Jasmine asked, panicking.

"You may want to …" he began, "you may want to fly out here as soon as possible."

Jasmine looked down at her leg. "Sure, Dad. I'll be there right away. May I talk to Mom?"

"She's asleep right now, but I'll call you when she wakes up, okay?"

Jasmine gave an almost inaudible "Yes," and hung up. Then she crumpled onto the floor in tears.

The flowers.

The text messages.

The voice mails.

Her weak voice.

"How did I miss this?" Jasmine glowered, as she buried her head in her hands. She opened the note card, which she was holding. She felt the desperation in her mother's words as she read the card again. "Why didn't you just tell me, Mom? Why didn't you just tell me!"

At last, she picked herself up from the floor, went to the kitchen table, and opened her computer to figure out how to get a last-minute flight. The first thing she did was to close every work tab that she had open. She didn't give a single crap about work right now. She felt sick and was frustrated and confused, all at the same time.

She found herself staring at the computer, not knowing where to begin. The thought of driving crossed her mind. *If I leave right now, I can get there in ...* Jasmine didn't know exactly, so she looked it up. "Thirty-three hours" Jasmine exclaimed. "I don't think I can do that."

After going from site to site to site, Jasmine finally had a last-minute flight booked with an airline she'd never heard of before. Her head was spinning and her mind was asking a thousand questions. She frantically packed her bags, and prepared for a long trip home.

She sat on her bed, ready to go, simply waiting for the time to pass. Jasmine laughed ironically to herself. Only a month ago, she had thought the same exact thing, and look where time had gotten her: sitting on the edge of her bed with her world continuing to crumble around her. Exhausted, Jasmine fell asleep on her bed.

Jasmine woke up early the next morning in extreme pain. It seemed all the poking around that the doctor and nurse had done the day before had aggravated her foot even more than she thought, or maybe something was wrong with it. But she didn't have time to check. She needed to get downstairs to be picked up by the airport taxi. A cold morning, she could see her breath in front of her as she made her way downstairs with her backpack stuffed full.

When she reached the bottom, she asked the taxi driver to go up to the third floor to retrieve her suitcase. He looked at her, seemingly irritated, but reluctantly headed up the stairs. Jasmine didn't care. She wasn't thinking at all, really. She was just trying to make her way to her mom as quickly as possible.

She sat in the back of the taxi with her cast up on the seat. It was the most uncomfortable ride she'd ever taken. She felt so alone and scared, and kept suddenly bursting into tears and then finding herself staring off into space.

At the airport, the taxi driver set her luggage on the sidewalk, collected his money, and drove away. Jasmine had flown several times before, but somehow this was different. She only really flew for work. She'd be dressed up, ready to get down to business as soon as she arrived. But today, she was practically in her pajamas and barely able to move. She couldn't rush to the counter as she had the other times. She struggled to get herself and her luggage inside the terminal, out of the damp cold morning. Several cars were pulling up to the curb, and people were jumping out and racing inside in a rush to get past her.

"A little help here," she muttered to herself, inching her way forward. The voice inside her asked, *Would* you *have helped?* Jasmine ignored it, knowing the answer, and kept moving.

Finally, she got checked in. No more luggage to deal with until she landed. Now, all she had to do was pass through security, which was a nightmare. Because Jasmine had packed in a hurry and hadn't had a chance to put her toiletries and liquids in a separate bag for screening, her bag was flagged for hand inspection. While the agent dug through her entire bag, she increasingly became more agitated.

She spoke out to the agent. "I have a broken ankle, and my mom is dying. If I don't make my flight, I may not be able to see her!"

This action alerted the TSA agent, and Jasmine was asked to wait until more officials came to check out the situation. After several minutes of waiting with one agent by her side, three more came around the corner.

"Follow me, ma'am," she was instructed.

Jasmine was escorted down the hallway, surrounded by agents, not knowing where she was going. All she could think was, *I can't miss my flight!* but she didn't dare say it out loud again. She followed the agents to a small room. She hobbled inside to find two women standing there holding wands, waiting to pat her down and to check to see if her cast was a stunt. Jasmine sat in a chair as the pat down began.

"All good."

Was all this really necessary? Jasmine thought in frustration.

After being released, Jasmine hurried back to retrieve her belongings. She put her backpack on her back and rushed to her gate as fast as she could.

As she boarded the plane, she hopped sideways down the aisle, trying not to bump anyone, carrying her crutches in her hand. When she got to her seat, the stewardess took her crutches and placed them in a closet for her. Jasmine was more than happy to be rid of them for a few hours. She plopped down in exhaustion, annoyance, and pain.

As soon as she was settled in her seat, her phone began to ring. Immediately, she dug it out of her backpack and saw the video call was from her dad.

"Hi Dad!" she answered frantically. "Is Mom okay?"

"She's awake and asking for you, Jasmine," he responded, sounding drained.

He turned the phone around to show her mom. Jasmine gasped at the sight of her mother's frailness as she tried to smile. Tears instantly sprung to Jasmine's eyes. *How did this happen?*

"Hi Mom," she called, beginning to cry. "I'm so sorry" was all she could say.

Her mother could hardly move, but there was a faint smile on her face. "It's okay, Jasmine," she said slowly, softly. "It's okay."

"I'm on my way, Mom."

Jasmine saw a tear roll down her mother's sunken cheek, and her father reached forward to wipe it off. The plane began moving, but she didn't want to end the call. All she could do was stare at the image in disbelief.

The captain was speaking. "Welcome to Flight 272. We will be in the air for about three hours and twenty minutes nonstop to Dallas, Texas."

"I'll be home soon," Jasmine said through her tears.

Her mom smiled. "I can't wait to hug you."

Jasmine hung up the phone, put her head in her hands and cried bitter tears, her shoulders convulsing in anguish. She knew she must look like a complete mess, and she was in a lot of pain. Against instructions, she took a double dose of pain pills, hoping that would kill the agony faster. Shortly after, she fell asleep.

She awoke to the flight attendant tapping her on the arm and handing her the crutches. Almost everyone else had already exited the plane. She jumped up in surprise, shaking her head, trying to wake up. She blinked her eyes then began to make her way off the plane and into the terminal. After checking her gate number, Jasmine made her way to the food court to begin her three-hour layover. She wished she could speed up time. Better yet, she wanted to sprinkle fairy dust on herself and fly away on her own.

As Jasmine sat, she watched the hustle and bustle of people walking about. Everyone was headed somewhere, most of them in a hurry. Everyone had a life they were in a hurry to live. *Not a single person in this airport knows I'm headed to see my mom on her deathbed,* Jasmine thought. At first, it made her feel lonely, then it just made her sad. She looked at every individual she could, wondering where they were going and what they were about to do. She thought of Victor's words when she first met him, when he'd said that things weren't always as we perceive them to be. *No, they definitely aren't. They absolutely aren't.*

Jasmine looked down at her phone to see if anything had come through from her dad. Nothing was there—just a blank screen with the time and the date: 1:13 Thursday, March 29.

How ironic, thought Jasmine. *I should be running around like crazy at work right now, frantically realizing that it's Thursday afternoon, and I only have a day and a half to finish up an entire week's worth of work, and the work of people who didn't carry their load, too. I should be worrying about preparing for my marathon. I should be texting with Bradley about what we're going to do after the race. I should be eating a big plate of carbs for dinner and getting a full night's sleep.*

She leaned forward, placing her head in her hands again. She couldn't ever have contemplated that she would be rushing to her dying mother's bedside.

What happened to you, Jasmine? she asked herself. *When did you become so selfish and so mean?* She exhaled deeply and checked her phone again. Nothing.

She thought about texting Sara. *How's she doing? Did she know Mom was sick? How could she know and not tell me? Why didn't Mom tell me?* She began to cry again.

Mom, why couldn't you just come out and tell me. "I'm sick, Jasmine. Come home." That's all you had to say. She continued crying softly.

Her phone buzzed. Instantly, Jasmine picked up her phone. It was a text from her dad.

It's not looking good, Jasmine. Mom is hanging on for you.

Jasmine squeezed her phone in frustration and checked the time.

I'm doing my best, Dad. I'll be there as soon as I can. May I please see her?

The FaceTime call came through, with the camera already facing her mom. Her eyes were closed, and her breathing shallow. Her lips were pale and Jasmine could see her hospital gown was draped over her shoulders. A fan was blowing on her mother's sunken face.

The entire world seemed to stop as Jasmine stared through the screen at this person she called her mother. "MOM," Jasmine wailed in anguish. "Don't leave me. I need you!" She was beside herself with grief.

Sara stepped in front of the camera and waved to Jasmine but said nothing. Her eyes were puffy with tears. The two of them just stared at each other as the tears flowed down their faces. Sara pulled the phone close to her chest in an attempt to hold Jasmine close, to be with her. Jasmine cried inconsolably. When she opened her eyes, the phone was again back to her mother. "I'm so sorry" was all she could say. "I'm sorry."

Jasmine stayed on the phone for a few more minutes. The next hour passed slowly. Her head was spinning a thousand miles an hour. She found herself completely unemotional and unable to process the situation one moment, then crying uncontrollably the next.

When it was finally time to board the next plane, she had a two-hour flight to Phoenix where she would catch a taxi to the hospital. She felt sick to her stomach. She wanted to snap her fingers and find herself back in the office, telling Shawn about her awful dream.

As soon as she landed, she turned on her phone. Her hands were shaking as she tried to force it to work faster. There were three texts: One from her dad and two from Sara. She opened the one from her dad first. *Hurry quick, Jasmine. Mom doesn't have much time left.* Her throat tightened as she opened the texts from her sister. The first one read: *Mom is asking for you, Jasmine.* The second was simply three crying emojis.

"NO!" Jasmine wailed. "No. No. No. No. NO! Get me off of this plane. NOW!"

⁓———

After arriving at the hospital, she slowly hopped into her mother's hospital room. She had the slightest shred of hope that somehow, in some strange way, her mom would be there, breathing, holding her arms open for Jasmine.

When she entered the doorway, she was met with crying and sniffling. Sara came running over and wrapped her arms around Jasmine in the tightest squeeze she could give her. All the animosity between them had vanished, at least for the time being, and the two of them embraced in unity, understanding the grief they were enduring.

Her brother, Jacob, stood in the corner. He looked so much older. Jasmine hadn't seen him in seven years, and she couldn't take her eyes off him while she hugged Sara. He gave her a smile that reflected her same question back to her: *What happened to us?*

Her dad was kneeling by the bedside in complete grief and agony. As if somehow he had failed her—as if this was his fault. She watched as he sobbed in anguish. Strangely, Jasmine had never seen her father cry before, yet here he was crying like a baby as he held his wife's hand.

As Jasmine made her way to the bed, her face was covered in grief once again. It was true. Her mother had passed. There she was, lying on the bed. Her mom, as she knew her—that very intense woman, that ball of energy and enthusiasm— was gone. She was still. Already she didn't look anything like herself. Jasmine twisted her body to be able to kneel down beside the bed and brushed her mother's hair with her hand. She gently took her mother's hand and held it, even though it felt rubbery and cold. She stroked it for a few minutes, then lightly kissed it. "Mom," Jasmine murmured softly. "I love you. I love you." Her tears were flowing. Years of memories passed through Jasmine's mind rapidly, and with each one, Jasmine felt more and more pain and sadness.

She bent her head to the railing of the bed and wept.

∽ TWENTY ∼

*J*asmine's parents' house was simple but beautiful: a typical two-story Phoenix mission-style house with a clay-tiled roof and a small yard. It wasn't large, but it was homey. In spite of her aching heart, Jasmine was somehow glad to be back.

There was a knock at the front door, and Jacob went to answer it. Jasmine saw her Aunt Lisa standing in the doorway with her arms full of food. When she was welcomed in, there was a string of people behind her, all carrying food for the family that was continually gathering.

Jasmine felt increasingly more uncomfortable as more people showed up. She felt in the way, as she was hardly able to get around and help with her crutches and broken ankle. Every time she found a more private spot, it, too, filled up with people, with every one of them asking her, "Oh no, what happened?"

Small children ran around the house, far too young to fully comprehend what was going on. Jasmine resorted to sitting on a bench in the dining room corner, too uncomfortable to engage in conversation. She leaned back against the old wooden-slabbed wall, watching and listening from a distance.

Sara approached her, and Jasmine knew she wasn't going to be able to squirm out of this conversation. She faintly smiled at her sister as she approached.

"You look like such a mother," Jasmine said, starting the conversation herself.

"Ha ha, thank you," Sara replied, looking at her children who were running about. "They're a lot of work."

Jasmine breathed in deeply, trying not to start crying again. Her eyes watered though, as she quietly asked, "When did you know?"

Sara's eyes filled as well. It was such a vulnerable time for the whole family—almost a free-for-all for anyone to ask anything. Everyone's emotions were so heightened and raw. Sara blinked and lowered her gaze. "Dad told me about three months ago." There was a long pause. "The doctors thought they had a handle on it. Mom was positive she was going to be okay." Sara began biting the inside of her cheek.

"Why didn't you tell me?" Jasmine asked, feeling hurt and left out.

Sara knelt in front of her little sister with teary eyes. Finally, she spoke. "Mom begged me not to tell you. She wanted to tell you herself, in person."

Jasmine looked away, remembering her mother's weak voice when she called, and the way that her mother had repeatedly tried to tell her. *How painful that must have been for her,* Jasmine thought.

Sara continued on, as if she shared her sister's thoughts. "Mom was a stubborn little thing." They both chuckled at the truth of it. "She wanted things to be done her way. I did call you, though, back in January."

Jasmine scrunched her forehead, trying to figure out what Sara was talking about.

"About a week after your birthday. I had a feeling Mom hadn't told you yet, and I wanted to let you know as soon as possible when I realized things were going downhill."

Instantly, Jasmine recalled Sara's phone call she'd missed as she sat in traffic and having to bring her groceries inside during the pouring rain. She recalled spotting an incoming call from Sara and purposely ignoring it. *How different things would've been if I had just answered the stupid phone,* Jasmine criticized herself.

Sara added, "Mom didn't want to ruin your thirtieth birthday, and she didn't know how to tell you."

A commotion at the kitchen table interrupted their conversation. Sara and Jasmine looked up to see everyone laughing. Curious about what was going on, they made their way over. Jasmine peeked over the shoulder of someone sitting down to see that Jacob had retrieved a photo album, and everyone was looking at a picture of her mother with mud all over her white-and-dark-green outfit. Jasmine snickered to herself as she made her way back to the living room, which seemed like the emptiest room at the moment.

She sat down and closed her eyes, remembering the day she took that picture as if it was yesterday. Her mother wanted to take Jacob's new moped for a spin and hadn't let him finish reading the instructions. She was in a grassy area, and the moped had spun out as soon as she gave it some gas. She ended up wiping out, straight down into wet mud. Everyone was unsure then whether they could laugh, that is, until she looked up, smiling in humiliation. While the entire group of family and close friends laughed, Jasmine had snapped the picture.

For the next few hours, Jasmine watched as a houseful of relatives sat around, telling stories about her mother. The aura was strange. Eruptions of laughter were followed by moments of intense crying, then back to storytelling again. *Mom would have loved this,* she thought to herself. *This is what she always wanted.* She kept finding herself looking at the house's old, heavy, wooden front door, waiting for her mom to enter and start delegating orders.

Jasmine smiled to herself as she continued to think about her mom. In her imagination, Jasmine was waiting for her mother's instructions to "get the plates," "make some coffee," or "do the dishes, would you, please?" It was ironic that what drove her crazy and made her move across the country was the very thing that she was now craving.

Abruptly from behind, she felt an arm around her shoulders and an index card thrust in front of her face. "Remember this?" Sara asked.

Pulling back her head, startled, Jasmine exclaimed, "Oh my gosh! Yes!" They both grinned. "'Seven Layer Cheesecake,'" she read out loud. "Where did you find this?"

"Mom's recipe box."

As Jasmine looked over the recipe card, Sara disappeared and came back with the old, worn, fabric-covered box. The two of them began to look through their mother's collection of favorite recipes acquired over the years.

"Look," Jasmine said with a fond smile on her face, "Mom's chili recipe."

"Oh my gosh, yes!" Sara remembered. Turning as her dad entered the room, she asked, "Does Mom still have all her chili trophies?"

He wandered over to find out what they were doing. "They're probably in a box somewhere in the attic," he said, putting on his glasses to read the card. "Mom sure loved to make that chili," he proudly responded with a fond smile.

The sisters continued rummaging through the recipe box, bringing back memory after memory. "Oh my gosh, remember this?" Sara asked excitedly, as she pulled out a card and showed it to Jasmine.

She took the card and read it out loud. "Cinnamon-dipped cheese blintzes."

Just then, they were interrupted by a tiny voice. "Mommy, I have to go potty," the boy commanded, tugging on Sara's long shirt, looking at Jasmine as if she was a complete stranger.

As her sister left the room, preoccupied by the needs of her young son, Jasmine stared at the recipe card, remembering the day she and her mom were in the kitchen together, making those cheese blintzes. Her mom made them every year as a Christmas treat, and Jasmine couldn't wait for her turn to be able to help make them. That year, she'd tried her luck again, repeatedly begging to be the one to cut the crust from the bread. To her elated surprise, her mother had finally obliged, and Jasmine went to work. She did her best to cut the crust carefully, and when she was done, she'd proudly waltzed into the kitchen from the dining room table and announced, "I'm finished, Mom!"

Her mom looked over from the kitchen counter. "Jasmine, what have you done!" she'd exclaimed in a tone that crushed Jasmine's young spirit. "There's no way I can use those! How can you be so dumb? Now what are we going to do?" Her mother had yanked the plate of trimmed bread from the table and shoved it down onto the counter in disgust. "They look ridiculous," her mom said to her. "I can't roll these. Don't ask to cut the crust if you're too stupid to know how to do it." Jasmine stood, looking at the bread, wondering what in the world she had done wrong. She remembered her heart pounding in fear, unsure of what to do or what to say, wishing she could somehow fix the situation.

It had gotten late, and Jasmine needed to go to bed. She made it up the stairs, then had to take a deep breath to keep herself from getting dizzy. She couldn't believe it had been more than seven years since she had last stepped foot in this house. She felt overwhelmed and didn't like it.

She went down the hallway to her old bedroom. It was painted over in light yellow, and several shelves were packed full of stuff. It had become the room her mother always wanted: a sewing room. Sometime in the last seven years, she'd made it happen. *What else happened while I was gone?* Jasmine wondered. She poked through her mother's things. The needles were still sitting out. Pins were still holding together two pieces of flannel that was solid green on one side and had bears and trees on the other. It must have been for Sara's oldest son, she thought.

She pulled open a few drawers, hoping to bring back any memory or reminder of her mother to hold on to her as long as she could. She found half-cut patterns and all kinds of fabrics. Jasmine could only imagine how much she must have enjoyed herself in this room.

A noise at the door startled her, so she turned around quickly to see who it was. It was her dad. His head was cocked slightly to the side, and there was a fond look on his face, as if he was happy to see Jasmine back in his house in her old room.

They stared at each other for some time, both speaking silently with their eyes until, slowly, he held out his hands and walked toward her. The moment they embraced, more uncontrollable tears erupted. He pulled Jasmine back just a little and looked at her face, as if he was wondering what had happened to his little girl but not finding the words to express himself. "I'm sorry, Jasmine," was all he could say, his voice barely an audible whisper. He held her close a while longer, then added, "Do you know where you're staying tonight?"

"I didn't plan that far ahead," she admitted. "Would you mind if I stayed here?"

Her father smiled. "You're always welcome to stay here, Jasmine ..."

Jasmine started to crutch down the hallway.

"Jasmine," he called out to her when she was about halfway down the hall, "we're meeting with the funeral director tomorrow. Would you like to go along?"

"Yes, of course," she responded.

Jasmine continued down the hall to the guest room, Jacob's old room. It felt funny, seeing his old blue-and-white baseball-themed room now painted a light pink with a flowered quilt on a queen bed. She was shocked to see some of her photographs had been placed on the walls. Each one brought back a specific memory.

That night, she laid in bed looking up at the ceiling, unable to sleep even in her exhaustion. She had her leg propped up by every pillow in the room to help the pain of the long day subside.

∽ TWENTY-ONE ∽

*J*asmine sat in the funeral director's conference room with her dad, brother, and sister. All of them were solemn, not knowing what to think or expect. They all sat around a large mahogany table in very comfortable, cushioned revolving chairs. A big bouquet of flowers stood on a stand behind it. Jasmine thought of the flowers her mother had sent her.

A coffee stand was located on the back wall, out of Jasmine's reach. She smelled the coffee and badly wanted a cup, but her discomfort kept her from asking for one. She imagined herself crutching over to the counter and pouring herself a cup of hot coffee with cream and sugar. *But how would I get it back to my seat?* she thought. *You could ask for some help once you get done pouring the coffee*, the voice inside her head answered.

"Jasmine?"

"Huh?" she said startled, looking up, not sure what the question was or why her name was being called.

"Would you sign here, please?"

"Yes," she responded, bringing her mind back to the conversation.

For the next several hours, Jasmine and her family repeatedly answered question after question. They discussed burial, ceremony, and visitation options; plus the wording of the obituary and other numerous things that she had never thought of or even considered she would be discussing at the age of thirty, and certainly not the day before she was supposed to be running a marathon.

Just when she thought they were finishing up, they began to discuss insurance policies, estate information, and payment and financial options. It was so much, and so emotional to talk about it all. As she sat listening and occasionally commenting, Jasmine remembered when a co-worker, Melisa, experienced a death in her family. She recalled how snarky she was toward Melisa when she returned to work after the funeral. *It's just a funeral*, Jasmine had thought to herself when she reminded Melisa about all her work that had gone undone while she was out.

The conversation continued onward, covering flowers, food, what cemetery they were using, which photo would be displayed on the memorial cards, service times, pallbearers, and so on. Finally, they finished up the arrangements.

Jasmine couldn't believe how much information was needed for a funeral. They'd spent the whole morning and part of the afternoon talking with the funeral director. She'd had no idea that so much thought and emotion would be required. Her father was tasked with providing so much information, and they all had discussed so many different topics and choices. It was hard enough as it was, without adding to their grief, and left them all emotionally drained. They had felt rushed to come up with information and solutions, and all of their emotions were running high. In the few funerals she'd attended, Jasmine had simply showed up, offered her condolences, and carried on with her life.

When they returned home, food was sitting on the counter. Jasmine hadn't been this happy to eat in a long time. She was starving. Where the food magically appeared from didn't concern her at that particular point. All that mattered was that perfectly creamy mashed potatoes were moving from her mouth to her stomach.

"Hey, Jas, would you like to help me dig up some of Mom's paintings from the attic when we're done eating?" Sara asked.

"Sure. I'm not sure how much help I'll be with this cast in the way, but I can at least keep you company and watch you dig around," she replied.

"Who knows what we'll find up there!" Sara exclaimed before she was again being pulled away from their conversation by a small hand tugging on her shirttail. She gave Jasmine a look that said, *Hang on, I'll be back.*

Jasmine nodded, wondering where in the world seven years had gone.

Once more, Jasmine sat in the background as people wandered about the house. There were aunts and uncles, nieces and nephews, cousins, and people she didn't even know present. She'd had no idea that so many people could even fit in this house. Sometimes she participated, but other times she sat back just listening. One thing was certain, she absolutely did not want to be there. She began to feel claustrophobic, ready to be left alone in the house.

Sara rounded around the kitchen corner with a mischievous look on her face. "Let's get out of here," she whispered, "before my kiddos find me. Adam said he'd watch them while we dig around in the attic for a while."

"Oh my gosh, yes," Jasmine responded. "I feel as if I can't breathe."

They headed to the back stairs and disappeared as quickly as possible into the attic.

"I haven't been up here in years," she claimed, remembering playing in the attic as a child "Oh my gosh!" she exclaimed, "that old china cabinet is still up here? It used to be my favorite place to hide!"

"Believe me, I know. I used to have to pretend I didn't know where you were," Sara admitted.

Jasmine took in everything around her. It was as if she traveled in a time machine and turned the clock back twenty years. There was so much to take in. "Why did Mom want us to clean out the attic anyway?" she asked Sara after she'd finally gotten settled.

"I'm not sure. I think she just wanted to see us all together. Maybe she just wanted to picture us as kids again before she passed?" Sara paused, then noted, "She just wanted us here."

An awkward silence occurred as the two of them remembered why they were there. They were strangers now, who didn't know much about each other's lives.

Sara started looking into some of the boxes. "I don't know where to begin to look for those paintings," she voiced, breaking the silence and changing the subject.

Jasmine didn't even respond. She'd opened a box that was next to her to keep herself preoccupied, and to avoid a potentially awkward conversation. She had found a load of pots and pans. Jasmine couldn't help but say, "Why in the world did Mom keep some of this stuff?"

"What is it?" Sara asked, relieved to have the subject changed.

"Old pots and pans! I mean, these couldn't be used if Mom wanted to!" They both snickered.

"That's the mother we knew and loved," Sara commented. "Old pots and pans up in an attic along with award-winning art." They shook their heads at the irony of it.

They continued looking through box after box, digging up old toys and memories. "Okay, okay," Sara said. "What the heck is this doing here?" she asked, pulling out pieces of their old dollhouse.

Jasmine laughed when she saw it. "It's broken, isn't it?"

"There are still pieces of tape on them!" Sara exclaimed.

"Well, with the number of times Mom taped it up, I'm not surprised."

"That needs to go in the garbage. It's not worth saving." Sara began moving more furniture around to reach another stack of boxes.

Jasmine closed her eyes as she recalled when the dollhouse was taped up. Every time the two girls would bicker or fight, their mom would tape it up so neither of them could play with it. She'd felt so misunderstood and …. Jasmine's thoughts were interrupted by her sister talking again.

"This looks like your stuff, Jas," she said as she opened another box. Sara had pulled up some old clothes and shoes that Jasmine only faintly remembered.

"Yes, those are mine," she said, wishing she could just get up and walk over to her belongings and go through them herself.

Sara continued to pull things from the box while Jasmine strained to see what they were.

"A diary?" Sara said, seemingly intrigued.

"What! Give it to me!" Jasmine gasped. "Don't you dare open it!" She stood up from the makeshift seat she had made for herself and hobbled as quickly as she could over to where Sara was working.

"Relax, Jasmine, I'm not going to read it," Sara fired back, a bit irritated.

Jasmine reached out her hand and grabbed the diary as quickly as she could.

Sara gave Jasmine a puzzled look. "What's gotten into you?" she asked accusingly.

"It's none of your business, Sara," Jasmine sharply responded. "Stay out of my stuff. Your job is to find Mom's paintings, not to go rifling around in everybody else's boxes." Jasmine turned to go back to her seat with the diary in her hand.

"Well, it would be nice to have a smidgen of help around here," Sara retorted. "I have a lot to do, and it doesn't help having you just sitting around on crutches, pretending you can't hardly lift a finger and do a single thing."

Jasmine bugged her eyes and her mouth fell open, unsure how to respond.

"It's not my fault you dumped all your junk in your parents' attic and took off, leaving everybody behind to clean up your mess."

"My mess! My *mess*?" Jasmine asked, flabbergasted. "That's easy for you to say, Mom's little pet," she accused bitterly. "We both know full well that Mom liked you better. Mom worshipped the very ground you stood on, and HATED me."

Her jaw was clenched and a tear trickled down her face. "She hated me. No one has ever cared about me. And then, she sends me some pitiful bunch of flowers, thinking that was going to patch up thirty years of resenting my birth."

"Stop being so dramatic, Jasmine. She didn't hate you and she didn't 'resent your birth,' … you know that. You're being the spoiled little brat you've always been, throwing a fit when you don't get your way. Grow up and stop making everything about you. There are other people in the world, you know."

Jasmine glared at Sara with her nostrils flaring. "Who's being the spoiled little brat here, Sara? It's not me. You're the brat. You've always done everything Mom wanted you to do. You had her wrapped around your little pinky, and she made it obvious she liked you better."

"Do you know why? Would you like to know *WHY*?" Sara shouted, "I was *afraid* of Mom, Jasmine," her voice trembling. "You got to do whatever you darn well pleased, and I was stuck, wrapped around Mom's little finger. Doing everything *she* wanted me to do. Having no say in how *I* wanted my life to turn out. No say in what *I* wanted to do with my future. And there you went, off to enjoy the world, leaving me behind. I've despised you since the day you left because you got to live whatever life you wanted to and weren't afraid to do it."

Just then, the back door opened, and they heard Adam calling to Sara from downstairs.

"You can clean your own mess. I have a life I have to go pretend that I love." Sara retraced the path she'd made in the attic to the door. As soon as she stepped around the corner, Sara saw her dad looking up at her with the most distraught look on his face.

$\mathcal{M}$r. Stone shut the door as the last guests said their goodbyes. Jasmine let out a big yawn, more than ready to retire to the guest room to rest from the day's activities. When she was safely tucked away in the guest bed, she pulled out the diary Sara had found in her pile of belongings that somehow had made it up to a corner of the attic. Her eyes began watering as she gazed at the cover of the flowered hardcover book in her hands. She recalled the exact day she'd received the pretty book, a thirteenth-birthday present from her mother. It was something Jasmine hadn't even known she wanted, though she remembered being jealous that most of the other girls in her class always got what they wanted for their birthdays and Christmas. But not Jasmine. Her mother didn't allow lists. She said she gave from her heart, and somehow she always found just the right gift to give her children. This was one of those perfect gifts.

A tear slipped from her cheek onto the book's cover and onto one of the petals of the massive pink rose bouquet. She opened the cover to the first page and read the very first line of her first entry.

January 9, 2003
"Seventeen years ago," Jasmine murmured.

Today starts the best years of my life.

Jasmine glared at the page. "Wow," she admitted, "I couldn't have gotten that one more wrong."

I don't even know what I am going to write in here, but I know that it will be good. Maybe I will be an author! I bet I will be so important that everyone will want to know me. Wouldn't that be cool?

Poor innocent Jasmine, she thought. *I would go back and give you a giant hug if I could. You were so full of hope back then.*

Well, my mom is yelling at everyone to get in the car so I guess I better go for now. I love you already.

Jasmine laughed at the clear picture the words had conjured up and wiped away a few tears. She couldn't help but turn the page and keep reading.

January 16, 2003

Hi there, I can't believe it's already been a week since my birthday. It's a little cold out today. I don't want to go to school today, but I kinda do because Joseph will be there. He is so cute. I hope my mom does not see this. How horrible it would be if my mom only bought me a diary so she could snoop around on me and see what I write about. If you're reading this, Mom, I caught you. Put it down. How does it feel to be told what to do? HAHA on you. Bye.

Jasmine laughed again at her thirteen-year-old self, wondering if her mother ever had actually read her diary. She slowly flipped through the pages, reading parts here and there.

There was a big storm today …

The doorbell is ringing, and Dad doesn't know who it is. I heard Mom say just leave it alone …

June 10, 2003

Today was Lauren's bday. She is thirteen now, too. We both feel like grown-ups now, and we can talk about grown-up stuff. But Mom doesn't treat me like a grown-up. She thinks I'm still a kid. Like the other day when she told me I couldn't go to Theresa's house. She acted like one of those stupid moms who treat their girls like garbage. Well guess what, Mom, I'm a grown-up, and there's nothing you can do about it. And, if you read this, you will really know I am a grown-up.

Jasmine cringed a bit at her own words. *Man, I was a sassy little thing*, she thought, remembering that day. She snickered at herself as she thought about the serious conversation they had had, about truly being all grown-up now. Jasmine continued turning the pages, reading random sentences to see if she could remember the moments that went with them.

Today was the math test. I don't know how well I did, but I do know that Joseph likes me. He told me today that my shirt looked nice. I think I will wear this shirt every Friday ...

Jasmine remembered the very shirt she was talking about. It was the one she got from Goodwill from the ladies' section, and her mom hadn't known that was where she got it. It was hideous-looking, with huge shoulder pads, and it was way too big.

September 5, 2003
Today was seriously a great Friday. My mom packed my favorite pudding in my lunch, and Stella was jealous that ...

Jasmine skipped over a few more pages, looking for something interesting to read. She became excited when she reached December 25th. *I wonder what I got for Christmas that year*, she thought with a smile.

December 25, 2003

Gramma was here for Christmas this year.

I remember that! Jasmine thought as she kept reading.

She's in the bathroom now and I'm waiting for her. I don't know how she got here, but she showed up at the door. Mom seemed to be mad at her, but I don't know how anyone can be mad at Gramma. She talks a lot and she knows pretty much everything. She always lets me sit next to her and do her puzzles in her book. She seems tired a lot, though. Today, she took a long nap in my room and I wasn't allowed in, which doesn't make sense, because it's my room.

Christmas was fun. I got a lot of presents, but Sara didn't seem happy that I got more than her. I am happy though. Maybe Mom is finally starting to like me, I don't know. I got

Slippers

Stationery card set

A watch

Nail polish

Pajamas

A sweatshirt

And a blanket from Gramma.

Oh my gosh! Jasmine thought, *I have had that blanket for seventeen years!* She grinned as she thought of her Gramma and the blanket she'd given her. It was the softest one she had ever had. *It's still my absolute favorite blanket, Gramma.* She sniffed a few tears back and kept turning the pages.

January 15, 2004

Daniel got his hair cut, and I think it looks terrible. I don't like school. I feel so alone. Sometimes, I don't like Lauren even though she is my BFF because she's so boy crazy. She always has to make sure her hair is perfect every time she sees a mirror. Like who cares, seriously. Anyways, I don't know how to tell her that I ...

The entry stopped, and Jasmine wondered what in the world she was going to tell Lauren.

Her leg began tingling. She'd been so wrapped up in reading about her teenage life that she hadn't noticed that it had fallen asleep under her. When she tried to get up, it was limp and tingly. She straightened it, then decided to read a few more pages.

February 2, 2004

I am trying really hard to listen to Mom and Dad, but it's so hard because they don't understand me and they don't even try. I was listening through the vent in the bathroom again, and I heard Mom saying to Dad that I always have an attitude now. EXCUSE ME????? I do not have an attitude. I am just misunderstood and unwanted. You're the one with the attitude, Mom, HELLO!!!! It's not MY fault that you love Sara and Jacob more than me. Can someone please explain to me why that is MY FAULT? I feel like crying, but I don't want my mom to think she wins.

March 13, 2004

So, I have my flashlight under my pillow. I feel like you are the only person I can talk to. No one likes me. Today in school, Beanna told me that my breath stunk. I mean, what kind of name is Beanna anyways? That name stinks worse than anyone's breath.

Anyway, whatever. I told Lauren, and she said well sometimes it does. Like WHAT? Did you really just say that to your best friend? I cannot trust anyone now. I think there is no such thing as a best friend. No one really actually cares about me—not even my mom and dad. The whole world is mean, including God (and yes, God, I know you are going to punish me for saying that, but I don't really care anymore).

The whole world is mean except Gramma.

Bye for now, my head hurts from holding the flashlight. I'm glad my mom got you for me, but I still don't like her.

April 24, 2004

Mom yelled at me today. I took some pictures with the camera, and when she printed the pictures from Walmart, she saw some of the pictures I took. She said they were nice, but I shouldn't have been touching the camera without asking. Right, because you want me to follow you around, waiting to ask you every little thing. Do I have to ask you to swallow, too???? This is stupid. I have to get out of here. I don't think I want to live here forever. Life here stinks.

P.S. Lauren and Beth came over today and helped me cope. They told me that we will be a secret group. Sometimes, I don't like them, but they do help deal with this craziness.

And also, I did take really good pictures. I think I will take some more, but I don't know how.

May 19, 2004

Dear Diary, I cannot stop crying. I hate this Earth, and I officially hate Chad Wilkerson. He is the meanest stupidest boy that has ever lived, and I don't want to ever see him again. We had Jess's party at Greater Skate today, and I learned something. I learned that people are awful and mean, and I cannot trust anyone. I am done with boys. I mean it. I want to tie them all to a tree and watch them whine and cry and never get away. I know that's mean, but that's really how I feel. Boys are just so rude and mean, and not one of them can ever be my friend again. WHY do they think they can BE SO MEAN to girls????

Jasmine touched the page she was reading. It was still crumpled from where tears had fallen so many years ago. Her eyes teared at the memory, though she slightly smirked and shook her head. She recalled with vivid detail the moment when Chad had told everyone at the party that she stuffed her bra with tissues so the boys would think she was bigger. She recalled the complete terror and humiliation she'd experienced that day.

She managed to lift herself up from the floor. A few hours had passed and she'd only read half the pages. She was absorbed by this story of someone she now barely knew. It seemed these events had happened a lifetime ago. She closed the diary and looked at the cover, running her hand over it. "Mom …," she moaned to the diary in agony. She couldn't finish the sentence, though, because a lump in her throat constricted her vocal chords.

～ TWENTY-THREE ～

$\mathscr{J}$asmine looked down at the piece of paper in her hand again. She traced her finger over the picture of her mother's face and read the words above it: *In Loving Memory*. Murmuring noise and slow soft music filled the room. She dabbed her eyes with the damp tissue that was scrunched up in her hand. Her crutches were under the pew in front of her, and she settled herself as she waited for the funeral to start.

It didn't feel right or real. She looked to the front of the small room and saw two large floral arrangements next to the casket. A photograph and a poem stood between the arrangements. A few candles flickered elegantly from large holders, and two oil paintings were displayed on easels.

Jasmine closed her eyes and imagined her mother laughing and talking, being full of life. She pictured herself talking with her on the phone, then went back in her mind to the very short bitter conversations she'd had with her recently. She swallowed the lump in her throat and opened her eyes, not wanting to think about those recent conversations.

A hushed silence spread as friends and family members meandered about the room, somberly hugging each other. Jasmine watched her dad from a distance, as he held himself together while speaking solemnly to relatives and friends. Just as she was about to turn away, her mom's brother, Uncle Reggie, came around the corner, and she noticed the grieving look on her dad's face. They embraced, then continued to hold on tightly to each other for several moments.

Jasmine's bottom lip began quivering, and she tried her best to hold back her emotions. She again tried to swallow the lump in her throat, but it was no use. She squeezed her eyes shut as she burst into fresh tears, reliving memories as well as regrets. Every time she began to think she had cried all the tears she had in her, more would emerge.

She took a deep breath and dabbed at the corner of her eyes. As she reached to the end of the pew to grab another tissue, she saw someone walking toward her, waving, with a baby in her arms. Jasmine panicked but managed to pick up her hand to wave. It was Lauren, and she was proudly holding her baby.

"This is Reagan Rose," she said with a big smile on her face. "She's three months old."

Yes, and I'm at my mother's funeral, Jasmine thought before responding. "Aww, congratulations," Jasmine said with a forced smile.

"It's so good to see you, Jas! How have you been? What happened?" Lauren asked, noticing the crutches and Jasmine's cast.

If one more person asks me that question, I will scream. "I broke my ankle," Jasmine said shortly.

"Oh, how did you do that?!" It was as if Lauren was picking up a conversation after a twelve-year break—like they were still BFFs.

"A car accident" was all Jasmine uttered.

"Oh no, I hope it wasn't your fault! Insurance can be a nuisance," Lauren remarked, then moved right into her next question. "How's life treating you?"

"Good," said Jasmine, not exactly wanting to engage in conversation.

"Whereabouts are you in Baltimore? How did you end up there anyways?" Lauren peppered her with questions as she shifted her baby from one arm to the other, bouncing her up and down.

Jasmine bit the inside of her cheek before answering. "I live in a very lovely neighborhood," she bragged. "In fact, I am neighbors with Victor Laubenstein. Have you heard of him?"

Lauren gave her a curious look. "No, I don't believe I have."

"Oh, he's a world-renowned neuroscientist," Jasmine replied, waving her hand as if it was no big deal. "And he's a best-selling author, too," she added, feeling important.

Lauren opened her mouth to speak, but Jasmine cut her off. "We're friends. In fact, he bought me my groceries when I broke my ankle and took me to the hospital for my checkup."

Lauren tilted her head and gave her an odd smile.

"So, I'd say life is treating me terrific," she fibbed.

"Great," Lauren said, seemingly unsure of how to respond. "So, who's the lucky man?" she pressed further. "You do have a man, right?"

"Oh yes, of course I do," she asserted. "His name is … Bradley. Bradley Copeland. He's super handsome. And rich," she added in with a whisper as she nodded her head up and down, trying to convince herself. "He's a guidance counselor for one of the most prominent schools in the area and an upstanding citizen in the community. Everyone loves him." Jasmine paused, then kept on going. "And, he treats me like a queen!"

"Wow, well, good for you," Lauren concluded, her bubbly chatter calming down a bit.

"It's a wonder he ended up with a nobody like me, you know, from a small nothing town," Jasmine said with a sly smile. "How have you been, Lauren? You still live here, right?"

Lauren stared at Jasmine, wondering what had happened to her friend

"Oh hey, Sara," Jasmine called, desperate to get out of the awkward conversation. She looked back at Lauren and said, "If you'll excuse me. It was great to see you again, Lauren. Thank you for stopping by."

"What was that all about?" asked Sara, seeming to sense the thickness in the air.

Jasmine shrugged her shoulders. "Not much has changed. I just didn't want to make small talk right now, and I felt attacked."

Sara put her arm around Jasmine. "You're lucky you're on crutches and can't walk around."

"Yeah, well, you're lucky you are not on crutches. You get to walk away from a conversation that you don't want to be part of." They both smiled, understanding each other. "How's Jacob doing?" Jasmine asked.

"I think we all have our regrets," Sara replied.

Jasmine nodded her head in agreement. "It's surreal, you know. This isn't what I had planned for this weekend."

Sara smiled. "Jasmine, look at me right now."

Jasmine turned her head and looked at her sister. She was breathing more heavily and was starting to cry again.

"I'm so very glad you're here. I know it's not ideal, but I really, really missed you."

They embraced, and another surge of tears streamed down their faces, as they connected on a deep emotional level. While they were still embracing, the lights dimmed and a video began playing. Up on a big screen, they saw their mother's smiling face, bigger than life-size. The slideshow started, and Sara settled in next to Jasmine, squeezing her hand. Jasmine felt a tap on her shoulder and turned around to see Jacob and their dad behind her. She smiled at them with an invitation in her eyes and scooched over to make room for them to sit.

The family watched the video, laughing and crying at the memories.

Just as the video ended, Jasmine heard her phone buzzing. It was another call from Karen. She rolled her eyes with irritation and mumbled something under her breath.

"Is everything okay?" Sara whispered.

"It's work," Jasmine said as she rolled her eyes again and shook her head.

⁓

Everyone gathered under the cemetery tent. It was a warm day, but a light breeze blew. A strange hush grew as everyone waited. Jasmine sat with a few family members in white chairs in front of the casket. The officiant quietly came to Jasmine and Sara, allowing them to choose a flower to place on their mother's grave. As Jasmine chose her flower, she remembered the bouquet her mother had sent her just a short time ago. She breathed in, trying to maintain her composure. She then reached out and grabbed Sara's hand, giving it a squeeze as she closed her eyes. Nothing in the world could have prepared her for this moment. Her heart was aching in a way she had never experienced before. More than anything in the world, Jasmine wanted the pain to go away.

The officiant started to speak. "Dearly beloved," he said, "we are gathered here together to honor and celebrate the life of Emily Stone. Today, we set aside everything that would otherwise demand our attention and are here to focus on the significance of the role that Emily Stone played in each and every one of our lives. Our hearts and thoughts are with the family in this time of loss and …."

It was Jasmine's turn to place a single rose on her mother's casket. She slowly walked to the casket, kissed the red rose, and quietly whispered, "Goodbye," as she lowered the flower into the ground. This was the heaviest sadness—the heaviest grief—that she had ever experienced. She sobbed uncontrollably as she hobbled away from the tent, wanting to be alone.

Jasmine went to take a bite of the food that the venue prepared for the reception. Just as she was about to open her mouth, she felt her phone ring again. *Oh my gosh, this is ridiculous.* She looked at her phone, noticing this time it was Brett. She let his call go to voice mail, only to have it ring again a few moments later. Tired of them hounding her, Jasmine finally answered. "Hi, Brett. What is it?"

"'What is it?!" he echoed her in a frustrated tone. "You aren't doing your part here, Jasmine. Karen has been trying to get ahold of you for days."

Jasmine stiffened her neck as she turned her head away from the table where she sat. "I don't work seven days a week, and right now I'm at my mother's funeral!"

There was a pause on the other end of the phone.

Brett cleared his throat. "Your mother's funeral?"

"Yes, Brett, my mother's funeral. I took a last-minute flight out of Baltimore and flew all the way to Arizona. Today was the funeral. Would you like some corn or peas? We've got plenty."

There was another pause. "I'm very sorry for your loss, Jasmine. I am, but you should have at least told me."

"It was last minute. I'm sorry I didn't have 'call Brett' on my checklist before I ran out of town."

"I understand," Brett said formally, "but Karen needs the master Excel spreadsheet of potential client contacts and conversations."

Now, it was Jasmine's turn to pause.

"That's *my* job, Brett. That's my position, and you can't take that away from me because I was out of town for a few days."

"Jasmine, that position is open to anyone who applies. You and Karen have both applied for the position, and one of you isn't pulling their weight. It's a travel-heavy position, and unfortunately ..."

Jasmine tuned out as soon as she heard the word "unfortunately." She couldn't believe her ears. *Applied for the job?* She felt the heat rise to her face. She wanted desperately to rip the stupid cast off her leg and run out the door, but she couldn't.

"I buried my mother today, Brett. Catch me another time," she retorted angrily and ended the call.

Jasmine looked around at her family who surrounded her. Sara waved from a distance and smiled at her. She was happier than she had been in a very long time, and yet, her world was still crashing down around her.

⌒

Jasmine wasn't sure what to do. Her whole life had been turned upside down in a matter of weeks. However, it was time to return home. She had her backpack and suitcase ready to go, so she headed down the stairs of her parents' house to say her goodbyes and wait for the taxi to take her to the airport.

Jacob was in the living room, sitting on the couch.

"Hey, Jas," he said when she finally reached the last step. "It was really good to see you."

Jasmine crutched over to where he was seated and lightly punched his shoulder. "It was good to see you, too, Jacob. Let's keep in touch."

"Sure thing."

"You got any plans for today?" Jasmine asked.

"Yeah, actually. Todd will be here in a few minutes, and we're going to go for a run."

"Todd?" Jasmine asked, surprised. "So, you guys are still friends, huh?"

Jacob smiled. "Yes, we are. He came into town for Mom's funeral, so we're hanging out before he heads home."

"Nice. Tell him I said hi."

"Sure thing," he said, tipping his head toward her. Trying to keep the conversation going, Jacob added, "How long do you have to have that cast on?"

"Oh geez, another three months at least," Jasmine said, rolling her eyes.

"What!" exclaimed Jacob. "From what I remember about you, that isn't going to suit you very well."

Jasmine chuckled. "You have no idea."

They talked for a few more minutes, then were interrupted by a car pulling into the driveway. "Well, I guess it's time for me to go," Jasmine said as she struggled to stand up. She headed toward the door, only to be surprised that the car wasn't her taxi but Todd. He was standing outside when Jasmine opened the door.

"Hi, Todd," she said awkwardly. "It's been a while!"

"Jasmine! It's good to see you! How have you been? I didn't get a chance to say hello at the funeral."

"It's been a ride, that's for sure," Jasmine replied, raising her eyebrows.

"I'm so sorry about your mom."

Jasmine smiled. "Thank you."

"You still enjoying your photography job?" he asked.

Jasmine accidentally laughed out loud at the ridiculous question. "No," she said emphatically.

"Really?" Todd questioned. "I thought you were dead set on that photography thing. I'm really surprised. Isn't that why you moved clear across the country?"

She gave him a forced smile while biting her tongue, choosing not to make a scene.

"I found an even better job," she fibbed. She pulled a bottle of water from her purse and took a sip.

"So, where are you now?" He continued with the awkward questioning, and Jasmine desperately wanted her taxi to show up.

"Oh, I still live in Maryland," she answered, without offering further details.

"Cool. I've got a buddy in Baltimore," he said.

"Oh really?" Jasmine commented, more interested. "Whereabouts?"

"The north part, near the Johns Hopkins campus and Wester High School."

"What! That's where I am."

"He loves that area. He works for Detracam. Do you know where that is?"

Jasmine tipped her head to one side. "No, I'm not familiar with it."

"Oh, you'd love it. It's a small little company—a research and development firm working with new camera design prototypes; puts them through their paces."

Jasmine almost spat out the water she'd just taken another drink of. "Near Johns Hopkins?" she inquired to make sure she'd heard him correctly.

He nodded.

"Interesting," she said.

"I've heard they're hiring, if you're interested in a new job," he said casually, "but it sounds like you like the one you have."

"Well, you can never have too many options," she said, careful not to make it obvious that she had fibbed about her current job.

"I can give you his phone number, if you'd like to talk to him," he replied.

"Sure. Why not?" Jasmine responded, hardly able to contain her enthusiasm.

A honk originated from outside just after Todd pulled out a business card from his wallet. While Jasmine reached for her crutches, she said to Jacob, "Would you mind grabbing my suitcase from upstairs?"

"Of course!" he said, and headed quickly up the stairs to retrieve it.

Todd handed Jasmine the business card.

"This is your buddy's phone number?" she asked.

"Yes, it is. His name is Manny."

"Perfect. Thank you so much," she said with a smile. "It was good to see you again, Todd. Have fun today."

Jacob handed the suitcase to the taxi driver, who was standing at his trunk waiting for them, and turned to face toward Jasmine. A sad smile appeared on both of their faces as their eyes began to glisten. "Come here, you," he requested, holding his arms open for a hug. "I sure am going to miss you, Jas." They embraced. "It was so good to see you again."

Jasmine leaned into Jacob's arms and sniveled. "I'll miss you, too, Jacob."

"Stay in touch, now. And heal up quickly," he instructed. He then helped her into the car.

The taxi backed out of the driveway, and she turned around to take one last look at the childhood home she was leaving once again. As she turned around, she saw Jacob standing in the driveway with his hands in his pockets, watching her ride away. She waved goodbye. Her family felt healed and broken at the same time.

$\mathcal{J}$asmine stared out of the plane window. Her favorite part of flying had always been taking off—feeling the plane move from side to side, while she watched the ground below get smaller and smaller. Now, she watched as Phoenix disappeared from view. Then she leaned back in her seat and closed her eyes.

Later, she felt for the business card that Todd had handed her, wanting to make sure it was still safely tucked into her pocket. She pulled it out and looked at it again. The front said "Brochenbrugh and Associates, Inc." Todd's name was below that, with the words "Mechanical Engineer" printed underneath it.

She turned the card over again and examined the handwriting on the back:

Manny Colle 888-555-3635. Good luck!

Jasmine arched her lips when she read "Good luck" again. She was excited about the possibility, but she also realized a dream job like this was most likely not going to happen for her. She returned the card to her pocket, then patted it to make sure it was safe and secure.

After an emotionally exhausting funeral and a ten-hour travel day, Jasmine finally arrived back home at her apartment. The taxi driver pulled up to the bottom of the three-flight staircase leading to her door. She opened the taxi door and was abruptly hit with cold damp air. She shivered as a chill traveled throughout her body. She hadn't realized how much she'd enjoyed the warmth of Arizona weather until she was back in the cool evening air of Baltimore.

The driver pulled Jasmine's bag out of the trunk and walked toward the stairs, asking which door was hers. She told him, pausing on her crutches and pointing to the top level. He tipped his head to her and proceeded up the stairs.

Exhausted from traveling, Jasmine moved slowly up the stairs. The driver passed her on his way back down, waving goodbye before she'd even made it halfway upstairs.

Finally, she made it to the top of the third flight of stairs. *There is no way this is good for my brain*, she thought, pausing to take a break and rest her armpits. As she made her way down the hallway, she noticed that there was still a trace of purplish stain on the cement. She laughed to herself, remembering that she'd once thought spilling a little juice equaled having a bad day. She sighed, also, when she recalled running up those stairs not very long ago, frantically digging out her key to get inside in time to answer the phone.

Jasmine reached her door and leaned her crutches against the wall, while she pulled her backpack from her shoulders. As she searched for her key, she noticed a tied white plastic grocery bag sitting beside her suitcase.

"Ew, gross," Jasmine fussed, wrinkling her nose. "That isn't mine."

She assumed the taxi driver had taken it out of the trunk of his car assuming it was hers. She kicked it to the side as she finished hobbling to her door. Once there, she noticed a small note taped to her door. Curious, she put her key in her pocket, pulled the taped note from the door, and opened it. In beautiful handwriting, she read:

Hi Jasmine,

You left your sweater on the table when we went to dinner a few weeks ago. I didn't catch you home twice, so I'm leaving it here in the bag. Somehow, I also missed you at the marathon. I'm so sorry I didn't see you. I've missed talking with you. Here's my new phone number: 888-555-9897

—Bradley

Jasmine's stomach flipped when she spotted his name on the bottom of the note, and she let out a squeal as she held the paper close to her heart. She quickly moved everything inside her door and collapsed in her chair with her phone and the note in her hand.

She reread the note, and let out another big grin when she read Bradley's name on the bottom of the small lined paper. She contemplated calling him immediately and looked at the time. It was 8:23 p.m. She looked from the note to her phone and nodded her head, then dialed his new number. As she waited for him to answer the phone, she suddenly wondered how in the world he knew where she lived.

"Hello?" she heard his manly voice answer.

Jasmine's stomach flipped again, and she swallowed her nerves before she spoke. "Hi, Bradley, it's Jasmine."

"Jasmine!" he exclaimed. "I'm so happy to hear from you!"

Jasmine let out an audible sigh. "It's not too late?" she asked, not sure what to say next.

"No, not at all. You're welcome to call me anytime."

Jasmine let out another audibly nervous sigh. "I just got home," she said. "Thank you for bringing my sweater by."

"Oh, no problem. I'm sorry it took me so long. And, I'm sorry I didn't see you at the marathon. I was looking all over for you. I wanted to congratulate you when you crossed the finish line, but somehow I missed you."

Jasmine wasn't sure how to tell him her news.

"Hey," he added, before she could answer, "would you like to grab some dinner with me tomorrow? I can explain what happened."

"Explain what happened?" she asked, confused.

"Yeah, why I have a new phone."

"Sure, I suppose that would be nice," she hesitated, her brows furrowing. "Where would you like to go?"

"Would you like to meet me at Bygone's?" he asked with a twinkle in his voice.

"Bygone's!" Jasmine repeated. "Um, that's a nice place."

"You deserve it," Bradley replied.

Jasmine hesitated. "Um, I'd rather not, Bradley."

There was a longer pause on her end of the line.

"Oh, okay," he said, sounding thrown off. "Would you like to meet me somewhere closer?"

"I can't drive."

"Cars, they can be a nuisance. Well, I can certainly come pick you up," he said, probably assuming she was having car trouble.

"Sure!" she said at once, though she wasn't sure what she'd just gotten herself into.

"Perfect. I'll be by at about seven. Will that work for you?"

"It will," she said, too brightly.

"I'm looking forward to seeing you tomorrow, Jasmine."

"Oh, one more thing," she said quickly, before he could hang up. "How in the world did you know where I live?"

Bradley let out a playful laugh. "Remember when we met in the park?"

"Yes," said Jasmine, picturing it vividly.

"You told me you lived in those apartments. When I didn't hear from you and I lost my phone, I decided to head over to see if I could figure out which apartment was yours. I saw the mailroom, so I went in and looked at the name on every mailbox until I saw a J. Stone."

"Are you serious?" Jasmine asked, feeling flattered.

"I did," Bradley replied. "The first time I knocked, a few days before the marathon, you didn't answer. When I came back a few days after that, I had already decided to leave a note if you didn't answer, and I left your sweater outside your door."

"Wait that was my sweater!" she exclaimed.

"In the plastic bag, yes," Bradley answered.

"That was sweet of you, thank you. I'll see you tomorrow."

Jasmine sat, anxiously tapping her fingers on her crutches, waiting for Bradley to arrive. Bygone's was the last place she wanted to be invited again. She had been through the conversation a million times in her head, explaining to Bradley what had happened the first and only time she'd had dinner there.

Her thoughts were interrupted by a knock on her door. She took a deep breath and nervously hobbled toward the door. She felt increasingly anxious as she turned the lock, cracked the door open, and moved her crutch out of the way before she could open it all the way.

"Hi!" Bradley said, his brows up in the air and a look of surprise on his face. "How—what—hi," he stammered before he finally let out, "What happened?"

Jasmine hobbled out of the way to let him in. "A whole lot," she said, "since we last saw each other. A whole lot," she repeated.

Bradley seemed unsure how to respond. "Are you sure you want to go out tonight?"

"Oh sure." Jasmine smiled awkwardly. "Sure, it's no problem," she replied, trying to convince herself. "I've learned how to get around," she finished with a forced laugh.

"That sounds like a no," Bradley concluded.

"No, no, it's fine," Jasmine pitifully argued. "You made the reservations."

"We can cancel reservations, Jasmine. It's not a big deal."

Jasmine let out a big sigh. "You wouldn't mind?" she asked sweetly.

"Not at all! We can always order takeout. It's been a while since I've had a good pizza," he said, and his smile was as handsome as she remembered. "You go make yourself comfortable, and I'll order us a pizza."

Bradley hung up the phone and moved the kitchen chair into the small living room. "So," he said, as politely as he could, "may I ask what happened?" As soon as he said the words, he seemed to instantly put together why he hadn't seen Jasmine at the race, and he let out a long breath. "Oh Jasmine," he said, clearly feeling pain for her, "this happened before the race, didn't it?"

"It did," Jasmine said, slightly shaking her head back and forth, while looking down at her ankle. "The good news is, I had the 'best' ankle surgeon in town. He screwed my bones back together quite well." She mixed sweetness with sarcasm.

"I'm so sorry to hear that."

She went on to tell Bradley about the car accident, and about what she'd done when she read his text while she was in the hospital. "I deleted your phone number right then and there, and threw my phone across the room," Jasmine said while she scrunched her face in embarrassment.

"Whew," Bradley said, shaking his head. "I can't say I wouldn't have had a similar reaction. I'm so sorry, Jasmine. You know, I've wracked my brain for the last several weeks, trying to figure out what I did wrong. Never would I have thought it was the text!" He smiled now that the mystery was solved. "How do you get around up here all by yourself?"

Jasmine laughed, then told Bradley the story of going to get her package from the mailroom and running into Victor.

"... so, he took me to my appointment and brought me back home, and that's when I got the phone call," she said, pursing her lips and trying not to cry.

"The phone call?" he questioned.

"About my mom" was all she could reply. There was a long pause as she stared straight in front of her. "She ... I didn't make it," Jasmine said as tears filled her eyes. "I didn't make it."

Bradley quietly moved over to her chair and kneeled down beside her. He put his arm around her and put his head on her shoulder, seeming unsure of how to comfort her, but understanding that no words fit the situation. He squeezed her arm and held her closer than anyone had held her in a very long time. Jasmine let out the loudest cry she had ever been able to. Loud sobs erupted from her mouth as she recalled every detail of the situation. As much as she'd cried before, her mother's death—this ultimate loss—was truly hitting home.

Jasmine wiped away the last of her tears. "I'm sorry," she said, feeling totally embarrassed. "I'm not sure what came over me."

"There's no need to be sorry, Jasmine, not for a second. Feeling and accepting your emotions and letting them out is one of the best things you can do for grief."

Ignoring his words, Jasmine tried to move past her embarrassing bout of tears. "What about you?" she asked. "You got a new phone?"

Bradley let out a flustered laugh. "Jasmine, a new phone doesn't matter right now. All that matters is that we're here together now—that I didn't lose you forever."

Jasmine smiled as butterflies fluttered through her stomach. The doorbell rang, and Bradley removed his arm from around her to answer it.

"Get yourself comfortable and prepare to eat the best pizza in all of Baltimore," he said, trying to cheer her up.

When they finally settled down to eat, Bradley asked, "So, if you don't mind my asking, what does this mean in terms of your job? I know you were really looking forward to the new position they were creating for you."

Jasmine sighed. "I have no idea. I'm working from home right now, but I'm not even sure I want to stay with the company."

Bradley looked up in surprise halfway through a bite. "Not sure if you want to stay with the company?"

"Turns out you were right, Bradley. Having those 'things' didn't make me important. As soon as they were taken away, so was my importance."

"Jasmine, I shouldn't have said that. It was uncalled for, and I was being very inconsiderate."

"No, you were right," Jasmine said. "But honestly, I have no idea what to do now."

Bradley paused for a minute. Then, he put down his pizza and moved his plate to the side. He looked intently at her and asked, "What is it that you *really* want to do? Put aside your circumstances and situation for a minute, and ask yourself what it is you really want to do. What's your dream job? What does your dream home look like? What do you *really* want?"

Jasmine put her plate aside as well and looked back at Bradley after thinking for a few moments. "I don't know," she said, shaking her head. "I honestly don't know what I really truly want."

"May I ask you a question?"

"Sure," she said, though she wasn't sure she was ready for what it might be.

"How can you know which decision to make and what direction to take if you don't know what you want? As a guidance counselor, I often remind people that if they don't know where they're going, how will they know when they're there?"

Jasmine shrugged her shoulders. "I mean, I guess I kinda know what I want, but it really doesn't matter what I want now, does it?" She looked up at a corner of the wall, then stared into space. "The Guy in control ultimately gets to decide for me." She paused again. "I don't like to voice what I want because He just gives me the opposite anyway. But enough about me," she said, feeling extremely uncomfortable. "What about you? How's work going for you?"

They continued with surface-level small talk until it was time for Bradley to go. She waved goodbye as he walked out the door and smiled contentedly after. There'd been something different about him tonight. She couldn't quite put her finger on what exactly it was, but she liked it.

When she closed her door, Jasmine glanced over at her bookshelf. She knew exactly what she wanted for a career anyway. She looked at the old camera box and smiled, remembering again the day she received it. There was no doubt that her dream job had been in camera design and photography. *But God had other plans for me*, she thought.

↬ TWENTY-FIVE ↫

*J*asmine peeked out her kitchen window, wondering how much time she had left to get ready. It was too late; the taxi was already there in the parking lot, waiting for her. She crutched over to the table, placed her leather bag over her shoulder and onto her back as she had practiced, and headed for the door. She turned around one last time to make sure she had everything she needed for the day, then let out a breathy sigh.

Considering this wasn't her first rodeo with crutches in a taxi, she quickly turned her back to the car, placed both crutches in one hand, removed her bag, held on tightly to the door, and lowered herself onto the seat, plopping down at the last second. She reached for her crutches and placed them across the back of the seat. She gave the address to the driver, and nervously prepared her mind for her first day back in the office after working from home for over two weeks.

What are people thinking? What have they been saying about me? She took a deep breath, desperately wanting to turn back.

She let out her breath heavily. She couldn't stand the thought of having to face Karen.

The taxi pulled into the office parking lot, and Jasmine immediately asked the driver to pull to the end of the lot. He gave her a funny look in the rearview mirror but obliged. "It's for exercise," she fibbed.

He gave her the same funny look.

She stood at the end of the lot, dreading the looks she would get when she walked in, but she was determined to show her commitment to work and to her new position. She made it all the way to the entrance, stopping a few times to adjust the crutches and to give her armpits a break. Tomorrow, she would have the cab drop her off at the door. This wasn't quite worth it.

When she exited the elevator and looked around, she sensed an eerie aura filling the space. She hobbled to her desk, remembering the last time that she had been here, rushing about in an unpleasant mood. Somehow, things seemed different. She had changed since the last time she was in the building. She realized that Victor had given her a new perspective.

Corbin meandered by her cubicle, and instantly stopped when he noticed her presence.

"Hi Jasmine! It's good to see you again!" He moved in closer. "We heard about what happened."

She put her head down in self-repentance. "I'm sorry for the way I treated you, Corbin."

Corbin jerked his head back and gave Jasmine an incredulous stare. Unsure of how to respond to her seeming kindness, he raised his eyebrows and walked away with a childlike smile.

Something had changed in her.

⁓

Jasmine was happy to be back at home after an unusual day at work. Just as she settled herself in her chair to eat her dinner, there was a knock on her door. Not expecting any company, she let it go. A few seconds later, she heard the knock again. Frustrated, she put her plate on the wooden TV table that Bradley had brought over for her and hobbled to the door.

She was pleasantly surprised to see Victor.

"I thought you could use some cheering up!" he said, with a beaming smile. "How are you feeling? How's the healing process going?"

"Come on in if you'd like," she said, moving aside. Victor came in and placed a small cake on the little table.

"You didn't have to do that," Jasmine said.

"Well, I wanted to check on you and see how you were feeling. I haven't heard from you in a while."

"Chocolate cake does sound good right now, to be honest," she commented. "Would you like to join me for coffee and cake?"

"Sure, why not? I could use a break. Would you like me to make the coffee?" he asked.

"No, you make yourself comfortable. I can get it." Jasmine hobbled to the kitchen counter, happy now to have company, and reached for some plates while the coffee was brewing.

"I'm glad to see you're doing so well."

She turned around and looked at Victor. "To quote a world-renowned cognitive and behavioral neuroscientist, things are not always as you perceive them to be," she said, allowing a touch of sarcasm to creep into her voice.

Victor chuckled. "No, they aren't, are they?"

"I wish I could change things. I wish things worked out better for me," she said her tone defeated.

"I'm sorry to hear that, Jasmine. Is there something in particular you're referring to?"

Jasmine took a deep breath. "It's nothing. Just work," she said, shrugging her shoulders as she poured the coffee.

Victor walked over to the counter and picked up both coffee cups. He then walked over to Jasmine's chair and placed her cup on the tray table, while she cut the small cake into pieces for them. There was an awkward silence before he spoke. "I keep hearing you say things aren't up to you. May I ask why you say that?"

Jasmine put down the knife and gave Victor a confused look. "Because it's not," she said. *Why couldn't he see how obvious it was?* "Because no matter how hard I try, things *never* work out for me. I know you like to think you live in a friendly universe, but the truth is, Victor, it doesn't work out that way for everyone. There are just some things that aren't good."

"How long have you felt that way?"

"It's just life."

"Can you give me an example of something that hasn't worked out for you?" Victor asked with curiosity.

"We've already discussed this, but crushing my ankle a couple of weeks before the marathon I trained thirteen weeks for is one example." She pointed to her ankle.

"So, what about that didn't work out for you?"

"I didn't get to run the marathon, Victor," Jasmine irritatingly replied. "What do you mean, what didn't work out?"

"Well, is it possible that was how you were able to go to the funeral without having any animosity toward your mom? Having the space to grieve without wishing you were somewhere else or blaming your mom for being in your way?"

Jasmine silently contemplated Victor's question. "Yes, I guess it's a possibility," she said, knowing full well that she would've been upset if she'd had to go to Arizona to the funeral instead of run her marathon. "But what about wasting those thirteen weeks training for a marathon that I didn't get to run? That darn well didn't work out for me."

Victor chuckled. "Jasmine! 'Darn well didn't work out' for you? If you weren't training for the marathon, you wouldn't have met Bradley!"

She warmed at the mere mention of Bradley. "True," she agreed, now understanding his point of view and softening up a bit. Her wheels began turning, and she asked the question she'd hesitated to address before. "But what about my mom, Victor? How is that working out for me?"

"Well, only you can decide that, Jasmine," he replied softly. "You tell me. What are some good things that came of you having the opportunity to go to your mother's funeral?"

"There's nothing good about going to your mother's funeral, Victor. Don't be ridiculous."

"Were you able to see your family?"

She immediately thought of the conversations she and her sister were able to have. "I was able to connect with my sister," she said reluctantly.

Victor smiled. "That's beautiful, Jasmine. Would that have happened without the aid of the funeral?"

"Most likely not," she said, shaking her head slightly. "No, definitely not."

"See, here's the thing," Victor explained. "You're perceiving and experiencing life through the lens of your beliefs, remember? You're seeing things through the lens of what you've chosen to focus on. You've believed for a very long time that the world is out to get you—that God is out to get you. Would you say that's true?"

"Yes, that's true."

"I bet," Victor said cautiously, "if you were to find a diary from your childhood, you'd find evidence of your beliefs over and over again. I'd venture to say that the things you struggled with then, are the same things you struggled with in college, and they're the same things you're struggling with now." He paused for a moment before he continued on. "And it's because of your belief system that you feel you have no say in what happens to you—what choices you make—because there's 'a man upstairs' who controls it all."

Jasmine contemplated what Victor was saying. She didn't want to argue with a scientist and decided to hear him out.

"Your belief system—what you believe *about* life—determines how you behave. That's why you think that no matter how hard you try, you always end up with the same results. It's because you have a fundamental belief that you're screwed from the very beginning. And, with that belief, what's the point in trying, right?"

"You have no idea how many times I've thought that," Jasmine reflected.

"Do you remember the reticular activating system that I mentioned before?"

"Yes, I do."

"The reticular activating system is the lens through which everything you think and perceive is filtered. It decides what information comes in, and what information gets filtered out. There's so much sensory information going on at the same time around you, that you would go crazy—you would bust—if you tried to ingest it all at once. So, the brain narrows down what you experience into a rather narrow band, and that band is based on what you believe. You'll always see evidence of the things you believe, and you'll automatically filter out any evidence of the opposite of that belief. Does that make sense?" Victor asked.

Jasmine shook her head 'yes'.

Victor kept going. "If you believe things never work out for you because God wants it that way, what do you think you'll find evidence for?"

"Well, I suppose I'll find evidence for the fact that things never work out for me."

"Yes," he said enthusiastically. "And that's what you've shared with me a few times without even realizing it. You've said things never work out for you—that you can't catch a break. And, when that's what you believe, that's what you repeatedly experience. You live life through the belief that nothing ever works out for you. That's where your specific perspective comes from."

Jasmine felt relieved and confused all at the same time.

"Each individual's perspective is based on their belief system." Victor stated. "But that's another topic for another day."

"Then, if I have all these beliefs that are supposedly sabotaging me, how do things magically end up working out for me?" she asked.

"Well," he said, "every single thing in your life always works out for you. You just don't see it because you're filtering those things out through your reticular activating system. The evidence that things are always working out for you is there, in the same way a forest has all its trees, but you only see the trees next to the well-worn path. You have a well-worn path to the belief that things never work out for you in your brain, so all you see is evidence to that, and it will be there until you choose to purposely focus on other possibilities."

"Interesting" was all Jasmine could say, as she tried to comprehend what she was hearing. "Cake?" she asked, holding up a plate. "And lukewarm coffee?"

Victor chuckled. "Sure, why not?"

They took a drink of cooled-down coffee and began to eat their cake.

"So, I was wondering," Jasmine said, her curiosity finally getting the best of her, "your wife, Clarissa. You said she's in Europe?"

Victor beamed at the mention of his wife. "My sweet Clarissa. Yes, she's in Europe, visiting her mother. When I was asked by the university to lead an extensive brain imaging study here on campus, my wife decided this would be a great time for her to spend some time back home in Germany, so I could focus my attention on the research."

"That sure was sweet of her," Jasmine said.

"It sure was. She has a charming soul, and I miss her dearly," Victor said, clearly thinking about his wife.

"Then I must ask," Jasmine said hesitantly, "why are you living here, in these apartments?"

Victor smiled. "I get paid a per diem, so I got to choose where I wanted to live for the duration of my work. Clarissa and I are planning a nice vacation together once we get back home to each other, so living here has allowed me to save up enough money for the trip."

Jasmine was relieved that she finally knew why such an amazingly important person was living in these apartments. "And it doesn't bother you to live here?" she again asked hesitantly.

"What kind of a question is that?" Victor asked with a laugh. "Not one bit. It led me to you, Jasmine."

She almost teared up at the thought. She shook her head without saying a word, feeling humbled.

"I'll be reunited with my love exactly two months from tomorrow," he added, his smile elated.

"Two months!" Jasmine exclaimed. "Well, I definitely want to say a proper goodbye before you leave. I know you're a busy important man, but will we have a chance to meet again before you go?" Jasmine asked. "Hopefully, I'll have this goofy cast off by then."

"I would love that. We'll be in touch," he said as he finished the last bite of his cake, then stood up and held out his hand to take both plates to the sink.

"Thank you so much for the cake and for coming up to check on me, Victor. You didn't have to do that."

"It was my pleasure," he said. "I'm sorry about your mother's passing."

Jasmine hobbled back to her room the second her front door closed. She was on a mission to find her diary, to see if what Victor had said was indeed true. She carefully moved over the clothes in her closet to reveal the diary, which lay on the wire shelf. She picked it up as if it was some kind of treasure and sat down on the edge of her bed.

She began to turn the pages, searching through them. It didn't take her long to find the first evidence of the belief of which Victor had spoken. There it was, plain as day, in the second entry:

How horrible it would be if my mom only bought me a diary so she could snoop around on me and see what I write about. If you're reading this, Mom, I caught you. HAHA on you.

Jasmine reread the entry. She put down the book and crashed face first onto her pillow. "I've never trusted anyone!" she blurted out loud. "And here it is—at thirteen. Wow."

She sat back up and kept reading.

I am trying really hard to listen to Mom and Dad, but it's so hard because they don't understand me, and they don't even try.

You love Sara and Jacob more than me.

No one likes me.

Wow, she thought. *I have been believing this for a very long time.*

I can't trust anyone now.

No one really actually cares about me, not even my mom and dad.

The whole world is mean, including God.

Jasmine read it again. There it was. Jasmine read out loud. "'The whole world is mean, including God,'" "How did Victor know this? How did he know that these very things would be in my diary?"

She kept on reading, fascinated by what she hadn't caught the first time around.

Life here stinks.

Jasmine snickered as she read that. "Life here stinks, too," she said out loud. *Victor was right. The things I struggled with at thirteen are the same things I struggled with in college, and the same things I'm struggling with now. But how the heck do I change it?* She was feeling desperate and lost. *Or am I just stuck with it forever?*

She kept reading.

I hate this Earth.

Jasmine stared at the words, shaking her head in disbelief while goosebumps formed on her arms. It was all becoming so clear.

I learned that people are awful and mean, and I can't trust anyone.

Things never work out for me.

There it was. Plain as day, right there, in her very own writing. *My gosh*, she thought. *He's right! I have believed this for a very long time.*

Jasmine finally closed her diary.

What do I do now? How do I change a belief I've been believing for so long? Will I be stuck like this forever?

⏤ TWENTY-SIX ⏤

*J*asmine returned to work for the fifth and final day of the week. She was in good spirits knowing that it was Friday, and even though she was used to being dropped off at the front door by now, the embarrassment hadn't faded. Every single time she crawled out of the cab, she lowered her head to hide, not wanting to see who was watching her.

Today was no different, but it beat walking from the back of the parking lot.

As elevator doors opened, Jasmine spread her shoulders wide to let herself off first. She was in such a hurry to get off that she didn't notice Karen standing at her desk, waiting for her.

"It's about time," Karen smirked, glancing at her watch. "You're usually a smidge earlier than this."

She paused, taking the time to fully stand up. "But I'm glad you're here."

Karen's abrasive smile filled Jasmine with animosity.

"I put the Excel reports on your desk," Karen pointed out, while she walked away with her head held high in arrogance. "Oh," she added, turning around, "I rearranged the format. I couldn't follow the way you had it laid out."

All Jasmine could do was bite her cheek and stare at Karen in disbelief.

Not long after Jasmine was seated at her desk, Brett hurried around the corner. "Hey, Jasmine!" he called out. "Ready to rock and roll today?"

"What for?" she questioned, not sure what he was referring to but willing to do anything to secure her position.

"It's spring, Jasmine. We rock and roll every day during spring campaign," he said, looking at her as if he was surprised she even asked the question. "Meet me in sixty," he commanded, turning around, and walking backward as he spoke. "I need to run a few things by you before the week is out."

Jasmine gave him a weak "yes, sir" salute, but he'd already turned around to scramble down the hallway.

She breathed deeply and closed her eyes for a few seconds to ground herself. She'd forgotten how fast-paced this place could be. When she opened her eyes, her index finger pushed the power button on the computer. She cringed as she hesitantly typed her passcode, knowing what would greet her on the screen.

I need coffee, Jasmine mused, staring at her desk. *I miss being able to do something as simple as carry a cup of coffee.*

There were too many emails to catch up on and too many loose ends from the week to tie up, and she clearly needed to go through the reports before "sixty." Jasmine dropped her head into her hands and started to ponder why she had put up with this place for so long.

With her head buried in the reports, she heard Brett's voice again, barking orders as he walked past. "Jasmine," he commanded abruptly, "I'll need the new Look book for the meeting. It contains some new designers that we need to discuss for the spring product launch."

Jasmine looked at the time. "I'll have to go get it," Jasmine called out.

Brett raised his eyebrows and cocked his head, signaling that she had better get going.

"I'll be right there," she called to no one, realizing she had only a few minutes before the meeting.

Jasmine packed up her bag, so she could grab it as soon as she returned from retrieving the Look book. She put on her backpack and crutched down the hallway, each movement digging into her already painful armpits. When she arrived to the copy room, she wasn't sure which Look book he wanted, so, in a hurry, she pulled off her backpack, stuck all three of the books she found in there, zipped it up, and headed back down the hallway to the meeting.

She heard inaudible voices coming from the conference room and knew she had to crutch faster. She didn't know how long they'd been waiting for her. She was a few steps away from the conference door when she heard Brett broadcast, "No, we're waiting for Gimpy." Everyone broke out in laughter just as Jasmine entered the doorway. She instantly came to a stop.

"Ah, Jasmine! There you are. Glad you could join us," he nervously said, obviously hoping she hadn't heard his insult.

Jasmine's chin dropped and her tongue rested against the back of her teeth as stared at him in disbelief. She proceeded to slowly place the Look books on the table, making it obvious that she'd heard. It was as if one could cut the air with a knife.

"Jasmine, it was a joke. All in good fun," Brett insisted, breaking the silence.

Jasmine peered around the room of people, looking at each one. Brooke. Karen. Derek. Brett. And an empty chair. She nodded her head, in agreement with her thoughts, waved goodbye, and clicked down the hallway on her crutches. Bradley's words rang through her head: *If you don't know what you want, how will you ever get there?*

She calmly returned to her desk, sat down, took a deep breath, and let out a long pent-up sigh. She reached into her desk drawer, and pulled out Todd's business card that had Manny's name and phone number on the back. She picked up her phone and nervously dialed the complete stranger's phone number.

"Hello?" a man's voice answered after the second ring.

Jasmine panicked. She wasn't sure whether to hang up the phone or speak. Finally, she squeaked out, "Hi, is this Manny?"

Minutes later, she hung up the phone and let out a quiet, excited "Eek!" She couldn't believe what had just happened. Her eyes glistened as she took in the possibility of what she hoped would be the next chapter of her life. She gave herself a slight pinch to make sure it was really true.

Jasmine heard footsteps advancing down the hallway. She felt like crawling under her desk to disappear, but instead, she closed the tab she'd been working on earlier and opened her email tab.

"That was a risky thing you did there, Jasmine, walking away from the meeting like that," Brett chided as he nonchalantly strolled around the corner at a much slower pace than he had an hour earlier.

"No, Brett, that was a risky thing *you* did there," she declared, looking directly in his steel-blue eyes. "I just finished filling out my two weeks' notice."

Brett swallowed and looked down at the floor, breaking their gaze. "Jasmine, don't do this," he pleaded, without even apologizing.

"It's too late," she let him know, "Gimpy has made up her mind."

As soon as Brett was out of sight, Jasmine picked up her phone, almost hysterical.

"Answer, answer, answer, answer, answer ..."

"Hello?" a manly voice answered.

She pressed a hand over her chest and instantly calmed down. "Hi Bradley."

"Hi Jasmine," he replied tentatively, noticing her heavy breathing.

"I know you are at work. Do you have a second?" She knew he would hear the worry in her voice.

"Sure, what's up?"

Jasmine squeezed her eyes shut and tilted her head back. "I quit my job," she whispered.

There was silence.

"What do I do now?" she asked him, opening her eyes.

Bradley oriented his thoughts before speaking.

"Well, I suppose you start looking for a new job," he teased, stating the obvious.

Jasmine didn't respond. She sat there, holding the phone to her ear, just wanting to hear Bradley's voice, still in complete disbelief at what she had done.

"Is there anything I can do?" he asked.

"I want to get out of here," Jasmine answered. "I feel like I can hardly breathe."

"I'll tell you what, I'll come get you as soon as possible. How does that sound?"

"That would be fantastic. Thank you so much. You're the best."

"Just hang tight, and I'll finish up here. I'll be there in a couple of hours."

Two hours had never passed more slowly. Jasmine glanced at her phone every few minutes to ensure she hadn't missed Bradley's call. So many things needed to be done, but she just couldn't concentrate. She was second-guessing herself every few minutes.

Finally, her phone rang. She'd never been happier to get a call in all her life. She picked up before the first ring had even finished.

"Hello?" she answered in a jittery tone.

"Hi, Jasmine. I'll be there in about fifteen minutes."

"I'll be outside waiting," she said tensely.

In a matter of seconds, Jasmine had packed her bags and was standing at her desk. Every nerve in her body quaked. She waited for Brett to walk around the corner and scold her, or for someone to walk around the other corner and dump a pile of papers on her desk.

Breathing heavily, she glanced around at everything that needed to be done. She looked at all the people moving about, meeting deadlines and frantically shuffling papers. She scanned her desk over one last time, before walking toward the elevator. She spotted the stack of reports that Karen had given her that morning. Carefully, she removed her backpack, placed the reports inside, and made her way to Karen's cube. She tapped the wall to let Karen know she was there.

"You're right," she quietly announced to Karen as she unzipped her backpack and handed her the reports. "The format *was* a mess. I'm so glad you fixed it." Her voice hinted sarcasm. Then looked at her watch. Without another word, she put on her backpack, adjusted her crutches, and hobbled toward the elevator.

She nervously waited for the elevator doors to close behind her. Everything seemed to be moving in slow motion. The doors closed and the elevator started down to the main floor. It felt liberating to be leaving work so early on a Friday afternoon.

Once outside, Jasmine let out a long audible sigh, looked around for Bradley's car, then glanced at her watch. Only ten minutes had gone by. With each passing second, she grew increasingly more anxious. She crutched nervously back and forth at the building's entrance, watching for his car, then decided to sit down on a bench to rest. She bounced her left leg up and down, trying to be as patient as possible.

Bradley's electric-blue Rav4 Toyota pulled into the parking lot, and Jasmine stood up and raced down the sidewalk to meet him. "You have no idea how happy I am to see you!" she gushed as she opened the door.

Bradley gave Jasmine a smile that warmed her entire body. "You okay, Jas?" he asked sweetly.

"I am now." She happily admitted. "Let's just get out of here."

"Where do you want to go?" he asked, driving past the building's entrance, looking for a place to turn around.

"You know what?" Jasmine replied, feeling free, "let's go to the park."

"Sounds perfect!" he exclaimed. "Have you had lunch yet?"

"I haven't had an appetite."

"I know the best place for club sandwiches. What do you say we grab a few and take them to the park?"

"That would be amazing," Jasmine affirmed, leaning back onto her seat's headrest in relief as they left the parking lot. At the stoplight, Bradley faced Jasmine directly and looked intensely into her eyes. "I am so proud of you, Jasmine," he said with a soft tone, staring into her eyes until the light turned green.

Jasmine's pulse raced and her stomach felt weak. She arched her back and continued examining his face, even after he had turned to watch the road.

It was a quiet ride to the sandwich shop, with both of them stealing glances and flirtatious smiles at each other.

"How do you know of all these places?" she inquired once they pulled into the lot of a hole-in-the-wall place.

Bradley let out a chuckle. "I've been here a long time, and I know a lot of students who tell me about them," he responded, giving away his secret. "I'll be right back."

Jasmine remained in the car and observed as she watched him talk to every stranger he passed. She kept her eyes on him while he stood in line, waiting to order. His smile lit up the entire shop. The woman behind the counter waved, obviously happy to see him.

Bradley returned to the car with the sandwiches, holding them up for Jasmine to see with a big grin on his face. He opened the door and handed her the bag. "Okay!" he interjected with enthusiasm, "off to the park it is!"

"I had another checkup," she shared as they drove to the park.

"And how did that go?"

"Dr. Peltos said I'm healing remarkably and should be off my crutches in another month or so."

"I know how ready you are for the crutches to go."

"You have no idea," Jasmine replied, and they both laughed.

"I just don't get it Bradley," she wondered, "a month ago, Brett and I were high-fiving each other as we celebrated a major deal, and now he treats me like the help." Her voice started to crack. "What was I thinking? Now, I don't even have a job. I was climbing the ladder, making it work. I'm thirty! What do I do?"

Bradley listened, hardly responding. It was as if he realized she wasn't actually wanting answers just then, and that the best thing he could do was to let her talk and get all her thoughts out in the open.

After he parked his car, Bradley helped Jasmine get out.

"Do you have a favorite spot?"

"I do, actually." She was pleased that he'd thought to ask. "Follow me," she instructed, with a mischievous smile. She led him to a bench at the entrance to the trails. "I love it here. You can still see the water, and it feels secluded enough to have peace and quiet."

"Secluded sounds great," he confessed, with a low, soft voice.

Jasmine blushed and put her head down, breaking his gaze. The two of them seated themselves on the bench.

"Are you ready to eat?" he asked.

Jasmine didn't respond. She just stared into his eyes and involuntarily arched her back with a suggestive gaze.

Bradley slowly moved closer to Jasmine without taking his eyes off her. He slipped his hand behind her waist and pulled her close as he leaned forward for a kiss. Her legs trembled under his touch, and her breathing grew faster and more audible. Her stomach tensed under his soft caresses. She tipped her head back and closed her eyes to better enjoy the intensifying sensations. The faint scent of the aftershave on his cheek made her lips want even more. She felt his fingers press into her ribs, pushing her head further back; his lips sampling their way down to explore her bared neck. With their bodies pressed against one another, Bradley moved his hips to turn his body closer to Jasmine, his foot shoving the sandwich bag further under the bench, and shifting Jasmine's broken ankle. She winced in pain and pulled away.

Bradley winced with her, feeling guilty he caused her pain. "I'm so sorry," he apologized, his furrowed brows moving his face into a frown. "I didn't mean to hurt you."

Jasmine chuckled. "It's okay. I'm fine. We're here for lunch anyways."

"I'm here for *you*," he declared, with a twinkle in his eyes, as he bent down to find the brown paper bag that held the sandwiches. When he handed Jasmine her sandwich, he pecked her on the cheek. "Let's eat."

"Oh my gosh," she exclaimed, "this seriously *is* the best club sandwich I've ever eaten." She pulled the sandwich out in front of her, trying to see what made it so good.

As they ate their lunch, they made minimal small talk, basking in each other's presence.

"Jasmine, you know what I enjoy most about you? You're so full of fire and life."

A tear of happiness formed in Jasmine's eyelid, and rolled down her cheek. Bradley reached out to wipe it away. She once again scooted closer to him, and he put his arm around her. She leaned her head on his shoulder and closed her eyes, feeling safe for the first time in years.

⟶ TWENTY-SEVEN ⟵

$\mathcal{J}$asmine didn't want their time in the park to come to an end. A day that had begun so miserably had just become the most magical one she had experienced in a very long time. As they walked to the car, Jasmine couldn't help but stop and watch a mother and a teenage daughter, who were arguing nearby.

"I didn't get to say goodbye," she said quietly.

"I can't imagine how you must be feeling, Jasmine."

"I feel lost. I didn't get closure."

"What would you have liked to have happened?" Bradley asked as they walked to the car.

Jasmine was silent for a few moments as they continued walking. "I just wanted to talk to her," she said, staring into space. "I wanted to have a conversation with her, asked her some questions."

"What would you have said? What would you have asked?"

She began to cry, not wanting to reveal what she would have said and asked.

Bradley helped her into the car, settled himself in the driver's seat, and reached over to place his hand on Jasmine's to comfort her. "May I offer a suggestion?"

She shrugged. "I guess."

"When you get home, take some time to write your mother a letter. Spill out onto a piece of paper everything that's in your heart. Start with what you were upset about. Tell her what you wanted from her, and what you loved most about her. Don't hold anything back."

The car was full of silence, except for Jasmine's sniffling.

Bradley reached into the glove box and pulled out a white napkin. Jasmine dabbed her eyes with it, as Bradley started the engine. When the car pulled up to her apartment, he asked, "Would you like some help upstairs?"

"No, thank you. I'll be fine," she said, drying her final few tears. "Thank you so much for today, Bradley," she added, this time with happy tears in her eyes.

Bradley leaned over from the driver's seat and gave her an awkward hug.

"I'm sorry I had to ruin it like this," she said, rolling her eyes.

"You didn't ruin anything, Jasmine. Not one bit. I'll call you later," he replied, giving her a wink.

She shut the car door, then headed toward her building's steps. When she reached the first flight of stairs and was headed toward the second, she looked down and saw that Bradley had gotten out of his car. He waved at her, and she smiled and shook her head. When she'd climbed the third flight, she again looked over the wall. He was still there, smiling at her and waving. "Goodbye, girl," he called out sweetly.

This was too good to be true, Jasmine thought.

Once inside her apartment, Jasmine sat at the head of her bed with a spiral notebook and a pen in her lap. She stared off into space, not sure how to even begin a letter to her mother. So many thoughts, memories, and ideas came to mind as she thought about her childhood and her teen years growing up in her parents' house. Yes, there were things she was thankful for and things she'd enjoyed, but there was also a lot of hurt and a lot of scars left behind as well.

"Hi, Mom," she said out loud. "Where are you? Can you hear me? I'm writing you a letter." She bit the side of her lip, trying to keep from giving into her emotions. "I miss you." Jasmine's lip began quivering, and when she looked down at the paper, her eyes were so blurry, she couldn't see to write. She looked around for a tissue and spotted a box across the room. "I need a tissue, Mom," she said, with a little chuckle.

She sat for a few more minutes before she started writing.

Why didn't you tell me you were sick? Why couldn't you have given me more time to say goodbye?

As the questions came to Jasmine, she began writing them down.

Dear Mom,

I don't even know where to start, but you had no idea how angry I was that you didn't tell me that you had cancer—that you didn't let me say goodbye.

Jasmine's eyes watered as soon as she wrote down the words. She reached for the corner of her bedsheet and used it for a tissue. Somehow, just getting it out on paper and admitting that she was angry allowed the dam to break. Tears rolled down her face in torrents, but she kept on writing, hardly able to see through her tears.

I'm angry that you died, Mom. I'm angry at you, and I hated you for bringing me into this world. I hated that you didn't care for me and protect me. I'm angry that you didn't hug me more often and hold me, even when it seemed like I didn't want to be held. I'm angry that you didn't like Gramma and Grandpa. I loved them. Gramma loved me. I'm angry that you controlled me and didn't let me live the life I wanted to live. I'm angry that you didn't follow your dreams and your passions. I'm angry that you weren't the role model that I needed you to be.

Jasmine had to take a break from writing. She grabbed her sheet again and buried her eyes into the fabric. The ache in her chest and throat were too much to bear. When she cleared up her eyes enough to be able to see again, she continued.

Oh Mom, she wailed out loud as she wrote. *I'm angry that you bottled up your emotions and always pretended that everything was okay even though we all knew it wasn't. I'm angry that you yelled at me the way you did when you got mad. You scared me. I'm angry that you gave me dirty looks when you disapproved of a choice I made. It hurt me. I'm angry that you grabbed my arm that day at the strawberry patch when I misunderstood your directions.*

Jasmine cried intensely as her mind returned to that day.

The look in your eyes, Mom, and the strength of your hand ... it hurt me. It hurt me on so many levels. In that moment, I felt so alone, so uncared for, and so unwanted.

It hurt me when you'd tell me to clean up my mess. It hurt me when I'd pull out crafts and projects to work on, and not only didn't you care about what I was creating, you called it a mess. It hurt me when you fussed at me for taking pictures and loving photography. It hurt me when you didn't have time for me. And, when you would yell at me and glare at me with those scary eyes. It would make me feel so very scared and alone. It hurt me deeply when no matter how hard I tried, nothing pleased you. I couldn't do anything right. It hurt me when I went to pick you up on my bike in the rain because you had gone for a walk, and you gave me that face and instructed me to go home, with your finger pointing at me. I cried so hard that day that the downpour of rain was no match for my tears. That day changed me. I know you didn't know it then, but that little twelve-year-old girl never ever forgot that moment. I loved you and tried to show you repeatedly, but my love was always rejected. You were too busy, too frustrated, too tired … it was always something. You conditioned that love right out of me. So much so, that I've never been able to love another person since that day. I remember feeling so alone, unwanted, and uncared for, that I promised myself I would never put myself in a position to be hurt again like that. And, you want to know something? I've never opened myself up like I did that day in the rain again. I can't. I wouldn't be able to handle the rejection.

And, while I'm thinking about it, why didn't you take my period seriously? I felt like such a grown-up woman the second I found out I had finally started my period. I remember calling you to tell you, and you said, "I'll be home in a few hours, ask Sara to help you." A few hours? Ask Sara to help you? How could you, Mom!

Jasmine again grabbed the corner of the bedsheet and covered her eyes. She was vividly remembering that day, when she was so proud of becoming a woman, just to have it shot down.

I learned how to hate during those years. I learned how to criticize and judge people to direct my intense pain—to project it onto someone else. It was simply too much for me to bear. I began to enjoy watching other people hurt. Can you believe that? I can't even believe I'm telling you this, but somehow it felt good to watch other people hurt. Somehow, it made the emotional pain more bearable for me. Everyone was my competition. I held people at arm's length and taught myself to trust no one.

Jasmine couldn't believe the words that were pouring out of her. She hadn't known these things about herself until she just let it flow outward.

You scared me. You scared me out of being able to show you and allow you to see who I really truly was and who I wanted to be. I wanted to go into fashion design and photography, but I didn't dare tell you. I did my absolute best to keep that secret from you until the very end, when I belted out to you that I was going to photography design school. The look on your face ... it was exactly as I expected it to be. I was scared to death of you. I was scared that I'd become you one day. I vowed I would never be like you. Some days, I would watch you. I would watch you walk around, and talk, and laugh, and do your thing, and I despised you, Mom.

Tears were hitting the paper that she was writing on. It felt terrible and liberating at the same time to be writing this letter to her mom.

I hated you, Mom. Somehow, you became my worst enemy, but I missed you at the same time. I became a stone wall that I vowed no one would ever be able to penetrate. And, I kept that promise ... until now. You have no idea how badly I wish I could take all those feelings back if it meant I could see you one more time. If I could just talk to you one more time.

Jasmine wept uncontrollably before she could move on. She picked up the pillow that was next to her, burying her head into it as she wept violently. Several minutes passed before she was able to sit back up. She stared off into space as she continued to explore her memories of her mom. Her body felt better just being able to spill out her feelings and thoughts. She started writing again.

I'm so sorry, Mom. I'm so sorry you were in so much pain yourself. I didn't know that. I'm so sorry, Mom. Why couldn't we have just been there for each other? I didn't know you loved me so much that you were afraid to mess up. I'm sorry I hated you. I don't hate you anymore. I'm sorry, Mom. I'm sorry I didn't thank you more. I'm sorry I despised you. I'm sorry I didn't communicate better with you. I'm sorry I was such a difficult teenager. I'm sorry I played a part in making your life difficult and miserable. I'm sorry I gave you those very same eyes you gave me. I'm sorry I took, and took, and took from you and never gave back. I'm sorry for the terrible thoughts I had about you. I'm sorry I didn't make it to your bedside. Mom, I'm so sorry. I want to take it all back! Will you please forgive me?

All I ever wanted was for you to love me. For you to hug me, squeeze me tight, and tell me that everything was going to be okay. I just wanted to be your daughter. I wanted to hold your hand and put my head on your shoulder. I wanted you to smile at me, laugh with me, and play games with me. I wanted you to look into my eyes and give me life. I wanted you to accept me. I wanted you to be proud of me. I wanted you to tell me "good job." I wanted your approval. I wanted you to tell me that I was beautiful. I wanted you to tell me that you loved me, Mom! I just wanted to hear "I love you." I wanted to hear you say, "I'm sorry." I wanted to see and feel your emotion. I wanted to be able to hug you and tell you that everything was going to be okay, but I couldn't! You hid everything from me! You were hurting so bad, and I'm so sorry. I'm sorry I couldn't be the person you trusted.

I know it's a little late, but thank you for birthing me. Thank you for the physical and emotional pain you endured. Thank you for everything you've done for me. Thank you for being the mom you were—good and bad, because it made me who and what I am. Thank you for the special and thoughtful gifts you were always able to find for me. Thank you for my diary. Thank you so much for my camera. I still have it, by the way.

Thank you for sheltering me and giving me a home to grow up in. I can't tell you how much I enjoyed being there after so many years. Thank you for giving me a brother and a sister who I can go through life with. Thank you for being my tooth fairy and putting fifty cents under my pillow. Somehow, you were always able to slip it in under my pillow without my noticing, even though I did my best to catch you.

Thank you for calling me every single year on my birthday and Christmas, even though I pushed you away. Thank you for the flowers you sent me; it got me back to where I wanted to be. I should have sent you a picture. They were beautiful! Thank you for the note you wrote asking me to come home and attempting to talk to me and say that you were sorry. I shudder to think what state I would be in if you hadn't sent that letter and at least made me call and say goodbye to you. Thank you for saying goodbye. Thank you for telling me that you loved me. It gave me wings.

I will forever love you and miss you.

—Jasmine

⟿ TWENTY-EIGHT ⟾

Jasmine scooted closer to Bradley as they settled into their booth at Bygone's. Seafood was one of Jasmine's absolute favorite foods, and she drooled as she looked over the menu. "Everything looks so good right now," she said. "Do you know what you're going to have?"

"No, I don't. It all sounds so good."

"So, Bradley," Victor said, "Jasmine tells me you're a guidance counselor?"

"I am. I absolutely love it. There's nothing I love more than providing young adults with the support they need to realize their potential and create an extraordinary life."

"That's amazing, Bradley."

"That reminds me," Jasmine commented to Victor, with a furrowed brow. "You didn't know this, but when you told me that I could probably find my beliefs in my diary that I actually found an old diary when I was home for my mom's funeral. I looked through it and was completely shocked to see what you'd said was totally true. What I was struggling with at thirteen is what I struggle with now. I couldn't believe it."

"Wow, it's amazing that you actually kept a diary, Jasmine," Victor commented. "It's such a simple thing. And once you realize your thoughts are what create your reality, things can change pretty quickly."

"But how? It left me feeling stuck and discouraged."

"The way I see it is, we all have the ability to respond, and it's our responsibility to do so. You can respond to whatever choices you make in your life. Can you give me an example of something you found in your diary?"

"Sure," Jasmine said, surprised. "Um, I can't trust anyone ever again. Those were the exact words I used."

"That's a great example, Jasmine. So, I'm assuming that something happened to make you feel that way, correct?"

"Yes!"

"Your brain, at that moment, was trying to protect you. You felt that the only way you could survive in that moment was not to trust anyone ever again. That's how you responded to that circumstance, right?"

"Yes."

"You can continue to respond to that belief through choices. You decided that the safest thing to do was never to trust anyone again in that moment. Do you have the ability, in this moment, right now, to decide that the best thing you can do is to trust again?"

Jasmine thought about what Victor had said. "Yes, I suppose I can."

He leaned in closer. "Then that's all you have to do. Decide. You decided at one point *not* to trust, so you can decide at any moment that you *can* trust. Because here's the thing: Remember we talked about the reticular activating system?"

She nodded.

"Your brain loves instruction, and it loves being told what to do. That's how it's designed to operate. The human brain has about one hundred billion neurons. Each one fires, on average, about two hundred times per second. And because each neuron connects to about one thousand other neurons, every time each one of them fires a signal, those thousand others receive that information."

Jasmine looked at him as if he was speaking a different language.

"What this tells us," he kept going, "is that our brains are made to change, and the way your brain changes, as a result of your mental activity, is scientifically called neuroplasticity. It means your thoughts and choices, which are your decisions, actually change the structure and function of your brain. As you change both, you actually begin to change your current reality and your future as well. When you find that a belief isn't serving you, you can simply change it," he said passionately.

"And how do I do that?" Jasmine asked, still feeling confused.

"Well," Victor said, "let's take this belief you mentioned, if you don't mind. Is the belief that you can't trust anyone serving you?"

Jasmine chuckled. "Absolutely not," she responded.

"Then you can change it to the opposite, or to something else that feels more empowering to you."

"Like what? I can trust people?" she asked hesitantly. "How about, 'it's good for me to trust people?' Or how about this, 'I trust the people my gut tells me to trust.'" Jasmine's face lit up when she said that.

"Bingo!" Victor exclaimed, pointing at her. "I felt your body physically change when you said that. Did you notice it?"

"I did!" Jasmine blurted out. "I did notice it. I feel lighter. Freer!" She buried her nose into Bradley's arm. "My gut told me to trust you," she said with a charming smile. Bradley leaned over and quickly kissed her on the cheek.

Victor continued. "Here's the most important thing for you to remember: Your belief systems actually determine your behavioral patterns. If you believe you can't trust anyone, your behavioral pattern will most likely push people away, or attract people into your life who actually are untrustworthy."

Jasmine laughed. "Yes, indeed. I'm a pro at pushing people away. And a pro at attracting untrustworthy people, too."

"Which is a result of you not trusting people. Your beliefs and your results, or your behavioral patterns—your habits— are always aligned," Victor explained.

"One thing I see quite often," Bradley pitched in, "is that, generally, when a student doesn't feel important or necessary, they tend to create drama or have some other way of getting attention to feel important."

"Yes," Victor agreed. "Often they compare or compete."

Jasmine sank into her chair without saying a word. *It's all making sense!* She thought to herself. She couldn't wait to dive into her diary for a third time to find her thoughts and patterns. "So, how do I find all the other beliefs I have?" she asked.

Victor laughed. "You have synaptic connections, so you have millions of beliefs that are wired into your brain. Through neuroplasticity, you can change those connections. You can decide which ones you want to strengthen or weaken. One of the easiest ways to know which beliefs are limiting you is to have clarity on what you want. Once you know what you actually want, you can know what's in the way of that. What's something you want?"

"Um, like anything?"

"Anything." Victor smiled.

"Well, I would absolutely love to travel," Jasmine said.

"Perfect! So, tell me, why can't you travel?"

"Um, because I don't have the money. Because I don't have anyone to travel with. Because I can't leave work."

"What you just described to me are your thoughts, Jasmine. They're the only things actually keeping you from traveling. I teach something to my students and clients I refer to as a 'thought model.' Your thoughts create your feelings, and your feelings dictate the actions you take, and your actions naturally produce your reality. So, if you *think*, 'I don't have money to travel,' how does that make you feel?"

"It makes me feel poor and kinda worthless."

"If you are feeling poor and worthless, what actions are you going to take toward planning travel?"

"Not much at all, really. I guess I'll just keep wishing I could be like other people who get to travel."

"That's right. And, what outcome or reality is that going to produce for yourself?"

"Everything, but what I actually want," Jasmine said, laughing.

"Exactly!" Victor chortled. "Now, let's look at what you want to do. Let's get clarity on what you actually want here. Where would you like to go? What's something you've always dreamed of?"

Jasmine considered for a moment. "It's been a while since I've given it much thought. Um, I've always wanted to go to Bora Bora," she said at last.

"When would you like to go?"

"I never got that far." She then laughed nervously.

"Can you see now why clarity is important?" Victor asked. "How much does it cost?"

"No idea."

"So, let's get clarity on that. Spend some time researching exactly what you want. When you'd like to go. Who you'd like to go with. Get all the clarity you can, then write it down. If you don't know where you're going, how can you actually get there?"

"That's awesome!"

"How do you feel now?" Victor asked.

"I feel excited! I feel like I have something to look forward to."

Victor and Bradley smiled.

"What actions will that produce?" Victor then asked.

"Well, the first thing I'm going to do is decide that I'm going!" Jasmine exclaimed. "Then, I suppose I'll look up some information, see how much it will cost, and find someone to go with me." She turned to Bradley, and he winked at her and squeezed her arm.

"And what reality will that create?" Victor asked.

"I'll be in Bora Bora!"

"That's how it works, Jasmine. That's the basic sum of behavioral psychology."

Finally, their food arrived at the table. Jasmine felt like a million pounds had been lifted from her shoulders and was famished.

⌒ TWENTY-NINE ⌒

A tight smile appeared on Jasmine's face and she pursed her lips with a deep, weighted sigh. Her eyes closed while she slightly tipped her head back, and then to the side, feeling the intensity of the surreal moment. She stood nervously waiting for her turn at the microphone. She let out a quiet "eek" as Bradley snuck his arm around her and softly kissed her cheek.

"Happy birthday, my goddess," he whispered with a wink. "You're going to do great. I couldn't be more proud to call you my wife."

"Thank you so much for being here with me. I'm so nervous."

"I wouldn't have missed it for the world," he replied, with his charming smile.

Someone onstage was introducing her. "Ladies and gentlemen," the voice commented. "Today we have the pleasure of having someone very special to speak to us. Someone who has helped to create new developments in camera lens design, which has aided in revolutionizing the photography industry. She's a regular contributor to the *Photographer's Journal* and has won this year's ADGI award. Give it up for Jasmine Stone!"

The crowd clapped and cheered as Jasmine walked out. Bright lights hit her as she made her way to the middle of the stage. She stood behind the podium and looked out at the audience. Instantly, her nerves got the best of her, and she could hardly speak.

"Hello," she said, as her high-pitched voice shook. She cleared her throat. "I feel incredibly grateful to be here today with all of you. Just like many of you, my love for photography and camera design has led me to meet some of the most amazing people on the planet, and I do not take this opportunity lightly."

Jasmine proceeded with her speech, until she shared something that no one expected.

"Have any of you ever felt that you just couldn't catch a break? Like life is just working against you? Maybe you've thought that if a particular thing hadn't happened to you, or if it had happened differently, you'd be happier. Your life would be better."

She gestured her hand up into the air.

"If that's you, then I know exactly how you feel. For several years, I lived my life feeling caged by my circumstances and the things that were happening to me. All of my life, all that I ever wanted to do was work in photography, and I thought that no matter what I did or how hard I tried, life was not going to let that happen. I felt that life just wasn't fair.

"On my journey, a dear friend shared with me a quote from Albert Einstein. He said 'One of the most important decisions you can make in life is whether you live in a friendly or a hostile Universe.'

"Let me illustrate it this way. Imagine a beautiful, decorative rug with amazing colors, patterns, and designs on one side and on the other side is a mix of knots, mismatched shapes, and random colors. The rug has two sides to it. It is up to you which side you choose to view and focus on. You could also look at it as a film negative. When you first look at a negative it is a jumble of shapes and colors, without any rhyme or reason, but within that seemingly 'ugly' picture is all the beauty of the original, the image just needed a bit of time to be focused and developed to show its true glory.

"I realized that I had been choosing to live in a hostile universe where everything was out to get me, and God 'punished' me whenever He felt pleased to punish me. But what I didn't realize, was that we as humans are the only species that have been given a free will, and we are responsible for how we choose to exercise that free will.

"Three years ago today, I was living in an apartment, alone, unhappy, and miserable. I was in a job I didn't like, and everything was out to get me, because I focused on the wrong side. I was caged by my own thinking. What I didn't realize was that there were opportunities all around me. What I perceived to be failures and unfortunate circumstances were actually the biggest blessings in my life. I just had to choose to see it.

"I had to decide if I lived in a friendly or hostile Universe. Just like you have the free will to decide if life is out to get you, or if life is working for your best interest."

She paused for a drink of water before continuing.

"I would like to invite each of you to go on a little journey with me."

Jasmine glanced over at the soundman and gave him the gesture. Soft music slowly filled the conference room.

"Let's close our eyes," she invited, "and plant our feet firmly on the ground. As your body relaxes into your seat, think with me for a moment about the lunch we all just enjoyed."

The music set the pace.

"Think of all the events that needed to take place in order for that delicious steak to make it to your plate. Think of the events that had to take place for those potatoes, and broccoli, and the bread, and the butter, and lettuce to be on your plate.

"There was a rancher who had to raise the cattle. There was a farmer who had to grow and harvest the potatoes, and the broccoli. There was another farmer who had to plant and harvest the wheat in order to send it off to a factory that could turn it into bread. Someone had to raise the cows that could give the milk that would be churned into butter.

"And then, someone had to start and open a grocery store so that we could buy this food. Someone had to cater the food. Someone had to make the plates that we used to eat our food. And countless other events and circumstances had to take place so that you and I could spend thirty minutes eating it, and getting to know one another.

"I invite you to take a deep breath and place your hand over your heart in gratitude for all that had to happen so we could enjoy that steak dinner.

"Next, I invite you to think of the miracle of you being in this room here today. So many things had to happen for you to be here. Take a moment to truly appreciate all of the events that needed to connect. Look at all of the coincidences that needed to show up to make sure that YOU were able to be here, today, on your journey. How did all of the events connect?

"We could go all the way back to your birth. Your childhood. What are the pains, the heartbreaks, the experiences, the challenges, the moments, the people you've met, everything— so you could be who you are today?

"You'll find that all along, life has been working for you."

Jasmine paused, and the music came to a close.

"While you open your eyes, I encourage you to acknowledge and fully appreciate how incredible your life truly has been.

"What I thought were tragedies turned out to be the best things that could ever have happened in my life. Looking back, I wouldn't have it any other way. For so many years, I searched for relief from my circumstances. Miracles were occurring around me every single day, but I couldn't see them because I chose to believe that life was out to get me. That God was a mean bully who controlled everything and everybody, and that there was nothing I could do about it.

"I've often found myself wondering what my life would have been like if I'd gotten the first job I wanted. What if I didn't have family issues and never left my hometown? What if my mother hadn't passed away so young? What if I'd never gotten the sales job I didn't even want? What if everything worked out the way I wanted it to from the beginning? Where would I be now?

"Even in my perceived mistakes, life worked for me. And, it's doing the same thing for each and every one of you.

"None of us know all the possible courses our lives could take, and maybe should have taken. What's important is that it doesn't matter—everything works out for you exactly the way it's supposed to; for your greatest growth, your greatest evolution, your greatest prosperity.

"Is it a possibility that miracles are happening all around you every single day, but you choose not to see them because you are out of focus and believe that life is out to get you?

"Is life always working for you, or is life always working against you? As you leave here today, may I invite you to see your life through a new awareness.

"See your life from a friendly, powerful place, knowing that every challenge, every hurt, every seemingly awful setback is all working *for* you, not against you. It's moving you closer to the person you are meant to become.

"Life is lovingly guiding you. You simply have to choose to accept it.

"Think of the thousands of people involved in the support of your journey. Who are you influencing? Who is grateful for you? You've had an impact on thousands of lives as well. Your photography talents and skills allow you to be a part in the lives of mothers who capture the smiles of their playing children. In the lives of husbands who get to capture the special moments with family. You create a space for creators to capture moments that inspire them. They can do this because of *you*.

"I invite you to let go of the negative thoughts and fears, to set yourself free of the cage you may have placed yourself in, to let go and go live! I want to ask you to recall those unfortunate circumstances and consider that they are actually your biggest blessings.

"Will you choose to believe and live in a hostile universe where life is out to get you, or will you choose to live in a friendly universe where life is corresponding with you to give you the best life possible, even when it may not seem like it?

"The choice is up to you, what do you choose to believe?

"Thank you, photography. This is my life. I'll continue to dedicate my life to the enhancement of the photography industry. And, I know that each and every one of your stories are amazing and beautifully unique in your own individual sovereign way. Thank you."

Jasmine waved goodbye to the crowd and quickly left the stage. Bradley met her with open arms and gave her a big squeeze. "That was amazing!"

"Thank you," she said.

"And I have a surprise for you."

She furrowed her brow, wondering what he could have thought up for her this time.

"Close your eyes and hold my hand," he said, a mischievous look on his face.

Jasmine gave him a questioning look, then closed her eyes and held out her hands. She felt a weighted paper drop into her palms.

"Okay, open your eyes!" His voice was excited.

Jasmine opened her eyes and there were two tickets to Bora Bora. Words escaped her, and tears trickled down her cheeks.

"It's true," she said. "The most important decision I ever made was that I live in a friendly universe, and every single thing in my life is working out for my good."

"I'm glad I get to be part of your friendly universe," Bradley pulled her close and the two of them held hands as they walked toward the crowd of people.

ACKNOWLEDGEMENTS

$\mathcal{I}$ would like to thank the following people for the roles that they've played in the writing, editing, and publishing of this book.

Thank you to Erin Minckley, Naomi Charalambakis, Rose Boots, Hilary Ross-Rojas, Jen Sugermeyer, Brendakay Hoyt, Janet Morris, and Kristin King, who gave me insights on their profession and expertise to make this story as realistic as possible.

Thank you to Maria Bentz, Sandy Gassett, Kristen Garcia, Traci Ronholm, Ellyn Boots, Kylie DeMarco, Iliyana Pavlova, and Kristi Battalini, for their valuable feedback in helping to make this book the best version possible.

Thank you to Margaret Craig who managed the editing process and kept all of the pieces and parts moving smoothly in the right direction.

A particular thanks to my husband who gave me the space to give my best to this book. Thanks for always being ready to run out with the kids or play with them, so I could have quiet time to write. Thank you for fixing dinner and doing the household chores. Thank you for believing in me and loving me when I doubted myself.

Thank you to my precious children who allowed me the time to write even when they did not like it or understand why mommy had her door locked—again. I love you beyond words.

Thank you to David and Carol Bayer who played a major role in the transformation of my life and introduced me to a world of possibilities and opportunities.

Finally, thank you to Ashley Mansour, my amazing writing coach, who often believed in me more than I did. Thank you for holding a space for me and for your belief in not only me, but the book as well.

This book would not have been possible without every single one of you.

EXPERIENCE YOUR
PERSONAL TRANSFORMATION

P erspective

I nsight

V ision

O pportunity

T ransformation

To learn more and access exclusive reader-only resources go to www.neuropivot.com.

ABOUT THE AUTHOR

 Andrea Stephens is an author, speaker, and life coach. In 2020, she founded NeuroPivot Transformational Programs in order to fulfill her mission of transforming lives, one mind at a time. She has dedicated her life to inspiring, empowering, and teaching women how to move into their power.

Before her work as a NeuroPivot Transformational coach, Andrea lived in Germany for three years and ran a successful e-commerce business. When she's not writing, coaching, or running her programs and events, you can find her walking and hiking in nature, traveling, and playing the piano. She currently lives with her husband and four children in Chesterfield, Virginia.